Smudged LINES

KRIS BUTLER

TATTOOED HEARTS DUET
PART TWO

Smudged Lines
Tattooed Hearts Duet
Part two
Kris Butler
First Edition: October 2021
Published by Kris Butler
Copyright © Kris Butler 2021

Cover design: © 2021 by Bookish Duet Author Services
Proofreading: © 2021 by Locke & Key Proofreading Services
Formatting: © 2021 by Bookish Duet Author Services

❀ Created with Vellum

Our love song has always been written in the stars.

loud and clear. Turning, I walked back to my apartment, a huge smile on my face.

.

PRESENT

I'd waited for a week before I started to freak out. And when school started, and I moved to Knoxville, I chalked it up to being all in my head. It wasn't until a few years later when I was visiting Slade in Nashville, that I saw her again.

That was the night everything changed. The night that haunted Slade and I, and I imagined Simon too, though, it was hard to know since I hadn't ever talked to him.

The night I discovered my mystery girl, my Kelly, was none other than Lennox James. The night I realized the voice in my head, the girl of my dreams, and the best kiss I'd ever had were one and the same.

Nox was Lennox, and I would never be able to be with her.

Not after that night, the guilt was too much to bear. But mostly, because it was clear my brother was in love with her. I hadn't always been the best brother, and I'd failed him the past few years. So, this was a sacrifice I could make for him.

Vanessa said I was being a martyr, punishing myself for mistakes of my past. She was probably right, but I'd denied myself true happiness for so long, it felt natural.

Coming to Africa, that had been good, though. It was easier not to cave in to stalking her on social media when I was this far away with limited internet access. She still lingered in my thoughts, her presence a

Our love song has always been written in the stars.

Contents

Blurb

My life had become full of scribbles and lies, the lines smudged too many times to know the truth.

Small town girl, eyes full of hope, I never thought my life would come to this.

It had started out so simple, and then somewhere between first loves and now, it went majorly off course. All the lies caught up to them, and I no longer knew who to trust.

Everything was muddled, and no one knew the full truth of what had happened the day when everything changed. We'd become too twisted in our pain to look beyond it, believing the lies we were told, or perhaps wanted to believe.

Our inked confessions began as a safe way to share our fears and hopes, but with this betrayal, everything was riddled with deceit, and I wasn't sure if any of us would ever find our way back to one another.

And yet, their love was a permanent tattoo on my heart, three smudged lines I couldn't erase, nor would I ever want to, no matter how deep the pain pierced.

But the music didn't lie, and my heart was nowhere near a love song. *He'd* made sure of that. When all you had left was your gut feeling, was it enough?

Foreword

This is part two of a duet. Part one must be read first. This will end in a happy ending. This is a why-choose novel, meaning the main female character doesn't have to choose between love interests. This is a contemporary romantic suspense with some dark themes including grief, mental health, and stalking. This is a medium burn with MM. This is an adult romance and is intended for readers 18+ due to language and content. Cuss words are used throughout, and sexual scenes are explicit.

To all those who loved Lennox's story, I hope you enjoy this conclusion. And may it help you find your inner sassiness, strength, and belief in love.
And also toaster tongs because they rock!

Chapter One

THANE

THE BARTENDER SLID a beer across the wooden surface, part of the foam spilling down over the chilled glass as he hurriedly passed it off. The club was busy tonight. The bass of the music pulsed through the place as the bodies moved to the song on the dance floor. A hand trailed up my arm, pulling my focus, and I looked up to find a beautiful statuesque brunette.

"Hey, handsome. Care to buy me a drink?"

Smiling, I motioned for the bartender to bring her one while she took the seat next to me. "Come here often?" she teased, and I laughed at the long-time joke between us.

"Just killing time until I meet the one." Chuckling, I twisted on the stool to face her fully, dropping the act as I took in my friend. "How was your day?"

The bartender passed her a beer, winking before moving on. She smiled coyly at him as she took a drink, glancing back at me. "Not too bad. Yours?"

"The usual. Long, hot, and tiring. The real question," I shouted, wanting to be heard over the noise. "Now that it's the last week, are you finally going to hit that?"

Vanessa's head fell back, the laughter rolling

through her at my question, not at all taken aback by it. "Who says I haven't?"

"Hmph. I think you'd be walking funny and bragging if you had," I said, teasing her.

Sighing, she rolled her head, sipping her beer as she looked longingly at the man. "He is dreamy. I should just bite the bullet and do it, shouldn't I?" Vanessa asked, some of her earlier confidence slipping.

"No time like the present," I agreed. "Besides, it's our last week here, and you need a story to take back home."

"You make a valid point, my friend. I think my dance card just got punched." She smiled, drumming her fingers on the surface as she tracked him with her eyes coming to a decision. Kissing my cheek, she slid off her stool. "Don't wait for me."

Chuckling, I nodded and watched as she headed off to the dark hallway to the side. The bartender who'd been serving me all night stood in the frame, a seductive look on his face as she approached. Happy for her, I grabbed the barely touched beer and downed it, not wanting the stuff to go to waste. Especially since I'd bought it at this overpriced establishment.

Though, as much as I grumbled about the cost, it was the best place in the city to wind down after a grueling week. As with most things here, you paid for the safety—both from disease and violence—without question, knowing it was necessary.

This wasn't just any bar in any club. *Neon* was a bar in Monrovia, Liberia. My home for the past two months. I'd been working with Vets Without Borders to advance human health and livelihood by sustainably improving animal health. Stopping diseases like rabies from being transmitted into their food sources and educating them on veterinary services. I'd been working to improve their wellbeing while also helping enterprise development and trade around them. It was hard work, but I enjoyed it.

Most people didn't know V.W.B even existed, but I was no stranger to the organization. I'd completed my first short stint in college since my school partnered with a university in Africa, and now, I helped lead the program. Once a year, I spent a few months at different locations assisting and training. It kept my perspective focused and gave my life a purpose. Something I'd needed to forget about the girl who'd captured my heart.

Yet, it was hard to forget about someone who was constantly on your mind. Even here, across the world, I still thought of her.

Lennox James was hard to forget. I still remember the first time she captured my heart.

TEN YEARS AGO

"What are you doing?"

"Don't worry about it. It doesn't concern you." Slade slammed his notebook shut, sliding it under the books piled on his desk. He narrowed his eyes at me, daring me to ask him about it.

"Yeah, because that's not suspicious." Rolling my eyes, I crossed my arms as I leaned against the door-jamb. "Dad's going to be late, so we're on our own for dinner. I'm headed over to a pool party at Carrie's."

When he didn't respond, I sighed and turned to leave before stopping despite my better judgment.

Slade and I had grown distant over the years, and I missed him. We used to be so close, but lately, we'd practically become strangers. I knew he blamed himself for the divorce and Mom's death, but I didn't. Never had. It sucked, but neither of them were his fault. It seemed like this last move had been the hardest for him. The school here was cliquey, and filled mostly with preppy kids. Two things Slade hated to his core. Add in the incident with the weed and me telling Dad… Slade had barely talked to me in months, hiding stuff from me now, constantly in that notebook of his.

"I know you don't like this school, but it might do you some good to try. It's our senior year, and I think this move might last a full year. I can get you in if you want to come."

The glare he sent me could've cut ice, it was so sharp. "Haven't you heard, Thane? I'm a *loser*. I wouldn't want to bring down your image by associating with the likes of me."

"You know that's not true. They… just don't know you. You spend all your time in your notebook doing God knows what, and you put off this 'stay away' vibe. No one dares to even approach you."

"Good, glad it's coming across correctly."

"Fine, Slade," I huffed. "I tried okay. If you want to be miserable, then be miserable. I'm tired of waiting around for you to brush that chip off your shoulder."

I kept going this time, but I heard his mournful mutter, piercing my heart. "I don't know how, but Mom would." Dropping my head, I took a deep breath.

Mom's words of sticking together had me wanting to turn around, but the chime of my phone pushed me on, vowing to try again tomorrow.

A few hours later, I returned to a vacant house, my brother was nowhere in sight. Hopefully, he wasn't out getting himself in trouble again. We were eighteen now, and I didn't think the judges, or our father, would be as forgiving now. Walking past his room, his door stood ajar, the space inside dark. The dark feeling I often ignored emerged, and I felt the tug to do something impulsive.

Most days, I could reign it in, run out my energy through sports or helping others. Other times, the need was too strong and I gave into the part of me that liked the rush. The high from doing something reckless. The impulsive freedom of not thinking of the consequences, of not having to be perfect for a single second longer. The tension between my brother and me had grown into a gaping chasm, and I feared it would never close.

I justified my thoughts on what I was about to do as an attempt to save my relationship with my brother. It couldn't be bad if I had a good motive.

Creeping silently into his room, I walked over to his desk and slid the notebook out from under the stack of papers. Sitting down on his bed, I sifted through it. There were a lot of drawings, some in comic form and others looked like they could be tattoo designs. Amazement soared through me at the skill level I saw. Slade's art had vastly improved over the years.

Flipping through, I found the motherload at the back.

Letters had been flattened down and shoved

between the last page and back of the notebook. There were quite a few, and I remember him talking about this years ago. It had to be the pen pal thing. Quite frankly, I was surprised he still did it.

It didn't feel as much of an invasion of privacy if I wasn't invading his, considering the letters were from the pen pal and not his inner thoughts.

Reading through them, I began to realize there were two people he wrote to. There were far more from Nox than Fish, and I found myself drawn to Nox as I read each letter. I started to sit the Fish ones aside, focusing solely on Nox. Lying back on his bed, I spread them out, finding a semblance of order, and read them all.

It was apparent she was a girl, her light and personality jumped off the page. I'd say she was around our age, maybe a year or two younger. She was funny, insightful, and kind, and I found myself sad when there were no more letters to read. Hearing a car door slam, I quickly picked up the letters, shoving them back into the notebook, praying they hadn't been in any specific order.

When I heard him enter the house, I knew I wouldn't have time to get out of his room if he came straight here, so I slid the journal back into his spot and waited at the door. I prayed he'd grab some food instead of heading straight here. When I heard the fridge open, I sighed in relief and bolted through the crack, making my escape.

That night, I laid in bed intrigued about this unknown girl. Binging on her letters, I'd gotten her words stuck in my head, almost like I could hear her, the words already becoming my favorite sound without even hearing her voice.

PRESENT

My obsession started that night, and I found myself jonesing like an addict to read more of her words. It wasn't always easy to sneak them, but I became a ninja, creeping in the night to stay up to date on my southern sunshine. I wouldn't admit that no other girl held my interest. I even forced myself to date a few girls here and there, but it never went far. It was hard to open your heart to someone when it belonged to the girl in your dreams.

I realized how insane I sounded. I'd fallen for a girl I'd never met. A girl I'd only known through her letters to my brother. A girl I'd never even talked to.

But the fact was, *I had.*

When I read they were switching to email, I was equally sad and delighted. There was something about holding her letter in my hand, her scribbles of ink and stationary that held a key to her personality. The faint scent of her lingered on the paper, and it felt like I held her in my hands each time I read one.

However, email meant better access, and I'd known Slade's login information since fifth grade. It had been the same since he first got his email, and I was desperate enough at this point to try anything to get more of Nox.

Of course, I felt guilty at first. *I did.*

My reputation as the golden boy with perfect grades wasn't hyperbole. I liked being the good kid, the star, and people praised me for my intelligence. In general, I was just trying to make it easier on my dad, my brother caused enough problems for the both of us. My role had always been the peacekeeper between them, especially once Mom was gone. But it was a lot of pressure to maintain.

Having this secret, this hidden indiscretion felt powerful. It had become an addiction, and like any junkie, I constantly wanted more. It wasn't enough to just read her responses to him anymore; I wanted to be part of it.

It was wrong to impersonate my brother, to lead her on and make her think I was him. I knew this, but I couldn't stop myself. I'd fully fallen into the black hole that was Nox, and I didn't want to find a way out. Every day, I would write to her and then erase my message, so it wasn't found by Slade. The truly complicated task was waiting for her response and hoping I saw it first. I'd gotten good at telling when it was obviously in response to me, and I would forward it to myself, then delete it before Slade saw it too.

There were a few times I slipped up, and I caught him asking her questions, confusion on what she'd meant about something. You think I would've stopped reading their messages since I had my own, but I'd become a voyeur to their letters. Now that I could read both sides of the conversation, I got to know my brother again. It had become just as compulsive to read his words as Nox's.

Each time I logged on and wrote to her, I felt more guilt line my soul and I'd vow to stop. It would last for a day, a week at the most. But something in my life would happen, and she'd be the first person I wanted to tell. Or Slade would be acting moodier, withdrawn and I'd itch to know what he was thinking. It was cheating, using his letters as a window into his soul. I coerced myself into believing I wasn't hurting anyone, telling myself it was all I had.

At the time, I could justify my actions, seeing the good I was doing, my own needs and curiosities met.

When it all hit the fan, as shit inevitably does, I realized how much I'd been deluding myself.

The fallout of my deception, and ultimately the fight between us, was catastrophic. I'd never seen Slade so hurt before. The betrayal had been thick, and I knew I'd finally done something I couldn't repair with a smile or good grades. *I'd royally fucked up.*

In an attempt to save my relationship with my twin, I promised to stop. He changed his password and locked down everything securely. I'd discovered this the few times I'd fallen off my detox of Nox.

I had to face the facts then. She was gone, and I had to move on.

The summer before I started Vet school at the University of Knoxville, I'd gotten a summer internship in Nashville, TN. One of my roommates pushed me to hang out one night, and I ended up at a 'Throwback Karaoke' night dressed as Zack Morris from *Saved by the Bell*.

It had been three years since I'd last written a letter to Nox, and my relationship with Slade was rocky at best, but he was still in my life at least. I hadn't met anyone during that time that had captured me the same way Nox had until that night.

THANE, 22 / LENNOX, 20

Going through the motions, I pretended I was having fun, despite wanting to do nothing but head home and study. Veterinary medicine had become my obsession and the only thing that occupied my mind outside the girl I couldn't have.

A voice sang out over the speakers, and I stopped in my tracks, turning to find the source. The melodious tune was like a siren song, pulling my feet closer to the stage. A dark-haired girl with lavender streaks sang on stage, and to my surprise, she was dressed as Kelly Kapowski. I couldn't take my eyes off of her. She was beautiful and radiant up there. She saw me standing at the front of the stage and winked, setting my heart on fire.

She was petite and had curves for days that could be made out in the iconic flower dress with puffy sleeves Kelly wore. I'd grown up watching the show on reruns and admittedly had a crush on the brunette beauty as a teen. This girl, though, blew Kelly out of the water.

When the song ended, she walked over to a table that had a few people, but I caught her looking over every few seconds. The charm and swagger I'd once had surged up in me, and I found my feet moving toward her. She watched me approach, a straw between her lips as she sucked down her drink.

"Hi, gorgeous. It looks like you're the Kelly to my Zack."

When she giggled, my cock perked up, liking the sound. "I guess I am. So, Zack, are we college years or high school? I just need to know what version of Kelly to channel."

Laughing, I cozied up closer to her, and we debated which was better, neither able to take our eyes off one another. I found myself inching closer and closer, needing our bodies to touch.

"I have an idea," she cooed.

"I can honestly say, I'll be up for anything you suggest." She spat out her drink in laughter, and I realized what I'd said. "Um, sorry, didn't mean for that to sound so suggestive. Here." Grabbing a napkin, I handed it to her so she could clean up.

"Well, Zack, I'd say that's the most forward thing someone's said to me, but unfortunately, it's not. But what I was going to suggest was a duet. You up for that?"

She grinned wide, and despite being a horrible singer, I found myself nodding. We sang a few songs together, danced to several others, and when the night ended, I once again found myself reaching for a napkin. But this time, to write my number on it. I was cursing the no phone rule of the event, resulting in having to use an old-school method. I kissed her under the streetlights up against the bar, and I was tempted to invite her back to my place, but when we pulled away, I knew she was something special, and I didn't want to waste getting the chance to really know her.

"Bye Zack, I'll call you."

"I'll be waiting until you do, gorgeous."

She walked off with her friends, one guy putting his arm around her as they grew smaller in the distance, and I wondered what the relationship with them was. It didn't seem flirty, but his arm screamed 'possessive' loud and clear. Turning, I walked back to my apartment, a huge smile on my face.

PRESENT

I'd waited for a week before I started to freak out. And when school started, and I moved to Knoxville, I chalked it up to being all in my head. It wasn't until a few years later when I was visiting Slade in Nashville, that I saw her again.

That was the night everything changed. The night that haunted Slade and I, and I imagined Simon too, though, it was hard to know since I hadn't ever talked to him.

The night I discovered my mystery girl, my Kelly, was none other than Lennox James. The night I realized the voice in my head, the girl of my dreams, and the best kiss I'd ever had were one and the same.

Nox was Lennox, and I would never be able to be with her.

Not after that night, the guilt was too much to bear. But mostly, because it was clear my brother was in love with her. I hadn't always been the best brother, and I'd failed him the past few years. So, this was a sacrifice I could make for him.

Vanessa said I was being a martyr, punishing myself for mistakes of my past. She was probably right, but I'd denied myself true happiness for so long, it felt natural.

Coming to Africa, that had been good, though. It was easier not to cave in to stalking her on social media when I was this far away with limited internet access. She still lingered in my thoughts, her presence a comfort. In less than a week, we would be heading back to the states, and I'd have to find something new to occupy me.

I could move away from Nashville, decreasing the temptation, but I wouldn't. A small part of me hoped that one day we'd naturally bump into one another on the streets of Nashville, sparking the connection back to life.

Maybe then I wouldn't feel so bad about invading her privacy for years or for feeling responsible for the epic fuck up on that night in question three years ago.

Maybe I was a martyr, but I was also a murderer.

One of which was easier to live with.

THANE TO NOX

From: blazetats@heartsemail.com
To: noxsmiles@heartsemail.com
Subject: Do fish dream?

Noxy girl,

I've been thinking about you, and wanted to see how you were. Nothing else, just a message to say hi.

I imagine if we knew each other in person I would never get tired of hearing your laugh, but I'd probably also never be this bold.

How is Noah? Any funny anecdotes to share? I sometimes wish I had a younger sibling. I think it would be fun.

Do you ever worry that no matter how hard you try that it will never be enough? Some things come so easy to me, but then I worry I'll never be good at anything else. Even when I do my best, I still feel like it's not enough. I feel guilty in a way for having things easier. Like I shouldn't be this lucky, I don't know if that makes any sense.

I think I like to test the margin of things I can get away with, to see what it would take to make people leave me. It's easy to know when you're good and perfect, but what about when I'm no longer that person, what if I was more of a black sheep? Would people still like me, or am I only useful for the things I give them?

Or, you know, that's what I wonder if my brother thinks. Being a twin is interesting. We used to be closer, but over the years, things changed and I feel like I lost him.

Did you hear the newest Mirrored Hearts single? If not, go and listen to it now! If yes, what did you think? Looking forward to hearing your thoughts.

Sing, Sing, Noxy girl,

Smoldering Blaze

LENNOX

"WHAT THE FUCK?" I shouted, the f-word rolling off my tongue with ease at the magnitude of the situation unfolding in front of me. Clenching my jaw, I seared him with my own look. "Explain everything. *Now.*"

For once, I was the one making demands, tacking on that *now*. Something shifted in his demeanor, my years of studying the man the only reason I'd noticed. But he'd softened, just a smidge.

"Are you not *Nox*, pen pal to *Blaze*?"

Swallowing as the memories surged forward, I nodded, never taking my eyes from his. "I was… until Blaze broke my heart."

"Broke *your* heart?" He scoffed, some of his hardness returning. "That's where you got it wrong, *Peach*. You broke mine first."

Shaking my head quickly, I started to hyperventilate, the memories of that night rushing forward. "No! You said…" but I couldn't get the words out. Everything connected to that night brought Duncan to the forefront, a pain so deep I'd buried it in order to survive. Thankfully, Simon stepped in since Slade nor I appeared to be budging from our stances.

"This is the problem. We're missing pieces of the

story. I think we need to all share what happened that day, as hard as it might be, Lenn."

Simon walked over and cautiously sat next to me on the couch. My feet had dropped to the floor, my arms braced on my knees as I hunched inward, trying to breathe. It hurt seeing them together; it hurt seeing Simon functioning at all. That sounded horrible in my head, but the past few months had barely felt manageable most days, and he looked unaffected. I wanted to see him suffer. Maybe then I'd know what we had was real.

And yet, my body craved the comfort of the best friend who knew me better than anyone, who'd been there with me through everything. It made me feel *weak*, but I wanted his hug. So when he scooted closer, our legs touching, he carefully placed his arm around me. I allowed myself to lean into him for a second, stealing his strength. Before it got too comfortable and I decided to toss the slight modicum of dignity I'd gained, I pulled away, returning back to staring at the floor.

"Maybe I should start?" Simon offered.

I nodded, not able to look at Simon or Slade. I feared seeing his glee at my weakness or his smugness at taking Simon from me. It wasn't something I wanted to face, not strong enough yet to deal with what I'd lost being paraded around in front of me.

"I remember Lenn getting a message saying Blaze was in Nashville and wanted to meet. She told me and invited me along. She, uh, didn't know I'd continued writing to you, though." Simon shifted next to me on the couch. His leg still touched mine, and I could feel his nervous movements. I wondered if he was looking at Slade, but I kept my face to the floor, not wanting the answer. After a pause, he continued.

"I was nervous the whole drive, wondering how I would get myself out of this pickle. But when we got to the Tavern, I pretended to have set up a date, not wanting to be the third wheel and told you to meet him first. But really, I'd chickened out."

This caused me to look up at him, the information new to me. "Where did you go?"

"I just walked around the strip after dropping you off. Popped into a place to get food and had finally talked myself into facing you both. When I returned to the restaurant, I found you running out of it. You were crying, and upset with me. I tried to chase you down, but you're wiley when you want to be," he said, chuckling. "You managed to evade me and it wasn't until I begged your father that I found you. I tried to explain, and bought you a drink, but you took off again, and yeah... I didn't find you until," he stopped, gulping. "Until I got the... call."

That was one way to put it.

Quiet fell around us in the room, me lost in my thoughts as I tried to align Simon's memories with my own. When Slade piped in, I jolted. "Wait, did you say the Tavern? That wasn't where we met."

My head popped up at his accusation, and I caught his eyes for the first time since I discovered he was Blaze. My brain couldn't reconcile the boy from our letters, and the man I'd worked with for three years as one and the same.

"Yeah, it was. You texted me right as we left my

house. You said it was too busy, so to meet there instead."

"That's right," Simon affirmed, turning to look at me. "We'd just gotten into the car when you got it. I thought it was strange but figured you hadn't gotten a reservation or something."

"No, that's not right." Slade shook his head, denial on his face. "I never texted that. I waited at Layla's like we'd planned. That's where your catfish approached me."

Screwing up my face, I looked at Slade like he'd officially lost it. "Catfish? What are you talking about? And you so did change the place! I remember it distinctly."

Slade began to protest, his hands clenching on the chair as his anger rose. "I'm not stupid—"

Simon cut him off, standing and placing his hands out between us. "Okay, it seems we've found something. Slade, why don't you start and then Lenn. Both of you will wait until the other is done," he stressed, looking between us both. "*Then* we can battle semantics. Okay?"

Slade gritted his teeth but eventually nodded, and looked at me. Anger had replaced the earlier grief, so I slouched back on the couch, folding my arms over my chest. There was no way he was going to blame this on me! Narrowing my eyes at Slade, I answered. "Fine."

"Let's see, I waited at *Layla's* like we'd agreed," he stressed, giving me a look that screamed liar. "After fifteen minutes, I was about to leave when 'you' finally sat down. Or so I thought it was you. Everything felt off. You acted bored and didn't know half of the things I spoke about. When the bill came, something came over your face, and you smiled at me. Or well, who I thought was you."

"I never met you until the day I walked into the tattoo shop."

"Lenn, you promised to wait," Simon sighed.

"Just keep on lying, *James*. You met me that night, just not at the restaurant. I guess the girl you'd paid to catfish me hadn't known all the details because she asked me if she'd been convincing enough to pass. Of course, I had no clue what she meant. When I asked her, she told me she'd been paid to be Lennox James."

"That doesn't make any sense!" I shouted, jumping off the couch. "You texted me and told me you'd been pretending! You-you-you!" I couldn't form words as my mouth hung open at his accusation. My heart rate skyrocketed at his story. Shaking my head, I crossed my arms. "No. I don't believe *you*."

My anger caused him to stand and stalk toward me. "Good to know you can't follow directions, *James*. Seems I'm not the only one you lie to, you also lie to yourself."

I moved to slap him, but he caught my wrist. My breathing had become ragged and I contemplated kneeing him in the groin next. The fury inside of me blazed to an inferno, my eyes feeling like fire. I wanted to hurt him for saying such hateful things. Simon stepped in between us, pushing us apart before I could take out any vengeance.

"As much as I've wanted to see the firework explosion between you two ignite over the years, even having dreamt about being in the middle of it, *this* isn't the time. Lenn, you said you'd wait. I believe Slade. I think something else is going on here. *Please*."

It was the final please that calmed my anger, and I stepped back, yanking my hand out of Slade's grip. Neither of us sat back down, though, our countenance agitated as we waited to prove who was right.

"Later that night, I found myself at that Honkey Tonk bar, and I helped you. You knocked into me and told me my tats were beautiful. Later, some guy was hitting on you, and I rescued you again and bought you a drink. We'd just started talking when Simon found you. You started arguing and ran off. Later, I found you in the hall. Some guy had you up against the wall. You didn't look right, but I figured you'd had a lot of drinks by then. I was walking toward you, going to break it up, when… " he paused, shifting his eyes, "some guy stepped in. The other guy knocked into me, and I was about to rearrange his face when… " he stopped again, blowing out a breath as he shifted on his feet. Throwing his head back, he scrubbed his hands down his face.

It was obvious it was distressing to him, and I wanted to feel bad for him, I didn't want to admit how most of what he said I couldn't remember. That night was… hard to recall, period.

"The guy stopped and laughed. He didn't notice my intention to pound his face when he started spouting off how he heard you'd been playing guys all over Nashville and were a huge slut, giving it up to anyone. When he saw me looking back at you, he told me I'd be better off staying away from *Lennox James*."

Shaking my head, I couldn't believe what he was saying, the words wouldn't form though as the memories climbed up my throat. I barely croaked out, "No, I, no," before Simon stepped in.

"What happened next, Slade?"

"When I realized who she was, I left. I figured you deserved whatever happened to you. Well, I left after you threw up all over me. Thanks for that, by the way. I never could get the stench out of my favorite shirt."

His words slapped me with force, the bitterness and hate so heavy in them that each one had felt like a slap.

"Deserved? You think I deserved what happened after that?" I wished the words had come out stronger, but they were weak. I was barely holding back my tears now.

"I didn't know any of that was going to happen!" Slade roared, his nostrils flaring as he pointed at me. I stepped back, the force of everything pushing me back.

"Okay, okay, we're getting off track again. Slade, was there anything else?" Simon interrupted again, attempting to keep it on track.

"Not from that night, no. I heard the next day about a wreck—"

"Stop!" I shouted, holding up my hand. I couldn't hold it back anymore, and I bolted for the bathroom, barely making it before everything I'd eaten that evening came up. Hands rubbed my back a moment later, pulling my hair back. "Ssh, it's okay, Lenn."

When my stomach finally stopped cramping, I sat back on my legs and peered up at Simon. "I'm really upset with you still," I hissed, "so incredibly angry." He nodded, wiping my face with a cold wash cloth. He handed me a paper cup with some water, and I swished it around, spitting it into the toilet. He made an eww face and I laughed. Handing back the cup, he offered me some mouthwash next and I gladly took it. Swishing it around, I spat it in the toilet too, laughing now at his reaction. Flushing it for the third time for good measure, I addressed him again. Simon had always been so good at taking care of me when I was sick. "Can I have a free pass for tonight? I just really need my best friend. I'll go back to being mad at you tomorrow."

"Of course, Lenn. Whatever you need."

Falling into his arms, I cried all the tears I'd been holding back for the past two months, probably for the past three years. We sat on the small bathroom floor, cramped in the space, but neither of us complained or moved, needing the comfort the other had to provide. When I finally lifted my head, his shirt was a hot mess of tears, snot, and makeup, and it only made me do one of these tearful laughs.

"You think you're ready to finish the conversation."

"No. But I'll do it."

Sighing, I stood, my body stiff from the position. Stretching out my muscles, I found Simon staring at me, hunger in his eyes, and I realized I'd practically put my butt in his face.

"Oh, um, sorry."

He grabbed my hips, pulling me into him, his hard erection rubbing against me, and I found myself wanting to strip off all my clothes right then and there to bury the pain I felt.

"Don't ever be sorry for being you, Lenn. It's just a relief to not have to hide how insanely attractive I find you, or how many times a day you turn me on."

"I do?"

He circled his hips into me, making his erection brush over my center, and I sucked in a breath. "What do you think?" He went to bend down, his intention clear, when a noise from the other room reminded us Slade was still out there. It was probably for the best. There were still a lot of things we needed to discuss, and a pass tonight didn't mean I could just throw those out the window and jump into bed with him.

Letting go, I took a deep breath and returned to the living room, sitting back on the couch. I didn't look at Slade but began with my recollection of events, not caring if he was ready or not. If the words were going to come out, it would be when I was ready.

"Like Simon mentioned, we got a text to meet at a different place as we were leaving. I waited an hour, sending you several messages. I ordered food while I waited, and the staff looked on with sympathy as it became clear I was stood up. When I was about to leave, worried something awful had happened, you finally responded back. Told me I'd been a joke, a prank you'd pulled with your brother. That you read all my letters out loud at school and you had some of your friends write to me too. The real kicker you shared was that Simon knew and was in on it because he'd never stopped writing to you. You called me a country bumpkin with a crazy mother. And then... you told me to smile because I was on camera."

"I didn't—"

"Nope. Her turn now."

"But she—"

"Slade, seriously. Just let her talk, and then we can hash it out."

When they both quieted, I started again, still staring only at the floor. "I ran out of the bar, and that's when I found Simon. I asked him, and when he didn't deny writing to you, I knew everything else was true too. I ran off, hiding in some bar. I had a drink and then started going from one place to the next. I don't even know the last place I ended up in. I'd called my dad earlier, and he'd told me... " I gulped, determined to say it. "He said he'd send Duncan." I sucked in a breath at the sound of his name and felt Simon pull me close. The tears started again, silently this time, and I stayed staring at the floor.

"I vaguely remember bumping into you now that you mentioned it, saying the tattoo thing, but I hadn't before just then. Believe me or not, whatever, it's the truth." I shrugged. Sighing, I prepared myself for the last part, the memories that hurt the worst. "Everything kind of blurs after that. Someone bought me a drink. I danced. I sang a song. I had some more drinks. I saw Simon, and I ran away from him and danced some more. It's spotty, a blob of things out of order. Grabbing drinks, dancing, spinning. I remember being in a hallway and things being in and out of focus. Someone handing me some water, and then waking up upside down, the lights flashing all around me ..."

When I met Slade's eyes, I was surprised when I didn't find anger there. But it was worse because instead I found *pity*. Fury rose in me, how dare he pity me! It pushed the rage back in. Standing, I grabbed the first thing I found, which unfortunately was a pillow, and I threw it at his big head. It wasn't very powerful, but it felt good to fling it at him, even if it did bounce off. He looked down at it, cocking that smile that screamed condescension.

"Are you happy *now*? Did I get what I deserved?" My fists clenched, my face burning with rage as the painful things slapped me in the face with their memories. I directed it all at him. "Do you want to hear how I found out I'd almost been raped by the person who'd taken me? Or how when I'd been rescued by my *boyfriend*, I watched him get hit by a car? What about how they still don't know who the driver was? Huh? Does that make *you* feel any better?"

At some point in my rage induced shouting, I'd walked closer, and when I needed something else to throw, I restored to poking him in his chest, *hard*. It was an extension of my anger spitting out of me.

"No, *Peach*. It doesn't," he spat. Slade's chest rose with each inhale. "Why do you think I gave you a job despite hating you?" he ground out through his teeth. "I felt partially responsible, so I suffer every day as I war with myself on *wanting* you and *hating* you. So *no*, it doesn't make me *happy*."

We glared at one another, our chests rising with our rapid breathing as our eyes locked in a fierce stand-off. Simon's words finally broke through the anger haze, and I turned, breaking the hold Slade held over me.

"What, Si?" I exhaled, defeat and exhaustion heavy in my question. My shoulders sank, and I could've collapsed right there on the floor, the fight leaving me.

"Don't you see it?"

"What? How much we hate each other? Yeah,

thanks for pointing that out." Rolling my eyes, I didn't miss the way he smiled at my sass.

"No, Lenn. You *both* couldn't have been catfishing one another. Something else is at play here, or more likely *someone* else."

I looked back at Slade, his expression reflecting the same surprise as mine, I expected. Was Simon correct, and we'd both been played?

"But how?" I asked, confused.

"*Thane*," Slade raged, his nostrils flaring.

Looking at him curiously, I couldn't understand what he meant. "Thane? How is your brother part of this?"

My question stunned him, and he took a step back, betrayal covering his face. "How the *fuck* do *you* know, Thane?"

It was my turn to step back this time, his vehemence thick as he directed it at me. Stretching out my hands in front of me, I shielded myself in protection from his words. Glancing at Simon, his confusion mirrored my own, helping to calm my racing heart.

"Because... I met him." I sounded it out slowly, not wanting to spook the raging Tatzilla in front of me. "When you ran off after we slept together, he came into the shop, or well, I met him the night before I hit my head actually."

"You slept together!" Simon shouted and I winced, remembering he hadn't known. Cringing, I gave an apologetic look to him, dropping my hands. "Oops." He didn't get to ask anything else because Slade drew both of our attention back as he shouted again.

"That's not possible!" The sneer had been flung at

us, and I held my hands back up. I couldn't deal with them both shouting at me.

"Whoa, tone it down. I can't take you both shouting." Turning to Simon first, I answered his question since he'd been the least grouchy about it. "Yes, sorry. It was the night we were stuck in the rain. We slept together, and then he ran off like a scared little boy the next morning. Sorry, I thought you knew with all of your combined secret keeping between you both."

Exhaling, I turned back to face Slade. His glare hadn't lessened any. "I first met Thane at Rookies when my date stood me up. We shared a pickled appetizer and talked all night. He kissed me at the end, but then I hit my head the next day, and with everything going on, I pushed it to the back burner. He showed back up a week later when I hit a cat. You were already gone at that point. When he walked into the store, he said he'd come to visit you, and was shocked to learn I worked there. My mom was at the shop, so she invited him to dinner. Simon came too. When I arrived in Nashville, I ran into him one night. I was drunk at a bar, and Thane helped me home. We've been hanging out ever since. We're friends. He was there tonight, at karaoke, but had to leave for emergency surgery right after you guys arrived. There," I sighed, my hands naturally going to my hips in defiance. "Does that satisfy your questions? Or do you want me to go into every encounter we've had since Nashville as well?"

It was clear by my tone that I was annoyed, and I almost wanted him to say yes so I could yell at him some more. I was tired of feeling like I was on trial, and

I would let him have it. Sitting down, I was glad for the decision a moment later when Slade dropped his bomb.

"That's impossible." He looked annoyed, like I was wasting his time as he massaged his temples.

"No, it's true. I was there for dinner," Simon offered. "He seemed nice. What does he have to do with this, though?"

"No," Slade said through gritted teeth. "I'm sure a *person* was there for dinner. I just meant it was impossible for it to be my brother."

"Um, well. Okay, whatever family drama you two have is between you. But I think I know when someone says, hey, I'm Thane Evans, Slade's twin. I wouldn't make that up."

Slade snorted, exasperation heavy in his stance. His whole body appeared like it might snap if touched. His jaw ticked as his breathing quickened, the muscles in his forearms flexing. When he calmed a hair, he finished filling us in. "No. I'm saying it's impossible he's my brother, because *Thane* has been in Liberia for almost two months with Vets Without Borders. He left a few days after we slept together. So you see, Peach, unless my brother has been lying to me about his whereabouts. It wasn't him."

Cold fear washed over me at what this meant. "But, but, but, no," I stuttered, violently shaking my head. "That's not possible." Turning to Simon, I tried to find some hope in him. "You were there. He introduced himself as Thane Evans. I-I-I..." I couldn't think anymore, the bottom had officially fallen out from under me. Simon's eyes were wide, and he looked back to Slade, realizing when I could no longer speak.

"If your brother is in West Africa, then who the Hell did we have over for dinner?"

"That's the question I'd like to know as well. I think…" he paused, sighing, his energy leaving him. "Maybe, Simon's right." I looked up at him, my head spinning from everything. Something in Slade's voice pulled me forward through the fog, allowing me to listen.

"Neither of us is at fault. We've both been played by this person, Peach. Someone has been toying with our lives for far too long. I don't know about you, but that royally pisses me off. Clearly, we have shit to work out," he stated, pointing between us both with his finger. "But I'm willing to listen… and accept I haven't given you a fair chance. If you are as well?"

He knelt down in front of me, taking my hands into his large ones. The ink on them covered mine, and they felt warm. The part of me accustomed to fighting with him for years wanted to junk punch him for good measure. However, if I looked closely, I could see how it covered a lot of hurt and pain even if at my own expense.

"Being nice to me now doesn't take away the pain you two caused me. I don't know if I'll ever get past that. I don't trust either of you."

He swallowed, and I noticed an emotion in his eyes I didn't want to acknowledge. He nodded, squeezing my hand. "That's fair. I haven't been the nicest or my best the past few years. Can we try to be friends at least? We were once the best of them."

I stared, not wanting to give in to the man who'd hurt me. But the girl who had been in love with her pen pal and then epically crushed on her hot bossnemy wanted to believe there was a different ending for her story that didn't end with her in tears and alone.

"Okay, friends," I agreed. "You have a lot of groveling to do. Can you answer me one thing first, though?"

He nodded, his thumbs circling my palms, and I found it soothing. "Why do you call me Peach?"

Slade gave a rueful smile, the corners lifting up as his eyes heated. "Because you're the prettiest peach there is. Your skin reminds me of peaches and cream, and it was the drink you had that night... before I knew who you were. I'd wanted to lick it off your lips, so it became a way to punish myself for wanting you so much."

"You wanted my skin?" I asked, confused.

"No, *Peaches*. I wanted to drown in your fucking cream."

NOX TO THANE

From: noxsmiles@heartsemail.com
To: blazetats@heartsemail.com
Subject: Only of coral. Prepare to laugh.

Moony Blaze,

I immediately downloaded the song and loved it! That was epic! How amazing would that be? To travel and sing, getting to do what you love? I mean, of course, assuming I didn't die of stage fright, or puke all over people. I could see that happening too.

So, funny story, huh?

Okay, it wasn't very funny for me, but you'll probably laugh. Because I don't know if I agree with you today that having a younger brother is better after this incident.

So, I'm taking a shower and Noah comes in. It's not totally uncommon, I mean, we share a bath-room and he's little and sometimes he has to go, so whatever. He comes in and is all cute and innocent.

"Lenny?"

"Uh, yeah, bud? I'm a little busy right now?"

"Do cats like to get wet?"

"No, I don't think they do. Can we, um, talk about this later?"

Instead of answering or leaving, he opened the curtain and launched the cat at me. So here I am trying to cover myself, and he's screeching in laughter, running away after tossing the poor thing at me.

Thankfully, I jumped out of the way and the cat landed on the tub, only scratching my leg in the process. Once my heart rate decreased, I was able to pick up the screeching thing and drop it out of the shower.

You're laughing aren't you?

Yeah, well, I hate you too.

I'm going to listen to the song again.

I don't really hate you,

Nox

Chapter Three
LENNOX

I STARED INTO MY MUG, zoned out as I waited for the one friend I'd made since I'd arrived in Nashville to show up. Exhaustion didn't even cover how tired I was today. Thankfully, it was my day off, allowing me a chance to sort out the mess my life had developed into overnight. Cheese on toast! What a doozy this was turning out to be. Slade's words echoed around my head in circles, the truth he'd spilled ricocheting off the reality I'd come to know.

Blaze. Blaze. Blaze.

It was like whack-a-mole to get them to go away. As soon as one would stay locked in its hole, another would pop up. I was tired, and didn't want to think about what they meant anymore.

There had been a small part of me last night that had wanted to let Slade and Simon stay at my apartment with me. But I knew I needed time to decompress the mess of everything or my head might explode trying to put the pieces all together. Plus, with both of them there, I'd be too distracted to sleep. Not that it mattered in the end, since I'd laid in bed staring at the stars on the ceiling all night thinking.

Where had everything gone so wrong? Could it all really be that simple?

Yet from the moment I started high school, my life felt like it had been sent off on a trajectory, the only direction, a crash course headed for disaster. Was the world out to get me? Or was I the maker of my own failures? Could it all be coincidental?

Questions and thoughts raced around my mind all night, and it was enough to make my head pound today with all the possible theories. My thoughts were a mess. It felt like all the drawers inside my head had been flung open, a strong breeze sent through and the papers scattered everywhere. None of it had any meaning and trying to find the one piece of information that would make it clear was impossible.

Sighing, I took another sip of the lukewarm coffee as I thought about what Simon and Slade had revealed. It all felt like a jumbled pile of goo, the lies a warbled mess of duplicity I couldn't escape.

Si texted me this morning informing me they were staying in town for a few days. I didn't know why it had surprised me, but I'd assumed they would've gone back to Kentucky having said their piece, running off into the sunset together. Of course, it wasn't like we'd spent hours last night catching up. I had no clue what they'd been up to, too afraid to know if they were together. For some reason, that thought alone, of whether or not they'd become a couple plagued me the most.

I wanted to know... but I didn't. Knowing meant accepting it.

When the booth jostled, I looked up from the mug and found a pretty blonde with sparkling emerald eyes smiling down at me. As usual in her presence, I couldn't help but smile back.

"Hey, Darce."

"What's up, hot stuff?"

Shaking my head at her, I waited for her to get situated and we ordered before I started in on my drama. Darcie had been one of my first clients at Equinox Ink, and when she'd invited me out to go dancing with her and some friends, I found myself agreeing. It had been a fun escape from everything that was Lennox James.

"How did your set go last night? Sorry, I couldn't make it, Damon called in sick, so I had to cover. I'm so gonna catch him lying one day, and then I'm going to ream his ass."

"I think you just want to boink him," I jested.

"Girl, no."

"Uh-huh."

Rolling her eyes at me, I noticed the smile that had tilted up slightly at the edges when she'd mention his name. Darcie could deny it all she wanted, but she wanted him. Smiling inwardly, I took another sip, wincing when I remembered its temperature. *Yuck.* Putting it down, I observed my friend as she attempted to avoid my discerning gaze.

Darcie was a manager at a line dancing bar, and despite her constant bickering about the place, I knew she loved it. She was too beautiful for her own good, though, always falling into bed with the wrong men. The fact she liked Damon but wouldn't admit it told me how scared she was of dating a nice guy. Not that I had room to talk. Clearly, I had issues when it came to dating myself, and avoidance had always been my solution. Not that it worked, my current state was a prime example of how hiding got you nowhere. In the moment though, it always seemed like the perfect solution.

Ignore. Ignore. Ignore.

Unfortunately, I couldn't ignore my problems any longer. Not when they slapped me in the face with reality.

"What's the deal with Thane? Your text sounded like something might've finally happened," she asked, her voice jolting me back to the present.

"Oh, well." I fidgeted, not sure how to explain. "*Something* happened, but not what you're thinking."

"Okaaaay. Quit being cagey and spill the beans already!" She laughed, making a face at me.

"You're so impatient, Darce," I chided, but found myself smiling. Her infectious personality had already begun to ease some of my stress. Rolling my eyes at her this time, I straightened my shoulders as I prepared myself to share.

"Ugh, okay. I'd asked him to come over afterward, you know, thinking about seeing if things could develop more between us. I know he's been wanting it too, waiting for me to be ready." She sat on the edge of the booth, eagerly listening, encouraging me to share. "Butttt... before anything could happen, Slade and Simon showed up."

"Shut the front door!" Darcie slapped the table, sloshing the cold coffee onto the surface.

"Yep." I nodded, wiping up the splatter. It was an excuse to drop my eyes from hers really, hiding my emotions again.

"Well, and? Was it epic? I bet it was epic. Did they sweep in and lay claim? Was there a fight? Are they all in jail? Is that why you're here and not shacked up in bed? What did Thane do?"

"Slow your roll, Darce. I swear you're like a freakin puppy."

She held her hands up, backing away from the excited stance she'd taken, after practically leaping across the table at me.

"And *none* of that happened. You watch too many movies," I huffed before continuing. "Slade sang a heartbreaking song, Thane left before it was over, and then I sang an anthem letting them know I wasn't the same ol' Lennox, and they couldn't just come in with their big dick energy and hypnotize me into forgetting how they broke my heart."

"Mmhm." She nodded, pressing her lips together to keep her words in. Sighing, I waved my hand in front of her face to tell her to go on. She popped like a balloon with too much air as it rushed out and she began her rapid firing of questions at me.

"That sounds soooo romantic. Did they look hot? I bet they did. Did you want to lick them? Why did Thane leave? What did they say? Are you seeing them again? How can you not see how in love with you they are? I haven't even met them and I know that! They can hypnotize me with their dicks any day."

She finally quieted, swooning in her spot at the notion, missing the waiter who brought our food drooling over her. He placed her coffee and pancakes in front of her as he waited for her to notice. *She did not notice.* This wasn't an uncommon thing. Darcie tended to like the guys who were unavailable. She'd yet to tell me why, despite me spilling all my secrets one night over ice cream. There was a story there, I just hoped she felt comfortable enough to tell me one day.

"Yeah, all yours." I waved, but my stomach turned inside at the thought of them with anyone else. I didn't even know if I *liked* them, or if I could even be with both of them. Not to mention, if I even *wanted* to be with both of them. However, the thought of them being with someone else, *even Darcie*, made me want to listen to angry music and thrash around a bit. Yeah, not a fan of that idea either. How was I supposed to figure this out if my own mind couldn't figure out what the fudge it wanted?

"Uh-huh, sure. Your *face* says otherwise." She chuckled before digging into her pancakes, a loud moan leaving her at the bite. Every male within hearing distance watched her with hungry eyes, and my beautiful friend ate on, clueless to the hearts she broke daily.

"Soooooo," she prodded, waving her syrup covered fork in my direction when I didn't answer her insane questions. Sighing, I gave in, knowing she wouldn't stop until she got what she wanted and began to tick them off with my fingers.

"It was *not* romantic. Unfortunately, they did look hot, but no, I don't want to lick them. Thane had a vet emergency. Simon said he missed me, Slade yelled a bunch, and *no* they're not in love with me. I think that covers it."

Lowering my hand, I hadn't paid attention to Darcie, so focused on dismissing her probes, I'd missed her reaction. So when I met her eyes, I found them huge, focused on something behind me. Confused, I tilted my head, preparing to ask her a question, but before I could open my mouth, a deep, sexy timber I knew all too well, breathed into my ear.

"I think you're leaving out a few details there, *Peach*."

My breath caught, my face flaming as Slade appeared to the side of the booth with Simon in tow a few feet behind him. Slade crowded me, squeezing into the booth, not caring there wasn't enough space for his large frame. His body pressed into mine, the heat of his touch searing into me. Slade ignored my stare, and reached across the table, offering his hand to Darcie. She was still frozen, her fork halfway to her mouth, the syrup dripping onto the table.

Despite the reason for her mishap being heartbreaker 1 and 2, it was quite humorous to see my usually unflappable friend stunned.

"Hello, I'm Slade, it's nice to meet a friend of Peach's."

Darcie went to shake his hand, forgetting it was the one holding the fork, and managed to shove her pancake into his outstretched palm.

Sputtering, I couldn't stop OJ from going up my nose at her reaction to him. In some ways, it was rewarding to see her just as affected by his alpha-male hotness. In others, I wanted to stab his hand with the fork and smush her face in syrup for the mere fact he was nicer to her than he'd ever been to me. Perhaps, I still had some aggression to work out where Slade was concerned. The angry music thrash-a-thon looked imminent for my future.

A napkin appeared under my nose, and I turned to see it belonged to Slade, as he looked right at me. There was a slight tilt to his lips as he waited for me to take it. This whole personality shift toward me was hard to reconcile. I mean, he was still a cranky buttmunch, but he no longer seethed hatred toward me. It was a slap to the face when I comprehended how much he *had* hated me in order to treat me like he did. It was sobering to think someone could despise you *that* much.

Snatching it, I wiped my nose, fighting the urge in me to say thanks. The laughter had died down in the meantime, and Darcie slid over, allowing Simon to sit next to her. I couldn't take Slade's body touching me any longer, so I picked up my purse against the wall and moved it between us. It gave my body some much-needed separation. However, the smirk he wore didn't go unnoticed from the corner of my eye. I hated he knew how affected by his body I was. Dagnabit!

"You were saying, *Peach*?"

"Nope. I said everything."

"Um, hi, I'm Simon," the other side of the heart-break duo offered.

"Darcie, LJ's Nashville Bestie. And I know all about y'all. I think you've got some 'splainin to do." I could've kissed her for giving it to them, supporting me despite the fact a mere ten seconds ago she was swooning. Girls unite! I had *so* needed a friend like her in my life.

"*Ouch*, you wound me with those words. Say it isn't so, Lenn. Have I been replaced?"

"Well..." I shrugged, not having it in me to soothe him. I held his eyes, and he nodded, accepting my words. His face fell, and I felt terrible, but one night of secret revealing didn't mean I magically forgave them for all the pain and events that had led to me being here in the first place. Darcie picked up on the awkwardness and, in her bubbly self way, jumped in to save the conversation.

"So, I know y'all have some things to work on, but any plans while you're here? Gonna check out the Wild Horse Saloon?"

"Oh, um. Not sure," Simon answered, finally dropping my eyes as he turned to her. "We hadn't really made plans other than to find Lennox."

"Well, that settles it then. We're all going. Tonight! I teach a class at 5 pm, and I expect you all to be there. Even you, grumpy butt." She lifted her eyebrows to Slade, who only smirked, not answering. He stretched and laid his arm on the back of the booth like he was some guy out of a romcom. The move was so casual and innocent, yet when he started playing with my hair, it felt like he was caressing my entire body with reverence based on the attention he gave to each strand.

Pull it together, girl! You will not be swayed with sexy boy magic.

He reached over to grab a piece of bacon off my plate, and I shifted out of his reach. Taking a bite, Slade held my gaze as he licked his lips slowly, dragging his tongue intentionally over a corner lip piercing. Hot jealousy rushed through me at the realization he'd gotten a piercing done by someone else done during my absence, or worse had replaced me at Emblazed Tats. The fact *I'd quit* was lost on me at the moment.

Scowling, I turned back to my plate, pulling the rest

of my food out of his reach. I couldn't stop the words from rising up out of me though a second later, spewing the visceral rage onto him.

"*Nice* piercing. Hope you checked their references thoroughly as you did mine. Though, it's a little off. Clearly you had to get sub par help in my absence. I'm sure they're not as qualified or as friendly as me." Sitting back, I huffed in annoyance, crossing my arms.

"Oh, this?" He brushed his thumb over it, carefully dragging it across his mouth, dropping the lower lip as he did. Hot chocolate lava cake, that was hot! The fart knocker was deliberately trying to seduce me! At this point, the rest of the booth and the restaurant faded away and I became lost in his espresso eyes, now so full of light at knowing he had me.

I didn't want to admit how hot and bothered it made me. Stupid boy! Stupid boy and his hot guy swagger! Clearly, I needed to put him in his place.

"No, the one on your dong, buttmunch."

The level of sarcasm in my tone was top notch, and I inwardly applauded myself for the zinger. In fact, it was so stellar, it took Slade by surprise, causing him to choke on the bite of bacon he'd just stolen. He coughed, his face turning red at the violent motion, and I worried I'd killed the dude. Wouldn't that be just the way it would go? Curse 2.0.

Breaking news! Lennox Elaine James, murderer! The weapon used? Sarcasm!

Thankfully, Darcie shoved a glass of water at him, and he drank it, saving himself from choking. Once he'd collected himself, he wiped his mouth and gave me a rueful look.

"James, I can't believe I'm saying this, but I've missed that mouth of yours." He leaned closer, moving my hair back so he could whisper into my ear. His fingertips brushed lightly against the pulse point in my neck causing my heart rate to speed up. His breath skated along my skin, goosebumps rising to the occasion as he spoke, and I concentrated on releasing my breath I'd unknowingly held. "Oh, the things I want to do to you. You'll cave first, *Peach*. You can't be mad at me forever."

The usual obstinance I felt in his presence rose, and I found myself laughing in his face. "We'll see about *that*, Evans."

Turning back to the table, I found Darcie and Simon watching us from across the table, heated looks on both their faces. When they saw me turn, Simon winked, not hiding his desire, while Darcie fanned herself with her hand.

"Oh, wow! I mean, I thought I knew what sexual tension looked like, but *nope*, that's the hottest thing I've ever seen. I think I need to go find a cowboy and save that horse, pronto!"

Shaking my head, I chuckled at her nonsense, she was too much not to love. "They're all yours, Darce. I gotta go anyway. I'll see you tonight, though."

Pushing on Slade's arm, he didn't budge, only lifting his eyebrows in question. Clearly he had no intention of letting me leave here. Too bad, Tatzilla. Tossing my purse strap over my body, I pulled out cash and placed it on the table, silence all around me as the three of them watched. Leaning over the table, I gave Darcie a hug before vaulting over the back of the booth.

Thane was all smiles, picture-perfect as usual, and Slade stood with a permanent scowl on his face glaring at whoever was taking the picture.

"When was this taken?"

"Oh, um, a few years ago. It was right after he opened Equinox Ink."

I dropped the phone at his statement, the sound of it clattering on the tabletop loud, and I cringed before looking up, eyes wide. "What did you just say?"

"That Slade owns Equinox Ink. I thought you knew?"

Shaking my head, I had no words. "Nope, can't say I did." Rage boiled to the surface as my face grew warm. Just how many things was Slade keeping from me? I didn't think I knew him at all.

"Yeah, well, he's had it for a few years. About a year before he opened the one in Kentucky, actually," he said thoughtfully.

Through gritted teeth, I spit out my last question. "Is there anything else I should know?"

"Just one thing."

"What?" I held my breath, not sure I was ready for any more bombs that might crush me.

"I uh, was there, that night too. I'd come to meet Slade, not realizing he'd made plans to meet up with you. Your hair was different then, you didn't have the blue ends, so it took me a while to piece everything together. But I saw him talking to you, and for once, I was jealous of my brother because he held the company of the prettiest girl in the place. I stayed back watching for a while, and well, I don't know how to say this, and I'm sorry for not saying it sooner. It's just that when you said you weren't going to see him again, I figured you were safe." Thane stopped, uncertainty now covering his brow as he watched me. I was getting tired of his drawn out stories and just wanted him to get to the point already.

"Just tell me, Thane. Get it over with." He nodded, biting his lip as he prepared to destroy me.

"I believe Slade was the one to spike your drink. In fact, I know he was. I saw him."

He handed me his phone again, and this time it was a grainy picture of that night. It was hard to see, but I spotted the outfit I'd worn that day, leaning against a bar talking to a younger Slade. Everything started rushing forward as the picture unlocked some of the repressed memories—the music, the smell of the place, the taste of the drink on my lips.

The picture depicted Slade grabbing some drinks. As I clicked over, it began to play out like a flipbook. In one, his palm was over the top. In another, he lifted it up to look at the bottom. Then one with him swirling the drink around, before the last one. Slade handing the drink to me. The one he said he named me after.

Touching my lips, I peered into Thane's kind blue eyes, sadness and understanding reflected there for me. Holding his gaze, I said the word that destroyed my heart.

"*Peaches.*"

THANE TO NOX

From: blazetats@heartsemail.com
To: noxsmiles@heartsemail.com
Subject: How many tacos can you eat?

Hello, my Noxy girl,

Okay, I admit it, I did laugh. How could I not? Picturing you shrieking as a cat was flung at you had me rolling on the floor. But afterward, I did wonder if you were okay? So, are you? As you discovered, cats don't typically like water, so I'm sure it wasn't pleasant for either of you.

I'm glad you like the song. I wish I could hear you sing it. Maybe someday?

I've been thinking that lately I might want to travel the world, see what is out there. I've traveled my whole life, but I still feel like there's more to see, more people to meet, and more things to enjoy. When we get to a new city, I always go to a local place and try the food. I walk around the

downtown streets and try to get a feel for the people and city. My brother doesn't join me anymore, it's hard to think about growing apart from your best friend, but it's happening. He hasn't really been the same since Mom died.

If I'm honest, neither have I, but someone has to be strong. Dad's trying, but he keeps moving us for his job, thinking it helps but we just need him in our lives. They weren't even still married at the time, but I think he feels guilty for divorcing her.

Guilt is a heavy thing.

Sometimes I feel guilty for being able to do things easier than my twin. When we were young, everything we did was together, and we balanced one another out. It's not like that anymore and our differences are even more prominent. I miss him though.

If you were to go to a new city, what would you do?

Hope you are well and smile a little when you read this. I do.

Laughable Blaze

Chapter Four

LENNOX

MY PLAN TO face things and quit running went down the drain an hour after I made it. The information Thane provided had me spinning, and I couldn't discern any of it. So, I turned off my phone and decided to go on a hike. Nature and fresh air were my solaces when my mind was too busy to focus.

Huffing, I made it to the top of an incline, the sun beating down on me, and I cursed myself for wearing jeans. It felt weird, but I hadn't been able to bring myself to fall back into the fun-loving Lennox I'd been. My heart had been broken, the pieces scattered all over the floor, and I didn't know if I could ever put them back together the same way again.

Sitting down on a bench, I looked out over the hills and valleys and felt peace for the first time in days. It shouldn't surprise me that I found comfort here. It had been one of my and Duncan's favorite things to do, and Duncan had always had a way of making me feel calm. It was his superpower.

FOUR YEARS AGO

"You want to walk up a hill... on purpose?"

"Yeah, it'll be fun. Come on, LJ. Just try it."

The cutesy nickname had me softening as Duncan turned his green eyes on me, and I found myself nodding in agreement. This was our third date, and things were going really well with us so far. He made me laugh, was fun to be around, and looked at me like I was the only girl in the room. Duncan had a way of making all the other noise disappear when I was in his presence.

"Well, I guess I better put on some different shoes. I'll break my ankle if I try to hike in these."

Duncan looked down at my platform wedges and cringed. "Yeah, do you have tennis shoes or hiking boots?"

"Uh, no to the hiking boots." I laughed. "I don't ever try to purposefully sweat, but I have some old tennis shoes somewhere."

Bending down, I started to rummage through the million pairs of shoes I owned. I never threw any of them out, and always insisted I'd organize it one day. Every time that day came, though, I never felt like doing it. A pained sound came from behind, and I froze. The slight draft I felt had me realizing my dress barely covered my panties from this angle.

"Um, LJ, I didn't realize it was show and tell."

Holding the back of my dress down, I backed out slowly, the tennis shoes clutched in my other hand. I kept my face to the ground as I attempted to keep the rest of me covered in the process. "Ha! It was a test, and you failed. Congrats."

Standing, I walked over to the bed, ignoring him as I took off one set of shoes and put on the others, but stopped when I noticed I'd forgotten to grab socks. A

pair appeared in front of my eyes, and I snatched them, looking up from under my eyelashes at him.

Duncan smiled adoringly at me, crouching down to look at me head-on. "I think you're the cutest girl I've ever met, LJ. You constantly surprise me and make me laugh, even when you're blatantly lying."

"I—"

His fingers pressed my lips closed, and I stopped, sucking in a breath. Duncan had been conservative so far in his physical touch, and this was the most hands-on he'd been. Slowly, he drew his finger away, trailing it down my jaw as he cupped it. He watched me the whole time, making sure I was okay. When he started to lean in, I closed my eyes, ready to feel his lips on mine.

They touched mine softly, a warm pressure against my own. Tingles raced down me as he held it there. When he moved, I met his efforts, and the passion exploded between us. What had started as a simple kiss, turned into an hour of intense making out, only stopping when we heard my parents returning home. I may be twenty-two, but I didn't need them walking in on me kissing a boy.

Fixing our clothes, we laughed when we realized we never made it hiking.

PRESENT

The memory of our first hike, or well, what was meant to be our first hike, had me smiling as I stared off into the quiet space. I'd never told anyone I did this, but every now and then, when I was struggling, I'd find some hill and sit, and I'd talk to Duncan.

"Hey, Dunc. I miss you. I hope you're holding down the fort and having a blast wherever you are." The breeze kissed my cheeks, and like always, it felt as if he was there with me, answering back. Tears sprang forward, and I let them fall, needing to let them out.

"So, I've made a royal mess of things. You're probably not surprised, though. You always said my special brand of chaos is what made your day. I never understood that, but I appreciated it all the same. It made me feel like I wasn't actually deranged or alone. But since you've been gone, I feel like it's been even worse. I no longer have an anchor keeping me grounded. I'm pinging all over the place, and I can't find my way. How do I even know what to trust if I can't trust myself or my own memories from that night?"

Sniffling, I leaned forward and grabbed a leaf that had fallen. It was mostly dead, and it crumbled in my hand as I played with it. I wiped my hands together, sending the dead leaf tendrils into the air, and I watched them as they floated away.

When I sat back, I realized that while I'd been playing with the leaf, deep in thought, an older woman had joined me on the bench. She didn't look at me or comment on my tears, just let me be, and I appreciated it.

Pulling my legs up, I balanced on my elbows as I continued to look out over the area. It had been around ten minutes or so when she spoke, her voice was soft and soothing.

"I love coming here. It always feels so peaceful."

"You come here often?" I asked, turning and looking at her, my head laying on my knees.

"Not as much as I'd like. It's harder for me to make it up the hill, but on good days, I do."

"Today was a good day then?" For some reason, I found myself engaging with her, curious about what brought her here.

"Oh yes, a wonderful day. I woke up to a visit from my grandchildren, and I felt a spring in my step. I just knew I needed to get up here. I'm glad I did. It seems I needed to meet you."

"Me?" I asked, sitting back as I touched my chest. She looked over at me, a kind smile on her face. Her appearance didn't give much to go off, with her grey hair, soft eyes, and wrinkly skin. She wore a purple sweater and jeans and appeared innocent and sweet. The woman was the picture-perfect version of a Hallmark grandmother. She let me inspect her, waiting until I was done before she responded.

"Yes, dear. I heard part of your message earlier. I didn't want to interrupt, so I waited. But when I heard you speak, the grief and pain were palpable in your voice, and I knew I was meant to talk to you."

"But why?" I ignored the fact this stranger had heard me bare my soul and focused on the crazy part. Did she believe in fate or angels? Neither had ever done anything for me. In fact, I was sure my guardian angel's wings had to be broken.

She scooted a little closer, taking my hand in hers. "I can hear your heartbreak and despair and how it's become this monster you're so scared of disrupting, that instead of facing it, you let it wreak havoc in your life."

"No, that's not it," I immediately said, shaking my head in denial.

She gave me one of those looks older women seemed to have a patent on, telling you how far-fetched whatever you just said was. I sighed, dropping my head, unable to bear her knowing gaze. "It's just, I'm so tired of being hurt, of being the one left behind."

Her free hand lifted my chin, wiping the tears falling from my face. It should've felt weird disclosing all this to a random stranger, but it was the south, and we tended to trust until we had a reason not to. Plus, her presence was comforting, and she made me feel cherished. How I had longed to feel that, my family was too far away to give me my daily doses.

"Oh, sweetie, that's one of life's hardest lessons. Every great reward comes with great risk. It's all a game of chance in the end."

"I don't think I have anything left to chance then."

"You know, I once loved a man who was all wrong for me. He was daring and impulsive, and he made me feel alive in a way no one in my sleepy little town had ever done before. My mama told me he was bad news, and I'd regret the day I ever met him. But I didn't listen, and when he asked me to run away, I did."

"Did you live happily ever after?"

"Oh honey, no." She chuckled. "My mama had been right about him being bad news. But she was wrong about me regretting it. Now, it was hard, don't get me wrong. I thought life was going to be one way, and when it didn't work out the way I'd planned, I panicked. I held onto something I didn't need for longer than necessary because of fear. But once I stopped and took a look around at my life, I found myself exactly where I needed to be."

"What if where I need to be doesn't exist? I don't know who to trust."

"The thing about trusting dear, we feel it in our bones. You just gotta trust yourself to know. Our body picks up all those hidden cues our brain stores away, the ones our heart chooses to ignore at times. Trust... it's more than a feeling. It's history and experiences, but most of all, trust is a promise. No one is going to be perfect, but you can't fake genuine emotions." She paused, letting her words sink in. When she felt I'd had time to digest them, she patted my hand. "How about you tell me what's troubling you, and I'll see if I can help."

Nodding, I exhaled and spilled my guts to the kind stranger I hadn't even asked the name of. I told her about my curse, about the letters, and about the night everything seemed to go awry.

"Now I'm having to look at everything and try to figure out who's lying. On the one hand, Thane hasn't lied to me since I've met him outside the letter thing, and Slade and Simon have. But on the other, I've known and loved Simon my whole life, and Slade's been nice to me in moments, even when he didn't want to. I can understand now why he might've pushed me away if he thought I'd been faking knowing him this whole time. But then that means Thane's lying."

"What if they're all lying and all telling the truth?"

"I don't understand how that would work."

"Well, in my experience, people tend to smudge the lines a little to put themselves in the best light. It's not even a conscious decision most of the time. It's much easier to think of ourselves as the hero in our own stories and not the villain. But what if we're both? We might be our own hero, but then does it make us the villain in someone else's? Until everyone sits down and talks things out, you're never going to know. You can't be in the middle of it this way, having to choose. Now, being in the middle of an S&S sandwich… Now, that sounds delightful!"

"Ma'am! I can't believe you just said that!"

"What? Just because I'm old, I can't talk about sex?"

"Well, *yeah*." My eyes bugged out at her, my cheeks heating.

"I'll have you know, I was a rebel back in my day. They didn't call it poly, whatever it's called now, but I once had two boyfriends."

"You didn't?" I gasped, giggling. "You sly fox!"

"Well, I don't like to brag," she started, before grinning wide. "Actually, I do!"

We laughed together, and I felt lighter, her infectious attitude the jump I needed to restart my own system. She was right about the monster. I'd hidden from it, hoping to appease it by not talking about the hard things, but in the end, I'd given it control, stepping on eggshells around it not to disturb the memories that were too hard to bear.

"Your other fella, he'd want you to be happy, even if that meant being with three men."

"Three?"

"Mmhmm."

"But I don't have feelings like that for Thane. I tried, but it's not there."

"Well, you never know, dear. But until you face that monster, you'll never be able to move forward. Regardless of who you end up with, or what the truth is. Tackle that beast, and everything else might be clearer."

"You're right." I nodded at her sage words.

"Ah, it never gets old hearing that, and I should know. *I'm old*."

Laughing, she squeezed my hand one last time before turning and looking out across the valley. "It sure was nice to get up here today." She turned back, a sad smile on her face now, and I felt like crying again. "Be brave, and jump, sweetheart. It's way more fun that way."

Nodding, I hugged her petite frame, pulling back as I wiped my tears. "I'm so glad I met you. Can I know your name?"

"It's Babs. Babs Taylor."

"Well, it's been an honor to meet you, Babs. I'm Lennox."

"I know, dear, Duncan told me."

"Duncan?"

She only smiled, getting up, and walked over to a man I hadn't realized was waiting. He looked like a home health worker, dressed in scrubs. He situated her in a wheelchair and began to push her down the hill, smiling as he passed. I watched, too shocked to say or do anything else. Had she known Duncan somehow? Was she actually delusional and spoke with spirits? Or had she simply overheard me say his name?

I turned back, taking a moment to shake off the grief, hoping the grief monster would start to dwindle and give me the courage to finally be brave and look at that night myself. Heading back down, a plan began to form in my head, and I turned on my phone, sending the same text to three people, ignoring all the others.

ME: I'll see you at the Saloon at 4:30 pm. Meet in the Cowboy Room.

NERVOUS ENERGY COURSED through me as I waited in the upper-level dressing rooms, watching for them below. Darcie was next to me, finishing up her look for the night. She'd teased her hair and had on some daisy dukes, cowboy boots, and a red plaid shirt tied under her boobs. She looked hot, but it wasn't her, and every time I saw her in this outfit, I couldn't help but giggle.

"Your hair gets bigger every week."

Darcie puffed up the ends, making a face at me in the mirror. "The bigger the hair, the bigger the tips, darlin'."

"I could never do this job. I'm not nice enough."

"That's where you're wrong, sugar plum! You're the sweetest. It's just your defense mechanism keeping people away."

"*Okay*, Dr. Phil." I rolled my eyes, looking back out to the floor. The line dancing hadn't started yet. A few patrons were below, flitting in and out, drinks in hand as they mingled. There were two classes a night and then dancing the rest of the time. Buck walked in a moment later, whistling at Darcie, and I turned to see what he was wearing tonight. When I caught sight of his outfit, I almost fell out of my chair at the sight.

"Oh my gosh, that has to be my favorite outfit ever!"

Standing, I bowed to his awesomeness. Buck preened, pumping up his arms in a macho man pose. Buck was known for his costumes, and despite being heterosexual, he played up his good looks and physique, pulling in a different crowd than what regularly entered the Saloon. Tonight, he was dressed in short lederhosen suspenders and a white puffy sleeve shirt. He had on white socks and boots, a fake mustache, and leather wrist cuffs.

"Thanks, LJ. I had to represent Oktoberfest. Any chance I can talk you into dancing with me tonight?" He begged, and I shook my head. Buck was a huge flirt and was always trying to get me to dance, go for a drink, or sing a song with him. Chuckling, I shook my head but shrugged in the end.

"Who knows, we'll see." He fake swooned, making Darcie and I chuckle.

"I'm afraid her dance card is full tonight, Buck," Darcie interjected. "You'll have to make due with me."

"Oh, now this is *interesting*." He moved over to me, and I could tell he wanted me to say more, but I ignored him, focusing back on the floor below. Simon and Slade entered together, and I simultaneously felt elated and rejected when I saw them. My feelings were all over the place, and I realized how right Babs had been today. I couldn't keep ignoring this, not if I wanted to move forward in life. Hiding only gave power to my demons.

"*Damn*. Well, at least I know it's not me."

"Hm?" I asked, turning to Buck, his face softening, and I saw real emotion behind his eyes.

"All this time, I thought you were just blowing me

off, but now I see your heart's already taken. I'm just not sure to which one."

"Yeah, me either," I mumbled. Taking a deep breath, I walked over to Darcie and hugged her, promising to be out later to watch her dance if things didn't blow up in my face.

"No worries, girl. Catch up with me if you can. Besides," she leaned in, whispering, "it looks like I might get to console Buck tonight. I think he was really crushing on you. *Who knew*?" She pulled back, winking, and I turned to look at Buck and caught him staring, a sad smile on his face. Waving, I walked out, not sure what to make of that. Hopefully, a night with Darcie would cure his feelings toward me.

I hadn't seen Thane yet, but it was close to the time, so I hoped he'd be here soon. I headed to the room Darcie had reserved for me, hopeful things would finally be clear.

THANE

Everything spun out of control as I watched Lennox walk down the stairs and head toward the room she'd texted to meet in. My breathing increased, becoming labored as I envisioned them touching *my girl*. I guess Lennox had decided to face her fears finally. Tugging at the ends of my hair in frustration, I paced the small alcove I stood in, debating my next move.

At lunch, I'd thought Lennox had finally been convinced to leave them once and for all. Her hurt had been so visible on her face, I didn't think she'd ever be able to forgive him. I'd hated to do it, but I'd been saving those pictures for the perfect moment to show her Slade's betrayal, the last thing in my grand plan to win her over to me.

Apparently, even his lies were more of a draw than *me*.

I'd wanted to do this the old fashion way. Boy meets girl, boy and girl fall in love, boy and girl live happily ever after.

But Lennox continued to make this harder than it needed to be.

If she proceeded to test me, then I'd have to remind her what was at stake. If she still didn't fold, I'd have to make her, even if that meant taking her.

It wasn't ideal, but it was better than the alternative. Lennox James would be mine. The amount of others who had to perish before it happened depended on her.

Stomping down the stairs, I couldn't wait to get out of the filth-ridden bar. In my haste, I bumped into Darcie before making it out of there. I didn't stop, though, powering down the stairs needing air.

I had plans to make, and playing Mr. Nice Guy wasn't in them at the moment. Quickly, I pulled out my phone and texted Lennox I couldn't make it. I had to forcibly stop myself from lashing out at her, asking why she brought them here. I'd punish her later for the subterfuge.

The crowded street blurred together as I focused on my new plan. It was time they remembered Lennox James was *mine*.

NOX TO THANE

From: noxsmiles@heartsemail.com
To: blazetats@heartsemail.com
Subject: 10, but I'm working on it.

Sweet Blaze,

Since you asked if I was okay, then you're forgiven for laughing.

I've never traveled further than a few hours from my home. I sound so boring compared to the life you've lived. But I like the concept of getting the feel for a place.

Here, that's Miss Patti's baked goods, the subs at Mancino's, and the lemon shake-ups at the fairs. It's the sound of the cannons on Friday night when a touchdown is made, and the band during their halftime show. It's the sound of Corvettes, and laughter at Beech Bend Park.

It's sitting on porches and swinging, catching fireflies with your neighbor, and taking a meal to someone when they're grieving. My town's small, but the people here have big hearts. It's the best part about the south.

Just look past most of my peers and all the gossipy women, that is.

The good people are there and I see them.

I couldn't imagine losing a parent. I complain about mine at times, but losing one of them, I don't know how I'd cope. What's your secret? How do you manage that pain?

There's a school dance this week, but I don't think I'll go. I made my dress because nothing at the stores that fit my body was cute. You won't know this, but the clothing industry is sizeist. They make clothes for curvier girls in either a block shape, or in heinous colors. Beware when it's both! Just because I have curves, doesn't mean I don't want to look cute, or want to be in fashion! But I digress... I made a dress, but so far, no one has asked me to go. Before you ask, I did ask someone and they said no. So, that sucked monkey balls.

It would be cool if you were closer and we could meet. Then maybe I wouldn't have to go to things alone. If you'd want to go, that is. What would you do if we had the day to spend together, but nothing else?

I think I would take you to Lost River Cave, or maybe even the dinosaur park! Oh, that would be the best!

I hate hearing how much you miss your brother. Maybe try asking him to join you? Go do something you both used to like doing? I have no real advice. Noah basically enjoys farting and coloring and one of those I agree to do with him. I'll let you decide which. It's not the farts.

Dancing with the fireflies,

Nox

What the ever-loving donkey balls! My mouth dropped open, the words fleeing as I stood, gawking at him, shocked by his statement. I hadn't expected him to be so disarming, and I didn't know if I could trust that this was him being honest, or if it was another mind game. Slade took my shock as an opportunity and sauntered closer, his cocky swagger on full display as he approached.

His finger lifted, and I tracked it as it came toward me. Slade closed my mouth, pushing my still open jaw closed, never taking his eyes off me as he spoke.

"*I'm all in, Peach.*"

Blinking, I reset my brain, working hard to stay up to speed with the racing thoughts running through my mind as they battled it out. "I don't get it. How are you capable of going from one extreme to the next? You hated me for years, and now you what? Love me?"

"You weren't listening, Peach. I said it would've been easier if I could hate you. Not that I did."

"Then why have you been such a butthole towards me these past couple of years?"

He sighed, hanging his head for a second. Slade's hand now cupped my jaw, a touch I didn't find myself hating. When he looked back up, he moved closer, touching our foreheads together.

"It was the only way I could stop myself from making out with you every damn day. You infuriated me with your sexy ass and your ability to walk around and be all hunky-dory when my heart had splintered. I thought you were pretending you didn't even know who I was, that I'd meant *nothing*. The simple fact you could ghost me and rub it in my face by how unaffected you were, well it enraged me. And I tried. I tried so hard to push you away."

"Yeah, well, you were pretty successful there."

He closed the last remaining space between us, invading me with his scent and sexual arousal. Both hands cupped my cheeks, and I sucked in a breath. Slade's dark eyes bore into mine, and for the first time ever, I saw all of him bared to me—heart and soul.

There was no way this was a lie. Yet, how did it explain the picture Thane showed me? How did it excuse him from stealing his brother's letters? My gut told me I knew who he was though. Even at his worst, I knew Slade Evans.

"I'm sorry, Peach. I'm so sorry. I regret never saying anything and believing my Starry Nox could hurt me that way."

It was the perfect thing for him to say. I closed my eyes, unable to look at him any longer. A tear slipped free, and my heart ached. It would be so easy to give in right here, to let Simon and Slade comfort me and distract me from the hole in my heart.

"Now that we have all the information, all the cards on the table, I'm not gonna let you walk away."

"I don't think I can give you, *either of you*, what you want," I whispered. His thumb brushed against my cheek, wiping away the tears.

"What happened during your time away then? If you came to that decision," Simon asked.

I stepped back, unable to keep my resolve if Slade kept being tender. "I uh, well, I first had to go meet with somebody, just to kind of see for myself."

"You met with *him*, didn't you?" Slade asked, his voice going heavy as his breathing increased.

"Yes," I admitted. "I met with your brother."

"*Not* my brother," he professed violently.

"Whatever your family drama is, that's between you two."

"He's. Not. My. Fucking. Brother," he bit out through clenched teeth. At least this Slade, I was able to distance myself from. "My brother is in Africa. How else am I supposed to prove that to you?"

"Well, he claimed you made that up, and that well, you were the one to steal his letters and spike my drink."

The room went silent for only a second before Slade stormed over, wrenching the door open, and stomped out. I stared, stunned he'd left. "Well, that makes it easier," I sighed.

Simon walked over, but before he could comfort me or say anything, Slade walked back in. His breathing was still quick, but he'd calmed some. The oddest thing was his face and hair were dripping with water, the top of his shirt also soaked through.

"Why would I make that up? That's the most random place to pick. I don't even know where Liberia is, for crying out loud."

Slade stared at me, asking and I realized he'd left to calm down instead of striking out at me. Something about him sticking around, and not lashing out at me showed me he was being honest.

"Yeah, I mean, I don't know, okay. Thane had a picture of you guys together at the tattoo shop. That's how I knew he wasn't lying about being your brother since you were clearly in it. Which, hey, one more thing you kept from me," I groused. Taking a few deep breaths myself, I focused on the current problem at hand. "Do you have a picture of him or you guys together?"

He sighed, closing his eyes, exasperation heavy in his tone when he spoke. "Peach, I have a fucking flip phone. I don't have pictures on it."

"That's right," I snapped. "You're so weird with your flip phone."

"I hate social media, so what do I need a smart-phone for? I have the Instagram account for the shop, which I pay Adam to manage because I suck at it. I suck at social crap. Satisfied?"

"You do have that one thing…" Simon started, before reaching over and snagging something out of the back pocket of Slade's jeans. They were tight, and I might've drooled a little as Simon's hand brushed his butt cheek to pull it free.

He waved the device in question and I focused back on what was safe to look at. It looked like a phone. It was skinny, silver, and precisely resembled an iPhone. Had Slade just told me a bald-faced lie to my face?

"What is *that* then?" I pointed. "It looks suspiciously like an iPhone to me."

"It's my mp3 player."

"Still looks like an iPhone, and what do you know, mine plays music too."

Slade smirked, enjoying my sass if the grin was anything to go by. "It's an iPod Touch, Peach. Music only, no phone."

"They still make those?" My eyebrows rose at the

revelation and I tried to recall if I'd ever seen him using it before.

"Yeah, well, it's old."

"Lucky for us then that the one thing you do care about is music and are willing to buy something decent for it," Simon teased playfully, sticking his tongue out at Slade.

I watched their interaction, enamored at seeing them flirt with one another. Slade's eyes twinkled, amused by Si's antics. Jealousy combined with the feeling of being left out of their exchange surfaced, and I swallowed as I tried to ignore it. I didn't want to feel that way toward them.

"Yeah, well, guess what? It has pictures on it."

I perked up at the information as Simon started scrolling through them, muttering under his breath. "Seriously, how many pictures of tattoos does one man need?"

Snatching it out of his hand, I spun as I started to scroll myself. "Simon's right, all I see are tattoos. Oh, look, more tattoos, and some more tattoos. Here's some girl's ass, and then tattoos, tattoos. Oh, look, another picture of a girl's butt. Ah! And here is one of her boobs. Geez, Slade, creep much? And here I thought you were above all that." I shook my head as I kept scrolling. "And more tattoos. Okay, you're officially boring."

I handed back the iPod, and Slade promptly shoved it in his pocket before responding. "Now first, did you really say *ass*, Peach? And second, it's not *some* girl's ass. It's *yours*."

"Why do you have a picture of my ass?" I shrieked,

planting my hands on my hips, avoiding the redness heating my cheeks at his admission.

He chuckled, the deep sound rolling over me like a tidal wave. Why the man had to look and sound so good was criminal.

"You didn't answer the question, *Peaches*."

His smolder hit me in the feel-good box, and I had to forcibly keep myself from moving my legs in response to the pulsing between them. The sexual innuendo had me all aflutter. Tilting my head up, I didn't care if I looked like a petulant child as I answered him. "I can say ass if I want to."

"It sounds so dirty coming out of your mouth. It makes me want to—"

Holding my hand up, I cut him off. "Stop your thought right there, mister. I do not need to hear it right now. It'll just scramble my brain with your alpha-sexy magic voodoo."

"Fine, at least you admit I'm sexy," he grinned, liking the effect he had on me. "And why do I have pictures of you? Because—"

"Because you need spank material," Simon interrupted.

"Simon!"

"What?" He grinned, not caring I'd called him out. Slade sighed, shaking his head at the two of us.

"Because," he emphasized, pausing to make sure we weren't going to interrupt this time, "I like looking at you, Peach. Okay?"

Throwing my hands up, I groaned. "I just, I don't know what to do with this information! We've hated each other, or well, you hated me. You told me... you told me I was *nothing*." I tried to ignore the way my lip had wobbled, or the emotion I'd let escape.

"Fuck. I'd hoped you hadn't remembered it after your head injury. I regretted it the moment it was out of my mouth. I hated myself for saying it even if it came from anger."

"Words still hurt, and I can't get over it as fast as you. I've been living with one version of you, I don't know how to live with this one. Plus, I'm not sure how I feel about you having pictures of my body."

"Those aren't the only pics I have. Most of them are of you peripherally, but I didn't want you to see how obsessed I was. There are only two of your butt, and the one of your boobs was an accident. I promise. I'd tried to take a pic on the sly and then had to move, and that's what I caught. I didn't delete it and I'm sorry for that."

Slade did look contrite, but it was so hard to rationalize it in my head. He moved closer in my contemplation, carefully touching my arms. "I'm not just getting over it, or whatever it was you said. Don't you get it, Peach? There was nothing for me to get over."

"I don't understand. None of this makes sense to me."

"I'm sorry for that, Peach. I really am. But for me, I thought you were pretending for years not to know who I was, and I struggled with my feelings about it. I hated you at first, but the more I got to know you, I saw the person behind the letters. My conflicting feelings have been warring within me for years, and it was why I acted so hot and cold at times. I couldn't stop the way I felt even when I needed to. I hate that I've hurt you in the process, especially once I realized you didn't know.

But it also freed me. It's just as easy as a switch for me because it set me free. I could finally quit lying to myself that I didn't love you, Peach."

His words hit me like a ton of bricks, and I sucked in a breath, taking a step back from him. Shaking my head, I held my hands up again, hoping to physically put some distance between those words and me. "I… I can't hear this right now."

"Then when?"

"I don't know, I um…" I trailed off, uncertainty and doubt filling my head. Simon stepped forward and grabbed my hands, rubbing small circles over them in a soothing pattern.

"What do you need, Lenn? Tell us what it is you need."

With his grey eyes boring into me, I found myself spilling everything in a rush. "I went and talked with Thane, and he had a different take about what happened. He uh, he made those claims, but they don't really make sense, like Slade stealing his letters and spiking my drink. It did make me realize I have to quit hiding from everything that's happened. So, I went for a walk, to a place where I felt connected to Duncan. I go sometimes to just talk to him about things, and it helps. Today, I met this really bizarre and totally amazing woman who was delightful. She helped me understand things aren't always what they seem, and that sometimes, people can be telling the truth and the lie. Ultimately, it made me realize something important."

I stopped, taking a breath, peering over at Slade. I kept waiting for him to throw shade at me or hurl a sexual innuendo that would push my button, but he stood there, listening. His eyes met mine, and I found softness there as he looked at me, the corners wrinkling.

"What did you realize, Peach?"

Swallowing, I held his eyes as I answered. "That it doesn't matter what happened that night, or at least in the sense of trying to figure it out step by step, I mean. Of course, what happened matters. Obviously, Dun-can died," I stuttered, the words hard to spit out. "And I was almost raped and kidnapped or whatever. I need to deal with it instead of ignoring it. So yeah, I guess it does kind of matter. I just can't let the monster get me. Geez, I'm talking in circles."

I shook my head, dropping it as I took a few breaths to slow my ragged breathing and hopefully my erratic speech. After a few minutes, I peered up and looked at both of them. I wanted to hate them, to rage at them for the heartache, but that was only a different form of hiding. I couldn't hide behind fear, any more than I could avoid the problem. It was time to slay this monster.

"I have to figure it out on my own. And until I do, I'm not going to be ready for any relationship, curse or not."

"So, what you're saying is, you're not ready? Not that it's a no?"

"I'm saying… I don't know if I'll ever be ready. But in order to try to be, I need to work on myself first."

"Does that mean we can be friends?"

"Yeah, I mean, I'd be okay with that. Are you guys okay with just being friends for now until I sort out everything in my head?"

"Lenn, if it means I get to be in your life, then I'm

okay with it. Of course, I want to be more, but I'm not going to push you. I hope it will return to how we left things, but I've always been your friend first, your best friend. And that's what I'll always be, no matter what."

"Thanks, Si, that means a lot to me." I smiled, my shoulders relaxing. Glancing between the two, I hadn't missed the fact Slade hadn't responded to my question yet. He stood there, staring at me with a level of heat in his eyes I wasn't used to. "I guess we were never friends, so I understand you not wanting to be Slade. So, what about you two?"

"What about *us*?" Slade countered, not answering or dismissing my question.

"Are you guys like, I don't know, together, now?"

"No." The vague responses were getting old. I was about to tell him where he could shove his answers when Simon filled in the silence.

"We haven't ever been what you would say 'together'," Simon offered, casting a glance over his shoulder at the silent statue masquerading as a man.

Slade's eyes flicked over to him briefly but then back down to me. I couldn't take his stare and everything he apparently thought he was communicating with his eyes, so I turned back to Simon. I didn't expect the hurt that filled my voice, but it was already out there before I could call it back. "Why didn't you ever tell me, Simon?"

"There's no good reason. I thought you guys hated each other. And I didn't want to rub it in your face that one night when he and I were drunk, we kissed, and then it developed into a mutual benefits thing on occasion."

I nodded, not really understanding his reasoning but accepted it. "Why didn't you ever tell me that he was Blaze?" This one was harder for me to accept.

He sighed, taking a breath, squeezing the hand I'd forgotten he held tighter. "Because by that point, I'd already been screwing around with him. I felt guilty enough as it was, and when he told me how he was convinced you knew who he was, I couldn't believe it. I vaguely remembered meeting him at the bar that night, so I assumed you knew, but didn't want to talk about it since it was connected to that night. Then... well it became something I didn't want to bring up, and it hurt you," he paused. "Selfishly, I wanted to keep him to myself." Simon shrugged, his cheeks tinting a little at the confession.

"Ahh, you like me, Si, you really like me."

"Shut it, Slade."

I giggled, covering my mouth with my free hand, not expecting their banter to be so cute. A whole new feeling of arousal hit me, and I focused on asking the one who was willing to give information. "Did it ever become more?"

"No," Simon answered, "because after having to lie to you about where I was going or who I was with, I couldn't do it anymore."

"It hurts that you guys kept it from me," I admitted, biting my lip. "I guess y'all kept a bunch of stuff from each other though." I sounded even bitter to myself with that comment, and I reigned in the passive-aggressiveness and focused on moving forward.

"I think it would be a good idea to set some ground rules if we're going to be friends, to even have the opportunity or chance to be more than that. We have to put everything out on the table and be honest. There can't be any more lies, no more secrets. I want to learn to trust y'all again, and I need to learn to trust myself. In order to do that, I need to know we're all working to be honest with each other if I'm ever going to get past it."

"I'm on board. I hated keeping secrets from you, Lenn, and it hurt keeping this one. I was miserable, and it only made it worse not telling you my real feelings."

"So, what do we do now? How do we move past it all?"

I looked at both of them, hoping they had the magic answer. Slade hadn't said anything in a while, so I assumed he was standing by his earlier proclamation that he was all in. When neither of them offered a solution, I resigned myself to being the planner of the bunch.

"Well, we have about ten minutes until Darcie's class starts. So, we might as well go and get a good spot. She's looking forward to teaching you guys the dance."

I wasn't surprised when Slade huffed, crossing his arms as he fixed his eyes at me. "You really expect *me* to line dance, Peach?"

"Yeah, I do, actually. I think it'd be fun." I lifted my chin in defiance, not backing down from the stare-off.

"Fine. I'll dance for *you*, Peach." He stalked forward, leaning down over me. "But I'm not gonna like it."

"I wouldn't expect anything less from you, Tatzilla." He smiled, almost killing me on the spot, effectively destroying my panties. Cheese on toast! It would be hard ignoring him if he kept that up.

"I've missed your sass, Peach," he rumbled.

Rolling my eyes, I stepped back, trying to alleviate the temptation and give my hormones a break, and probably why my response came out sounding juvenile. "I'm sure, probably about as much as I missed your face."

"Ah, I knew you liked me, James."

Sighing, I ignored him and his too-cute smile and was thankful when Simon walked closer, wrapping me in his arms. I held him close, breathing his clean scent in again, needing to fill up my Simon bucket after missing him for months. Slade moved closer to us both, his body heat announcing his presence.

It still felt odd having him this close and acting friendly. My body responded to him, but my heart reminded me what was at stake—itself. So with great strength, I pulled back from both of them and crossed my arms, needing the protection.

Slade cocked a smug grin, his crooked smile becoming my new favorite thing until he leaned his arm on Simon's shoulder, and the two of them side by side became my favorite thing. Wowzers! The familiarity and comfortableness between them was evident, making my mind wander into naughty land.

"Before we participate in the torture, we really need to discuss Thane. I don't trust whoever this dude is pretending to be my brother."

"Why do you think he's pretending? Like *who*? What?" I jerked my head in confusion. "What's the purpose of impersonating someone? I don't understand why he'd do that and lie to my face."

"Obviously, to get closer to you."

"Why would they want to get closer to me?" I

scoffed, not buying Slade's reasoning. Simon didn't say anything but didn't disagree either. "They could come up to me and be themselves. It's not like I'm scary. Thane isn't pretending. There's no purpose."

"You're right, you're not scary, Peach, you're intimidating as fuck. You're crazy beautiful and don't even realize it. You're dude kryptonite."

"Pfft," I rolled my eyes. "Don't try to sweet-talk me now, Slade."

"Oh, is that what you think sweet talk is? How about I show you what sweet talk really is, Peach."

He stalked closer, and my breath caught from the mere look in his eyes. I had to remind myself I didn't trust him for the millionth time, that I was still mad at him, and that I wanted more for myself. Now was not the time to be thinking with my vajayjay, so I pushed him back before he could touch me.

"*Friends*, Slade. Boundaries."

"Sure, sure, Peach. I'll show you boundaries."

Changing the subject, I focused back on what we'd been talking about. "Well, I guess Thane's not showing up," I acknowledged, sadly. I'd really hoped to settle this tonight.

"Why would he show up? He can't. He's not the real Thane. My brother is abroad, and faker knows he can't face me or he'd be outed. Think about it, Peach. Did he know I was going to be here?" He had one of his self-satisfied smiles on his face, thinking he was right and I was the dumb one. I wanted to wipe it off so bad.

"No. I just told him to meet me here. I sent the same text I did to you guys. I didn't say anything about who would be here."

"Still fishy. He's lying to you. I'm gonna call my brother next time and prove it."

"Fine," I exhaled, over this topic already. "We'll figure it out later. I just, I don't understand why he'd lie to me. He's been nothing but nice. He even helped me save a cat once. Why would someone save a cat and lie to me about this? It doesn't make sense. Crazy people wouldn't do that!"

"Doesn't have to make sense to you," he shrugged, confident in his assessment.

Groaning, I threw my head back. "Come on, let's go."

Finally, we walked out into the main area near the bar. It was a lot fuller than before. I spotted Darcie up above, and she gave me a wink before giving me a look asking how it went. I shrugged my shoulders and smiled. While I still didn't know exactly what happened that night, I would get there when I was ready. Right now, I was at a place where I wanted to breathe and work my way there. And I would.

I found an open spot and pulled Simon and Slade with me, placing myself in the middle. After a few minutes, Darcie came out on stage hyping everybody up. She clapped her hands above her head, her hips wiggling back and forth as she danced. Buck followed her out, and I didn't know who the whistles were more for, her or him.

"Howdy, folks! How y'all doing tonight? Y'all here to learn some line dancing? Well, if so, give me a holla!" She cupped her ear, waiting for everyone to respond.

"Yee-haw!" rang out around us, and already I felt

lighter, the atmosphere penetrating my sadness and pushing it away for a moment.

"That's how you do it, folks! Okay, let's get to it then!"

The music started, and she showed us a two-step. I learned instantly that Slade was a horrible dancer, and Simon was a decent one. Mostly, I found myself laughing for the first time in months. While things weren't perfect, heck, things were nowhere near perfect, I still felt like maybe there was a light at the end of the tunnel.

When they walked me home that night, I remembered to check my phone and found a message from Thane.

Thane: Sorry, Cherry. Emergency surgery. Can't meet tonight. Drinks tomorrow?

Something Slade had said wormed its way to the surface, sinking into my consciousness, and for the first time, I doubted Thane. So I didn't respond, figuring I'd wait to see how I felt in the morning. Pushing it back in my bag, I regarded the guys when we made it to the shop.

"I guess I'll talk to you guys later. Are you staying or heading back?"

"We have one more day. Maybe we can have lunch tomorrow before we go?" Simon asked, hopeful.

"Yeah, I think that'd be okay. I have to work tomorrow, but I'll let you know when my lunch break is."

"I'm sure the boss will give you a night off if you ask nicely."

"Ah! That's right!" I exclaimed, smacking Slade on the shoulder. I'd forgotten earlier in the barrage of questions he hadn't answered. "Why didn't you tell me you own this place too? And how come I could get an apprenticeship here but not back at Emblazed Tats? Hmm?" Once I started, it spewed out of me, and I found myself on a roll. "And you wonder why I don't know how you feel about me! Because of stuff like this!"

He held his hands up in a placating gesture, but it made me want to smack him more. "Sorry, I didn't want to give you a chance before as a way of punishing you, and that wasn't fair. I was an asshole, Peach. Okay? You already know this about me. I held a grudge and took it out on you for making me want you so damn much. I'll probably always be apologizing because, let's face it, once an asshole, always an asshole. When you moved here, I told your dad you could stay in the apartment as a way to make it up and keep you safe."

"Wait, it's your apartment too? You're my dad's buddy? Has there been anything truthful?"

"My feelings for you."

His face was serious, and I couldn't deny he meant what he said even if I didn't trust it. My anger deflated, and exhaustion covered me from the emotional whiplash I'd experienced today.

"Fine."

"Since we said we're starting over, cards on the table, and all that," he paused, nibbling on the lip piercing. It wasn't intentional this time, more of a nervous gesture. "I named it after you."

My mouth hung open, and he immediately leaned

forward, using my stunned silence to his advantage to kiss my forehead before walking away. Gaping at Simon, I searched him for any answers.

"I didn't know that, and I promise, no more secrets on my end."

He kissed my cheek and then jogged to catch up to Slade. Walking in, I climbed the stairs in a daze at the implications.

Equinox. Nox.

Emblazed. Blaze.

Fudge, he really was Blaze then. So, Thane had lied?

Too tired to think of what that could mean, I stumbled in the dark as I undressed, not even turning on the lights as I climbed into bed.

When an arm wrapped around me a second later, my eyes popped open and I screamed, scrambling out from under the covers. I slid across the floor, bumping into the wall as I tried to slow my breathing and find my pants where my phone still was.

Son of bee sting! Slade was right again and someone was after me. I needed to call for help, I needed to get out of here! Moving toward the door, I kept the bed and imminent danger in front of me. Unconsciously, I froze when the lamp next to the bed flicked on.

My flight or fight reflex kept me immobilized and I sat on the floor, watching as feet touched the ground. Bare legs followed, and when they came into view, I stared up at my predator, and found hypnotizing blue eyes staring back.

THANE TO NOX

From: blazetats@heartsemail.com
To: noxsmiles@heartsemail.com
Subject: I'm glad you're here

Dear Noxy girl,

I made a big decision today. It will affect the next four years of my life, and hopefully more. It felt scary doing something different than my twin, but I think it will be good. We've grown apart over the years, and maybe out of one another's shadow, we can shine more. When I hit submit, I couldn't wait to tell you though.

I started reading the book you talked about last time and I have to say, it's great. Maybe we can share book recs and talk about them? I really like the characters and story building.

I was thinking also, what if we did a version of truth or dare? We trust one another to go through with the dare, providing evidence as needed. Or putting the truth in writing.

I'll go first, truth or dare, Nox?

Thanks for being there to celebrate with me, even if only electronically. My dad will be happy, but he also expects it, not caring about the stress, and my brother doesn't care about me at all anymore. My friends are superficial, so you're the only one who will understand the risk I'm taking.

Until next time, how are you being brave today?

Truthful Blaze

Chapter Six

SLADE

STALKING OFF, I quickly made myself leave my heart, knowing if I stayed, I would kiss her until she couldn't breathe or say something to get me slapped. Neither needed to happen; kissing her wasn't an option with how things were at the present, and I didn't fancy getting slapped today. So I left, needing space to breathe. Shoving my hands in my pocket, I made my way down the street. A minute later, Simon caught up to me, panting slightly at my brisk pace.

"What are you thinking? I know you're over there devising some scheme."

I peered at him from the corner of my eyes, gauging his expression. In some ways, I knew Simon inside and out, but in others, he was still a stranger to me. Our relationship was complicated. It had been filled with duplicity and smeared lines more often than not.

"I'm thinking," I finally answered, "I need to figure out who this asshole is that's pretending to be my brother."

"Ooh, spy mission!"

"Simon, it's a good thing I like you." I chuckled, shaking my head at his nonsense. "You're so fucking weird, man."

He merely shrugged, a smile covering his whole

face, and I registered how little he'd done so in the past few months. Lennox's absence had affected him more than I'd wanted to admit, my denial and anger covering my own sadness at her vacancy.

"Yeah, but you like it."

"Yeah, I do."

I found myself agreeing, as I reached over and took his hand, watching to see if he would be okay with it. When he linked his fingers with mine, I relaxed, a giddy excitement filling me at holding hands with the boy I liked. No one on the street batted an eye toward us. The city was progressive and had a large LGBTQ+ community. It was the south though, and Nashville was the epicenter. Outside of it, flaunting our relationship would be riskier. Acceptance of all love was one of the things I missed about the west coast, well that and the ocean.

So taking the moment for what it was, I soaked in being able to hold Simon's hand for once. I'd never grasped how freeing it would feel to have everything out in the open. Si and I didn't have to hide from anyone anymore, not even ourselves.

"So, you're thinking he's an imposter?"

"Definitely an imposter."

"Then it's decided. I think we need to do a stakeout. See when she's going to meet with him next."

"As much as I want to figure out who this asshole is, I don't want her around him again, or to lie to Peach."

Simon thought it over as we walked, dodging other couples as we made our way down the block. It was getting late, meaning there were more drunk people on the streets as the town started to wind down.

"You're sure it's not your brother? You've never talked much about him."

I nodded, not wanting to admit there was a small percent of doubt. I wanted to trust my brother for once. We'd worked hard to get our relationship back to this level and I didn't perceive him to be someone who would throw it away now.

"When I met him at dinner, this Thane, he fit every detail I knew about him from your letters over the years. If it's not your brother," he paused, glancing at me, the worry creasing his brow. "Well then, I'm scared it's much worse than we want to admit. This guy knows details, enough to convince me."

I considered his assessment of the situation, something tugging on my consciousness. "I know I haven't ever wanted to talk about Thane, and I'm kicking myself for that at this moment. I won't deny things haven't been difficult for us over the years, because they have. But one thing I know to be certain is that Thane and I don't lie to one another anymore. Especially about whether or not we're even in the country. There's no fucking way he's back in the city without messaging me. No, I don't buy it."

"Do you think it's just not wanting to face the fact he could've been lying to you this whole time?"

"No. I won't even entertain the thought without proof."

"Okay, then we figure out who it is and get proof for Lenn."

I stopped, realizing how much I'd needed his support on this. "Thank you for trusting me. I'll call him right now. The time difference is weird, so hopefully, it's a good time."

Simon nodded, and I kept hold of his hand, using my other one to pull my phone out and hit his speed dial number. It might be a flip phone, but it worked. Unfortunately, it went straight to voicemail.

"Damn, he must be in an area without a signal."

Sending him a text to call me, I pocketed the phone and found Simon watching me closely. Concern and desire swirled in his grey eyes, and I found myself falling into their incredible depths. Swallowing, I knew I had to have hearts in my eyes as I stared back. Swiftly, I schooled my features and cleared my throat as I began walking again.

Fuck, I was getting in way over my head too soon. I'd felt the gauntlet of emotions today from pure relief to regret, and lastly, determination to win Peach back. It would be easy to fall into Simon's arms, seeking comfort without any solid commitment, but we deserved better. Deciding to be mature, my new declaration in relationships, I brought up the topic I'd always been too scared to ask, afraid he'd pick Lennox over me. After all, my twin brother had at one time.

"What is this between us? We both told Lennox it wasn't anything serious but is that where we're leaving it? We never talked about the future before."

My heart hung in my chest as I waited for his answer. I knew he'd always pick Lennox first. He'd loved her his whole life, and honestly, I didn't blame him. I would too. Lennox was an integral part of my heart. I hadn't been able to let her go even when I thought she'd broken mine. Knowing now that she hadn't, that we'd all been played, made me want to kick myself for never giving in sooner and talking to her. My stubborn pride and my innate belief I would always be discarded had kept me from loving her sooner.

Simon was important to me, too. He'd been my friend first, and then over the years, we'd confided in one another our confusing feelings. He became my confidant, my sounding board, and someone I'd come to genuinely enjoy being around. And when you were a surly bastard like me, there weren't many people I could say that about.

He blew out a breath, peeking over at me. I kept him in my peripheral, a trick I'd perfected over the years to watch Lennox. I didn't know if he intended to, but he squeezed my hand before he spoke, and it comforted me.

"I think it's something I'd like to talk about. Something to discuss with Lennox, even. I just didn't know if you wanted to wait until things were more settled down the road?"

He bit his lip, and I snapped, my Simon kryptonite flaring to life inside of me at the sight. Pushing him against the building, I crowded his space as I leaned my body into his. Simon sucked in a breath, fueling my fire for him, his noises and submission my weakness.

"I don't," I purred. "I'm tired of waiting for life to settle. It's always been a 'wait until' or 'when we get to this point', and I'm over it. I've already wasted years being angry. I don't want to wait for us to figure this out either, just because we're scared. But," I stepped back with forcible effort as Simon groaned, "I know I want to figure it out with Lennox."

"You mean that? All of us together?"

I nodded, and the smile that had seemed to light my world on fire lit up his face again, and my heart took off, soaring.

"I dreamed of us all being together, not having to choose, but I didn't think it would be a reality. Are you sure you could share her with me?"

The hope in his voice killed me in the best way. Groaning, I turned, adjusting myself, and grabbed his hand, needing to get home before I lost it on the street. I pulled him down the sidewalk, walking fast as we weaved in and out of people. Simon held on tight, though, following me wherever I led him.

When we made it through the front door, I pulled him hard into me, crowding him again. "Being with you both would be my everything."

I kissed him, not able to hold myself back from both of them tonight. My hands cupped his face, his stubble scratching my palms as I moved them up, grabbing onto his hair like a lifeline. Our lips found one another, fitting together in a way only Simon and I could. It was aggressive and violent, our teeth-gnashing as we wrestled for dominance. Fueled by passion, the savage kiss melted into a frenzy, and I found myself thrusting my hips into him, rubbing my erection as I looked for some relief. Somehow, I managed to pull back a few minutes later, our breaths heavy as we stared at one another.

"Let's do it right this time, Simon. If we're getting a chance, let's do it in a way that makes every love song and sappy movie jealous. You're my Fish, I caught you, and now I'm not letting you go."

"I forgot how sweet you could be. I'm digging this

possessive side, though." His eyes searched mine, his hands still clasped on my hips firmly. "I finally see the man I've always known you to be. It's like I'm getting the best versions of you now. I get the sweet boy of my past who I madly fell for through his words and the man my body craves with unbridled passion in ways I've never experienced before. If I get the whole of you, I'll go as slow as needed, jump through whatever hoops to have it. I think we can all be what we need. You, me, and Lenn. I'm all in, too."

Grinning, I kissed him briefly before letting him go and walking away. "I think we should enact a no more touching clause until we talk with Peach just so we reduce temptation because I really want to turn you around and fuck you against that wall right now."

Simon swallowed, eyes fixed on me. They started to travel down my body, lingering on my tight jeans. I rubbed the outside, and he moaned. Spinning on my heels, I quickly made my way to the room I was sleeping in, slamming the door behind me. Leaning against it, I breathed heavily, laughing as I heard Simon cursing under his breath too.

It was one night. I could do this. Locking the door for good measure, I fell onto the bed face first, hoping it would suffice for my cock.

It did not.

Before falling asleep, I found myself stroking my still hard dick, imagining Peach and Simon, all three of us together and naked. I came so fast that I almost worried something was wrong. It was my ultimate fantasy, though, and one I'd denied envisioning for fear of being too tempted or disappointed when I couldn't have it.

Sated, I fell into a deep sleep, my dreams happy for once.

THE MORNING LIGHT crept through the window, blinding me as the sun rose. Squinting, I threw an arm across my eyes before rolling over on my side. The nightstand was directly in front of me, my phone charging on it. Reaching out, I pulled it to me, unhooking the cord as I fumbled with it, my eyes remaining closed.

Pulling it close, I saw there was a message I'd missed last night before I'd called my brother.

Bro: Battery almost dead. Will call when in the city.

Not caring, I pressed the call button, but it went straight to voicemail again. Groaning, I tossed it onto the bed, the device offending me with it's inability to give me the answers I wanted. For the first time, I wished I had one of those smartphones so I could track his ass down. Maybe I'd go get one today and get Si and Peach off my case. It wouldn't hurt to upgrade anyway, and perhaps now I could keep real pictures of Lennox on my phone. The desire to have access to her at all times surged through me so fiercely, I sat up, knowing I needed to make this happen.

Having my Peach in my life meant broadening my horizons, especially if the payoff was more of her. I didn't think she quite understood my obsession with her yet, how savagely I loved her, but she would. There hadn't been a day since Nox came into my life that I hadn't thought about her in some shape or form.

Taking a shower, I got ready for the day, the determination from the night before still coursing through me to make this the future I wanted to happen. The fantasy I'd had before bed started to filter back in, and I smiled, the sensual scene had felt so tangible, and I'd been filled with happiness imagining the two of them. It only confirmed my feelings.

I wanted them both, and I wouldn't stop until I had them.

I'd never liked school, but I'd learned to work hard, and owning two tattoo parlors might not seem like a lot for some, but at the age of twenty-eight, it felt significant to me. My father had given me my college fund to use as a down payment once I'd completed an apprenticeship. He'd given in to the fact I wasn't going to school and had told me I could use it for whatever made me passionate as long as I showed him commitment.

It had been the best conversation we'd ever had, and for the first time in my life, I felt seen by my father. He wasn't trying to make me into my brother but had accepted me as my own person. He'd even come and visited the shops, impressed with what I'd grown. It had taught me I could be successful in things I felt motivated by, that I could work hard and earn recognition. Motivation had been something I'd lacked in school, but once I discovered it in myself, my whole perspective changed.

Obviously, my demons still plagued me, or I wouldn't have believed I wasn't worthy of love, frozen in my fear and belief I wasn't good enough for three years, punishing myself for a night I'd wish had ended differently.

THE REST OF THAT NIGHT

"Starry Nox?"

The beautiful girl, who'd stolen my heart in the few moments we'd spoken, concentrated on saying something, but when she opened her mouth, vomit spewed out, hitting me, the putrid smell filling the cramped hallway. A door sounded, and I stood, a scowl on my face as I tried to shake the puke off my hand.

"Fucking gross," I muttered. Lifting my eyes, I was surprised when they landed on my brother. He froze, a cup of water and paper towels in his hands.

"What the fuck are you doing here, Thane?"

Scowling deeper, I grabbed some of the towels out of his hand, wiping my hands clean. Looking down, I realized it had gotten on my clothes and shoes. Fucking great. I'd worn my favorites, wanting to impress Nox, who was supposedly the passed out girl on the floor.

When Thane hadn't replied, I peered up at him, finding his face still stuck on that expression as he gaped at me. I heard the liar on the ground mumble something, Thane's eyes finally moving to look at her, but I was past the point of caring what the hell this shit show was. Pulling Thane into the men's bathroom, I washed my hands and then wetted more paper towels, attempting to wipe it free of my clothes as best I could.

"*Thane*. Start. Talking."

"I uh, it's not what it looks like."

"And what does it look like? Hmm? Enlighten me, please."

"That I'm trying to take advantage of a drunk girl."

Tossing the useless paper towels into the trash can, I spun, bracing myself against the sink, and crossed my arms. Staring intensely, I waited to see if he'd say more.

"I promise, I just came across her in the hallway. Some guy was assaulting her, so I stepped in to help."

I knew this part, having watched it, but I was curious if he knew *who* she was. "So you decided to help some random stranger?"

"Well," he hedged, then deflated. "I know who she is. I met her a few years back, but then we lost touch. I was coming out of the restroom when I stumbled upon the scene and stepped in. You have to know I would never take advantage of a girl like that."

I watched him and realized he was telling the truth about this, but I wasn't sure how far it extended. Rubbing my chin, I debated what to say. *How* had he met her exactly? Was he in on her whole catfish scheme? Had they devised this plan together to hurt me? Or had she chosen him over me like so many others had? Was he the one Nox had been dating, and things were getting serious? So many thoughts swirled in my head, the alcohol adding to the disorientation, making them chaotic.

"Why are you here? At *this* bar?"

Thane's brow creased at my question. "I was going to have a drink with Adam. He just finished his shift, and had texted me to join him when I got off work. Why are you here? I figured you'd be out with Nox."

Thane said it innocently, but his betrayal had made

me question everything, and I hated it. "How did you meet her out there, then?"

Thane didn't like that I wasn't answering his questions, his huff of annoyance evident as I continued to ask my own instead. When I stared, not budging, he breathed out a long breath before answering this time. "Before I started school at UT, I met her at that throwback party Adam had dragged me to. You were too cool to come, remember?"

"It sounds vaguely familiar. Your point?"

"That's where I met her. She was Kelly to my Zack."

"And you haven't seen her since then?"

Rolling his eyes, Thane had gotten to his limit with my line of questions. "I'm not sure what your deal is with that girl, but no, I haven't. I gave her my number on a napkin. The party made us leave all modern technology in our cars or at home. But she never called after that night. I was just as surprised to find her out there as finding you. Now, have I passed whatever test you're giving me so I can tend to the drunken girl out there?"

"So, you have no idea she's Nox?"

He stopped, his back ramrod straight. He'd been moving toward the door before my question. Thane spun around, and the emotion on his face was so genuine I knew he hadn't. He looked stricken as a wave of emotions passed over him at the news. I relaxed, nodding as I walked forward and pulled him the remainder of the way toward the door.

"Nox? But how? Why was she with some other dude then?"

I stepped out into the hall, not answering him, determined to get to the bottom of the epic cluster fuck myself. Unfortunately, when we cleared the door, the hallway was now empty.

"Fuck."

Taking off, I pushed my way through the sweaty bodies, looking for her. I saw what could possibly be her being helped out the door, a guy in a hoodie next to her. Shit. I wasn't sure if she was Lennox, my Nox, but I didn't want her to be taken in her state either. Walking to the bar, I smacked it to get one of the bartender's attention. Adam was nowhere in sight, but Thane had said he was off, so he could be anywhere in the crowd. When a bartender saw me, they looked over relieved, and walked over with a card in hand.

"Oh good, I thought she'd left. Can you give your friend her card back? Thanks."

They handed it to me and walked off before I could reply. The receipt was long as I looked at the tab. Slowly, with trepidation, I glanced at the name on the card. I didn't know what I wanted it to say, honestly. But when I saw the name, *Lennox James*, it felt like a knife pierced my heart. The guy had been right. I scrunched up the receipt in my fist and stalked out of the bar. I bumped into a few people who weren't fast enough to get out of my way, not caring as I plowed them over in my rage. Thane chased me, catching me once we were outside.

"Slade, stop! What's going on? Where did she go?"

He grabbed my arm, and I twirled, slapping the card to his chest, my anger getting the better of me as I bit out my words. "Her fucking name is Lennox James. Congratulations, you were right. She's been catfishing me. I was just a joke to her. So much so, she sent an actor to play her tonight, not able to continue the facade. Of course, my luck was to come face to face with her hours later and feel a true connection with her. Joke's on me though, she's a liar and a fake, and I want nothing to do with her."

I stepped back, the card dropping from my hand as I walked off, leaving everything to do with Lennox James in my rearview.

When I woke the following morning, it was to a slew of Thane's texts and a link to a news article of a crash that ended with the death of a cop as the scene. I found myself rushing to the bathroom, emptying the contents of the night before into the porcelain bowl after reading it.

Had I done that? Was I to blame for her fate? Was my role in life to curse the women I love to die? My anger had seeped out of me last night, almost a tangible toxicity permeating the air. Had it reached out, taking on a life of its own in the process? Everywhere I went, I created havoc around me, and once again it appeared my rage had taken another life from the world in come-uppance. Just as it did with my mother years prior.

Guilt weighed heavily on my soul all day, and I found myself driving up to Bowling Green with the excuse of returning her card late that afternoon. I'd found it on the kitchen counter once I'd ventured out of the bathroom, Thane having placed it there. It gave me the excuse I needed though to attempt to assuage myself. It took two hours for me to build up the nerves to enter the hospital. When I walked down the hall, I found an older man sitting against the wall outside the room the nurse had given me. Based on his age and looks, I gathered he was Lennox's father.

"Um, hi. How… is she?"

He looked up, meeting me with tears in his eyes, and I sank to my knees, devastation settling in. I realized I might hate Nox at the moment, but I also loved her, and the hate didn't make love vanish overnight after being forged over eight years. A pain, unlike anything I'd ever felt, punctured me deeper than even the night before. Peering up, I found the man watching me, a look of recognition coming over his face.

"You're Blaze, aren't you?"

"*What*? *How*?" I stuttered, falling back from shock.

He smiled kindly, the corners lifting up slightly. "Son, I'm the chief of police here. Do you honestly think I didn't look into who my daughter was writing to for all those years? Once I knew you weren't a middle-aged man, I stayed out of it, but I knew she was going to meet you last night, and then something happened."

Accepting what he said, I nodded, liking his easy manner. He didn't judge, or overstep, but let her make her own choices. I liked that about him. "Is she… is she okay?"

The smile dropped, and I worried I was about to be crushed beyond repair for the second time in my life. First, my mother's death, and now, the girl who'd breathed life into me all those years ago.

"She's alive, but I doubt she'll be okay for a while."

"What… what do you mean?"

"The man that was killed…" he stopped, swallowing, tears falling down his face.

117

"Yeah, I uh, saw that on the news. A police officer on the scene, right?"

He nodded, collecting himself. "He wasn't just any police officer. He was her boyfriend."

The knowledge knocked into me like a blow. I blinked at Lennox's father as a tidal wave of grief cascaded down on me. Fuck. I hadn't wanted this.

"What happened?"

"All I know right now is there was a wreck, and when Lennox was being loaded into the ambulance, Duncan had walked back to possibly help on the scene, I'm not really sure. But he was walking backwards, and that was when the car jumped the divide, striking him. The paramedic said Lennox watched the whole thing, and they had to give her a sedative to calm down. The car sped off, didn't stop at all, and was found abandoned a few miles down the road set on fire."

"Shit, that's… "

Thane's messages flicked across my mind as things began to connect, reminding me how nothing good ever lasted in my life.

Thane: I'm sorry, I didn't know she was Nox. I promise I haven't gone behind your back.
Thane: I'll fix this. I'll make it up to you. Don't shut me out again. Please, Slade.
Thane: I'm doing something crazy, but I think you'll thank me in the morning.
Thane: I'm sorry. *News Link*

Nervously, I thanked Mr. James for the information, saying I hoped Lennox recovered okay, and handed him the card. I walked out of the hospital on shaky legs, and drove back to the apartment. I never asked Thane what he was sorry about, tucking it away into the far recesses of my mind.

PRESENT

The memory of everything that had occurred the entirety of that evening and Thane's texts had me wondering what he'd been sorry about. Had I read his messages incorrectly this whole time? What if he'd been sorry, because he was the one who'd been driving? *Shit.* The small percent of doubt I'd tried to quell, fought to rise up again.

Swallowing, I pushed the thoughts out of my head, not ready to face those without talking to him first. Plus, I didn't want to focus on them now when things were headed in the direction I wanted. I wouldn't distrust my brother until I knew.

Focusing on the present, I decided to go back to my roots. Now that the lies had been shed, and the pain had lifted, I could allow myself to admit the truth; the one I hadn't wanted to share with Lennox when she asked, not entirely anyway. Yet, I needed to show her how I felt and to do that, I needed to remind her who Nox and Blaze were to one another.

Pulling out my notebook, I wrote a letter, something I hadn't done in years, but as I sat there, pouring out my heart, it came back to me quickly. I'd initially won her trust and love with my scribbles and ink confessions, and I'd do it again, no longer hiding behind the smudged lines of fear. This was the way to win her back. I knew it.

SIMON POKED his head into my room, a curious look on his face as he noticed the guitar in my lap. He seemed content to watch me, so I kept playing, working out the last chords for the song I'd been working on. Once I'd scrawled down the words on my heart, creativity filled me again. Letters and music had always been connected to Nox; how I hadn't noticed it until now only proved how shielded I'd been to accepting her influence in my life. I hadn't wanted to admit it, but Lennox was my muse. She was my sunshine, and without her, life had become bleak, a dark shadow cast over me, hindering my ability to see what was in front of me.

I punished myself every day for the outcome of that night, for not letting go of my own anger and helping out someone who was intoxicated and in need of assistance. Lennox had connected with me before I even knew who she was, and *I liked her.* That alone should have meant something to me. I never liked anyone.

I became consumed with the what ifs and guilt of not doing more to stop the events that unfolded. What if I had tried harder and had put aside the pain? Maybe then, Duncan would still be alive. The part I didn't like to admit was how it made it easier for me, and the shame of that knowledge was what spurred me to punish myself day in and day out with her presence as a reminder of my own happiness at her pain. Anger and doubt had clouded my judgment, and I excused it because I was hurt.

I hadn't known Duncan, and while I hadn't wanted her to be in a relationship with someone else, it didn't mean I wanted him to die either, *especially* the way he had. The thing that kept me up at night, the piece that let me punish myself just to be around her, and would go out of my way to make sure she was always safe, was I never wanted her to have to experience anything else so tragic. If I could give her a moment, a second, where she wasn't thinking about him, then I would. Even if that meant she was sassing off to me, or angry with my commands.

I'd watch her, and I'd see her smile slip, something reminding her of what she'd lost, and I'd feel guilty all over again. Of course, I was an asshole, so I took it out on her for making me still care, lying to myself. I never said I was perfect, but I did try to make her life better in the ways I could.

I'd finalized the shop plans for Bowling Green, helping to relieve some of my guilt. I'd stayed in touch with her dad in the guise I was concerned about her. He gave me brief updates, and when I told him I was moving there and opening a shop, I asked him to keep our meeting private, not wanting her to think the job offer was charity. Yet, she walked in, acting like she hadn't known me, and all the guilt turned to hatred. Eddy, her father, told me it was to be expected, the trauma of the event blocking her from remembering.

I wanted to believe him, but when I found her watching me at times, I felt that same connection and didn't know how she didn't. It could only mean she was lying to my face, pretending she didn't know. Eddy and Simon both felt I was wrong over the years when they put the pieces together. They urged me to talk to her, but I was too scared to learn if I'd been wrong all those years. They'd respected my wishes to keep it between us, though they never agreed with my choice. It was another choice to add to my regret column.

"What's up?" I asked, laying the guitar down once I'd finished.

"Just wanted to see if you'd heard from Thane?"

Shaking my head, I stood up and rechecked my phone, but there still weren't any messages. "He sent one saying his battery was dead that I'd missed, but nothing else. Fuck. What if I'm wrong, Si? I don't know what to think anymore. I thought we were past this. I mean, at one time, I wouldn't have blinked an eyelash considering that he'd done it. But I didn't think he'd betray me again, not after rebuilding our relationship over the past five years. We're almost back to where we were as kids. We've been supportive of one another and communicating. I mean, I'm still an ass to him, but that's just me, and I hate to doubt him now."

Simon walked in, taking my hand. "Then don't. We'll deal with it. No jumping to conclusions until we have the facts, remember."

Pulling him into a hug, I relaxed into his arms, finding comfort for once. I released him a few minutes later, not wanting to tempt myself too much. I'd instilled the no touching boundary for a reason.

"You know, you are your own special form of asshole."

"Oh? Please, tell me more," I taunted, walking over

to the dresser and grabbing my wallet and keys as he laughed behind me.

"You have that 'I'm rough around the edges' thing going on about you, but where you're secretly a softy on the inside."

Scoffing, I rolled my eyes. "There isn't anything soft about me, Fish."

"Deny it all you want, babe. You're abrasive to a fault, but it's how you show you care because under it, there's always a line of thoughtfulness, your delivery just sucks. Good thing you're not DoorDash, or you'd have a 1-star rating."

"Har-de-har-har." Turning, I took in his frame as he leaned against the door. Simon was dressed in black jeans that had holes in the knees and a blue shirt that made his eyes stand out. I caught myself licking my lips, and I lifted an eyebrow, running my thumb across my chin as I assessed him. "There isn't anything 1 star about my performance, Fish. And I think you'll find my satisfaction rating is off the charts. What I want to know is, why you think I care?"

He pushed off the wall, walking forward with a swagger I didn't know Simon possessed. His hips swayed a little as he did, and I felt myself grow hard as I watched him approach. Fuck, this dude had always been the one my heart had melted for. When he reached me, he placed his arms on the dresser behind me, trapping me. Simon wasn't taller than me, but he was able to dominate a little at this angle. Needing to gain some control, I grasped his hips, pulling him closer, our lower halves melting into one another.

"I know because I know you, Slade."

"Oh, is that so? You think you have me all figured out, huh, Fish?"

"I think I know you better than most people," he whispered, his breathing ragged as we held our position, eyes locked on one another.

"Hmm, I'd say you're correct there. You always were one of the few people I could be myself with," I growled, nipping his nose. His whimpered moan had me groaning, and I pushed him back, putting space between us. "You're too tempting, though, and I don't want to screw things up. Must. Talk. To. Peach," I panted, shoving my hands in my pocket to keep from reaching out to him. "Then, we can fuck until neither of us can move. Deal?"

"Why do you have to say things like that? It just makes me harder," he groaned. He stepped closer, barely brushing up against me, and my eyes rolled back at the briefest touch. "*Please*, Fish," I pleaded.

"Okay, okay." He stepped back, putting space between us, and I could breathe again.

"So, um, where do you want to meet Peach for lunch?" I asked, attempting to change the subject.

"I have a place in mind, but it doesn't open for a few more hours. It was nice, you know, to hear you play."

"Thanks, it's been a while. I've always enjoyed playing. Just not really in front of people. But Lennox… kind of changed that."

"She has a way of doing that." He chuckled, his eyes going misty.

"Yeah, she does."

"Since we have a few hours, want to play Xbox, or is that still too risky?"

"Yeah, sure, let me pack this up, and I'll be out there. I emailed the owner as well to extend our stay a few extra days, and got Bubba to cover the shop. Are you okay with that? I know you said you had a million vacation days, but I don't want to assume."

Simon grinned, nodding as he left, and giving me a cheeky wink. Picking up my stuff, I read over the song again, and I realized how quickly it had flowed from me. Things were changing in me, and I liked it.

Walking out to play, I realized how nice it would be to do something casual with Simon. Over the years, we'd wanted to hang out, but we were always afraid, feeling like we had to hide, or in Simon's case, choose.

There was always a level of secrecy, which made it hot at first, but increased our guilt. I didn't want to admit to Simon that having him keep this from her had eaten away at me. I knew of their connection, having witnessed it on paper for years and in person as well. It got to the point in the end where I'd shut him out to save their relationship. I pushed him out the door as soon as things were over, throwing up those barriers left and right. Shit, I needed to make things better with Simon too. It was time I owned up to my feelings and accepted responsibility for the mistakes I'd made. No time like the present to make better choices.

When we left to meet Lennox later, I felt hopeful that, for once, new things were on the horizon, eclipsing the bad, just like they both did in my heart.

Dear Peach, ♡

I decided to show you that I'm me in the way I know best... words. It's funny that face to face, I struggle with the basic things like telling you my feelings or being honest. But when pen touches paper, I'm not able to hold back from you, never was. On paper, we poured our hearts out, not understanding the connection we were forging.

Every week I looked forward to your fun envelopes, the stationary changing as you ran out, but when I saw something bright or girly, I always knew it was from you. I think that was when you started being my sun. You radiated positivity and sunshine into my life, your exuberance and joy grabbed me from the pages. I started staring at the stars because of you, and ended up loving the view. It felt fitting to name my first shop Equinox. You were my sun, my nox. I wanted you to be part of it, and having my sun and stars for the same length of time felt right.

I never would've had the courage to step out of my father's plans for me or believe I could do something if you hadn't encouraged me.

I'm sorry for all the times over the years I hurt you. I thought I could handle being around you and I felt guilty for leaving you alone, and I blamed myself for the events that transpired. I didn't want to admit that to you. It was easier to hate you instead of myself.

But I never hated you.

How could I?

I REGRET THE WAY I ACTED AFTER THE NIGHT WE WERE TOGETHER. I PANICKED, REALIZING I'D NEVER BE ABLE TO BE WITH YOU, AND HATING MYSELF FOR GIVING INTO THE TEMPTATION. YOU WERE EVERYTHING I ALWAYS IMAGINED YOU TO BE, AND SO MUCH MORE. YOU ARE THE EMBODIMENT OF SEDUCTION, YOUR BODY CALLING TO MINE IN A WAY NO ONE EVER HAS. I KNOW IT'S BECAUSE OUR HEARTS HAVE BEEN LINKED FOR YEARS, THE KNOWLEDGE ONLY INCREASES THE INTIMACY. I COULD COUNT THE WAYS OF HOW SEXY YOU ARE, BUT I THINK I'D PREFER TO WAIT UNTIL I HAVE YOU NAKED AND KISS EVERY INCH OF YOU AS I DO.

BECAUSE I WILL HAVE YOU AGAIN, PEACH. THERE'S NO DOUBT IN MY MIND.

YOU ARE MINE, AND YOU ARE SIMON'S. YOU'RE OURS, AND I'M BOTH OF YOURS.

AND I WON'T QUIT UNTIL YOU'VE FORGIVEN ME AND LOOK AT ME LIKE YOU DID THAT NIGHT WHEN I WAS JUST A TATTOOED ANGEL.

GET READY, PEACH. YOU'RE ABOUT TO GET THE FULL SLADE TREATMENT.

Love,
Your asshole

Chapter Seven
LENNOX

"ZA-CK?" I managed to stutter out, shock giving way to my fright as I took in the half-dressed person standing in my bedroom. His mouth gaped open like a fish as he took me in too.

Standing, I ran to the man I hadn't seen in years, throwing my arms around him exuberantly. "Oh my gosh! It's you! I thought I'd never see you again. But wait…"

Pulling back, my excitement and surprise fell away as I realized it still didn't explain his appearance in my apartment in the middle of the night, or in my bed. Looking around the room discreetly, I double-checked I was, in fact, in my room. The familiar stack of books on the floor, my sketchpad, and even the several pairs of shoes I had lying around confirmed my whereabouts.

Stepping back, the recognition he hadn't hugged me back settled in me. In fact, Zack still stood frozen in shock. He rubbed his eyes, blinking at me. It felt as if he expected me to disappear into thin air. When he still didn't say anything, I tried a different approach.

"Not that I'm not happy to see you or anything, but care to explain why you're in my bed?"

"*Your* bed? But that can't be right."

Half-naked Zack rubbed the back of his head, his face scrunching up in confusion as he looked at the bed in curiosity. I had to keep my eyes up, or I'd fall down the sinkhole his happy trail inevitably led to. You know, the one where I sank to my knees to explore it? Closing my eyes, I mentally scrubbed all the things I didn't need to be thinking about right now from it.

"This is my brother's apartment," he said indiscernibly, practically muttering at the end. But I heard the words and it froze me solidly to my core.

His brother. His brother. His brother.

But that meant… Slade owned Equinox Ink, making this *his* apartment. But that couldn't be right because Thane was his brother. Unless…

Everything began to spin, and I found myself sitting down on the bed, barely stopping myself from passing out.

"Lennox?" His gentle prodding had me blinking up at him, and that was when I realized he called me by name. My *real name*. The one I'd never given him. Scurrying off the bed, I placed my hands out in front of me as I slowly crept backward, inching my way out of the room. Unfortunately, my angle had been off, and I hit the desk behind me instead of making it to the door.

"How do you know my name?"

His face paled, and I watched his Adam's apple bob as he forcibly swallowed. "I can explain. It's not how it looks."

Huffing, "I'm sure that's what every psycho in every book has stated! But guess what? It's always how it looks!"

He laughed, and then smiled at me, the grin so beautiful I wondered if I'd accidently taken a hallucinogen or something earlier. I stopped, not expecting his behavior.

"Why are you laughing? Are you going to turn into that gif of the little girl making the creepy smile? Was this part of your plan all along? *Was it you*? Or are you the one messing with things, now?" My questions sped out of my mouth, the implications of everything had started to hit me full force, and I began to panic, sending my breathing into hyperventilation overdrive.

Zack's face dropped, and he took a step forward, almost like he was worried. The move had me scrabbling behind me as I reached for anything to use as a weapon. Wrapping my hands around the first thing I touched, I pulled it forward and held it out in front of me, pointing it at him menacingly.

Zack stopped at my motion, before he burst out laughing. His reaction confused me again, and I felt quite like I'd been transported into an episode of *The Twilight Zone*. Glancing at the item in my hand, I inwardly cursed at myself when I saw it.

"I didn't know you recently graduated from Hogwarts. Are you going to *Petrificus Totalus* me?" he asked, raising his eyebrow.

Smirking, I leveled him with a glare. "I was always partial to *Stupefy* myself, but *Tarantallegra* is my favorite."

Narrowing my eyes, I lowered my wand to his legs, waving it around as I threatened to perform the dancing charm on him. I hadn't meant to grab the wand. I'd been hoping for a letter opener or a pair of scissors, but if it came to it, I could stab him in the eye with it. But when he laughed some more and then danced a jig, I found myself lowering the wand instead. If he knew obscure Harry Potter spells, how malicious could he be?

"Gah, you're adorable." He smiled, and this one lit up the whole of his face. Holy Guacamole! I'd forgotten how charming he was.

"Answer the question, or you're toast!" I threatened, trying to gain some control. "I can run fast, and I'll have one of the burly guys from downstairs beating up your pretty face before you can blink."

He sobered, nodding. "Right, and that's a good plan. Would you feel more comfortable if you also grabbed your phone and had 911 on speed dial?"

"Just get to it, and we don't have to mess with anything, buddy!"

My adrenaline had skyrocketed, and my legs shook from fright, but I held my ground despite having to casually lean against the desk for support. I gripped the wand out in front of me, and it gave me courage despite not being an ideal weapon. Instead, it was as if I was channeling Hermione and all the other kick-butt women in the series, their confidence filling me.

"I know your name because Slade told me. The night you guys met up? I was there at the bar. I was the one who helped you in the hallway."

His words had me dropping my wand as I tried to focus on the memory and what he said. Had he been there? I remembered blue eyes and being called gorgeous, but that was it until a flash of Slade smacking me awake before I vomited on him. He could've been there, but it didn't prove anything yet. Plus, I wasn't convinced he was the real Thane. He couldn't be. Because if he was, then it meant the man I'd known and trusted for the past few months was a liar.

"Nice try, buddy, but I already met *Thane*, and you're not him, *Zack*."

His face screwed up at my words, and he took another step toward me, making me lift my wand again. "I don't know who you think you met, but I can assure you, I'm Thane. We did meet years ago as Zack and Kelly, and then you never called me."

My face heated at the reminder, and I couldn't mistake the hurt I heard. "Uh, yeah, well, I suck at keeping track of things, and I lost the napkin. I went back to the bar a couple of times, but I never saw you again."

"I started school at UT the next week."

"Ah."

"So, you were planning to call me?" He smiled softly, hope in his eyes, and I didn't want to admit it made me feel things. All the butterflies from that night rose to the surface, and I found myself shifting my legs. I nodded. It was all I could get out.

"That's a relief. I thought about you all the time and wondered what happened to you. Then when I was visiting my brother, I found you at that bar with some asshole towering over you. I threatened him, and he left, thankfully. You hit your head on the wall, and I went to get you water. When I returned, Slade was there. You um, got sick, and Slade and I began to argue."

"Why were you arguing?" I found myself asking, completely leaning against the desk now. The adrenaline had left me as the arousal had risen. I crossed my arms, no longer feeling the impending danger as I waited for him to make sense of things.

Zack blew out a breath, the movement making the hair in the front lift slightly. He was more gorgeous than I remembered. His dirty blonde hair hung in waves around his head, mussed from sleep and only adding to the whole sex appeal he had. His eyes were a calming blue, the shade of a summer's day. It was the dimple and scruffy beard that got me every time.

I traveled further down, his shirtless torso as distracting as I'd expected at a closer inspection. I sucked in a breath when I found only a pair of boxer briefs below. Biting my lip, I discovered he was barefoot as well, his tall frame on full display. A clearing of a throat had me lifting my head, ensnared by his captivating eyes once again. One side of his mouth lifted up, making the dimple pop. Mother trucker, he was too good-looking.

"You get enough?"

Rolling my eyes, I motioned with my hand to carry on, hoping to cover my embarrassment at being caught.

"It's a long story. One I need to tell you, but if I start with it, then I'm afraid I'll never get the chance to show you who I am."

"Well, that doesn't sound convincing at all, *Zack*."

"I really am who I say I am. And I know it's not the best way to start a conversation. I have a lot of sins to bear, things from my past I wish were different, but I learned long ago I couldn't go backward, and living in the past isn't a life at all. I can only acknowledge my failures, my mistakes, and vow to be better, and I think I have, or at least I'm trying to."

"Yeah, well, I get that, but it doesn't excuse things either."

"I know. I was young and stupid, and then... desperate. Neither makes for excellent problem-solving methods."

"You're putting me into a weird position because I feel I need to know what I'm dealing with here to trust you're not going to murder me, but you want me to get to know you first. How can I get to know you if you don't tell me things? Plus, I'm not convinced you're Slade's brother."

"Okay, you're right. That's fair, and I think if I share some of the past, it will prove I am Thane. How about... I tell you something good and then something I'm not proud of. Maybe it will give a better reflection of who I am."

"Why didn't you deny you were going to murder me?" I asked, focused on his answer.

"Because it's obvious I'm not. One, I was already asleep when you came here. I just got off a really long flight, and jet lag kicked my butt. If I wanted to kill you, I would've been lying in wait, not half-dressed and drooling."

"Ew! You drooled on my pillow?"

"Sorry." He shrugged and fiddlesticks if it wasn't the cutest thing. "Speaking of... could we maybe both put on some clothes? You're really distracting, half-dressed."

I looked down for some reason, double-checking

what I was wearing, and then looked up to him. His hands were casually placed over his lower half, and I wondered if he was attempting to hide something. I didn't know why the thought excited me. A potential killer/stalker was in my room, and I was drooling over his abs and dimples. Clearly, I was the deranged one.

"Yeah, sure. But like, at the same time. I don't want to take my eyes off you."

"Oh?" He smiled again, his dimple popping, and I fell into the trap it created, taking a while to understand what he was smiling about.

"No! I didn't mean it that way. Geesh." My face flamed, and *Zane*, as I decided to call him now, gave me a knowing look.

"Okay."

His gentle statement let me off the hook, and it reminded me of Duncan for some reason. For the first time in years, I wasn't hit with an overwhelming sense of grief. Perhaps, opening up and crying had helped after all, making the grief monster shrink. Instead, I felt Duncan's gentle guidance and assurance to trust myself and my gut.

I took a step and waited for him to take action. Once he did, I took another and another. This continued as we crept toward our pile of clothing, and then both pulled them on piece by piece. Once I had on my sweatpants and an oversized hoodie, I did feel better. It could be because Simon's scent still lingered on the hoodie or that I'd snuck my phone from my jeans pocket as I'd been dressing. Take your pick.

We were still across from one another, facing off in the small room. Zane observed me, and I found myself continuing to soften to his presence. I'd wondered about him for years, and to see him across from me now, altered my perception of things.

"Okay, we're dressed now. Time to start talking, *Zane*."

NOX TO THANE

From: noxsmiles@heartsemail.com
To: blazetats@heartsemail.com
Subject:

Brave Blaze,

I'm so thrilled for you! I don't know what it is, but if you made a decision and are excited for it, then of course I'm happy for you. It takes a lot of guts to step outside of your comfort zone and I admire you for that. I need to be more like you in that sense. How is your place? Are you liking Arizona? The desert sounds like an interesting place to be.

So, I have a funny story to tell you. My best friend, well he tried to teach me how to drive a stick shift today. To say it didn't go well is an understatement. I nearly ran off the road, and then I mowed down a bush, and knocked into one of those lawn ornament things. I've never seen his face so pale before. He basically told me he was never riding with me again until I could successfully drive. Can you believe that? It wasn't like his life was in peril! The way he's acting, you'd think I swerved into oncoming traffic! I swerved, but there weren't any cars coming, so really, he needed to get over it.

There's a talent show coming up and I've been thinking about singing, but one of the mean girls started a petition to not allow me to. She gave it to me as I finally braved the table to do it. It was so humiliating standing there holding this paper with hundreds of signatures from people who didn't want me to sing. I don't know if I'll ever be able to get on a stage again.

I try not to worry or care about what they think. But that was tough. They can talk about my size, or clothes, but my voice is more personal, more raw. It felt like they were attacking me as a person. I wish I was as brave as you, though I know you feel the same way about singing in front of people. This is one of those moments I wish you were here and you could play your guitar and I could sing. Maybe together it wouldn't be as scary?

I'm intrigued by the truth or dare concept. Okay, I'll bite. I'll choose dare first. Did you read that book I suggested? Would you want to read something together?

Thanks for the smile,

Nox

Chapter Eight

LENNOX

HE LOOKED AT ME CURIOUSLY, his eyebrow lifting before asking, *"Zane?"*

"Well, yeah, I've only known you as Zack, and you're claiming to be Thane, so I decided to make you 'Zane' in my head."

He chuckled. The sound reverberated through my body, making me shiver. Fudge! I liked how his laugh sounded and the way it felt rolling over me.

"I like it. Okay, so time to prove to you I'm who I say I am and tell you something good about me," he mused, rubbing his chin. "Alright, so the good thing first. Well, I just spent the past two and a half months in Liberia, helping them learn how to keep their animals healthy and increasing their production of healthy food and water."

I nodded, trying to ignore how sweet that actually was. Shifting my weight, I looked at him, "And the bad thing?"

He sat down on the corner of the bed, bracing his elbows on his knees. Placing his head in his hands, he looked at me, a look of pure devastation on his face. "This is going to make me sound horrible."

"Isn't that kind of the purpose? To share something?"

"Yeah, it's just…" he trailed off, sighing. He sat up straight, rubbing his palms on his legs. "Okay, I guess it's better to spit it out, right?"

"Yep, get it over with, buddy. Just spit it on out there."

My encouragement made him smile, and I found myself walking over to him and sitting on the other corner of the bed. He turned, placing one leg up on the mattress, while the other stayed on the floor. When he began to speak, he looked straight at me, and I admired his courage. He might be ashamed, but he wasn't hiding from it. Something about that made me soften to him more, wanting to believe him despite what it could mean for me. It was also a good example of not hiding from the truth. I admired him for it.

"Well, when I was about 17, I was desperate to understand Slade. At that point, we hadn't been getting along for over a year. The last move had been hard on him. It was probably the sixth move we'd made since our mom had died, and I think he'd been writing to you for about a year. Your letters were one of the only things he seemed to enjoy. I know Slade blamed himself for her death. He felt guilty for telling Dad what he'd seen, placing the guilt on himself for the divorce," Zane disclosed, stopping for a moment to take a deep breath before restarting. I was transfixed as he spoke, hanging on every word.

"Life became difficult, and we were passed off between one parent to the next, but we at least had each other. Slade withdrew, and became so angry at Mom. He didn't even talk to her for a few months. I don't remember how long it was after the divorce when mom was diagnosed with cancer, but it changed something in Slade. He became her constant companion and would always make sure she was okay. He drew her special pictures for chemo days and made her special snacks."

"Why is the thought of prepubescent Slade making snacks so cute?" I mumbled, blushing when I realized he'd heard me. Thankfully, Zane only smiled before continuing again.

"He was the one with her... when she died. I had a baseball game, and Slade and I had fought before it about whether or not I should go. But Mom told me to play, and get her a home run. I was 12, I didn't really understand everything, and sports were more fun. At home, it had become sad, and I felt bad I couldn't do anything. Our dad's house wasn't much better. He'd buried himself in work, avoiding his own feelings. Slade became a nervous wreck anytime we were away for long periods. In a way, he'd taken on her sickness, carrying the burden of care and recovery as his job. Part of me was jealous of their connection. I'd always connected more with dad anyway with us both liking sports, and Slade had with mom, getting her artsy gene."

I scooted closer, turning in the same manner as Zane with one leg propped on the bed as I listened. It felt like getting insider information into someone I'd known forever. Zane smiled at me, but kept talking. Once he'd started, it seemed to want to flow out of him, only needing a listener.

"Being a twin is weird, and while there were a lot of

benefits like having a best friend around all the time, it was odd in the sense you didn't always know who you were, a single entity or a double partnership. This was the first time in our lives we weren't in sync on something, and I felt invisible. At least at dad's house, we could focus on me. It sounds so awful to say it out loud, but that was the case. I liked being adored."

He took a minute, blowing out a breath, and I found myself unconsciously reaching out a hand to him. Zane's emotions were tangible, and I could feel his grief as he recalled these memories. It spoke to something inside of me, calling me to comfort him. Zane effortlessly took my hand, squeezing it, and the connection I'd felt years ago sparked to life.

"When I was dropped off home after the game, there was chaos all around our house. Lights flashed from nearby ambulances and a police car. Running toward the house, I found Slade sitting there, on the porch, staring off into space. He had one of those shock blankets wrapped around him. I ran to him, dropping my mitt and bat on the ground as I fell to the concrete, grasping his knees in my hands. I yelled to get his attention, but it took me shaking his legs for Slade to finally look at me. I'll never forget the words he said to me. *'She's gone. Hope your game was worth never getting to say goodbye to your mother.'* I remember falling back in shock, the news and pain at that moment hit me square in the chest. I cried and screamed at him to tell me it wasn't true, that it was a sick joke, but he'd entered back into the zoned-out state, ignoring me. Dad showed up then, his grief written all over his face, and I knew, I knew right then I couldn't fall apart because they both needed someone to be strong. During the divorce, we'd been cast into roles, and I bore mine like a coat of armor, accepting my fate. Part of me liked it, being the one to be the peacekeeper, the one who had it all together."

"But you were twelve! You should've been allowed to grieve your mom."

"I know that now, Noxy girl, but at the time, it was how I managed." He smiled, but it didn't quite reach his eyes this time, though he seemed comforted by my ire at what he'd experienced. I couldn't imagine losing my mom at that young age, and I grieved for him and Slade. Some of my Tatzilla's flaws made sense now, his hesitancy to commit, his fear of losing people.

Thinking over his words, something about one of the familiar endearments Blaze used had slid off his tongue, tugging at my memory. When he started to talk again, I let it go, focusing on Zane in front of me.

"The hard part was, I'd stepped so far into that role, I lost who I was along the way, and it destroyed my connection to my brother. Being the good child, the peacekeeper, pushed us further apart. It was too late by the time I realized the divide my actions had created. So, by our senior year, we were practically strangers, barely speaking to one another. I missed my brother so much. On the outside, it looked like I had all these friends, the life of the party, and good grades, but I was disappearing inside. I'd become this fake person. I thought if I could maybe connect with my twin again, the other half of me, then maybe I'd remember who I was. But no matter my intention of why I did what I did, it doesn't excuse it. I know that. I'm not trying to make excuses, I'm just hoping if you understood why I did it, the desperation I felt, it might not sound as creepy."

"Okay." I nodded in response, because I got it. I'd hidden behind my rock for years, pretending the pain I felt at the loss of Duncan, and even Blaze, wasn't there. I'd convinced myself it hadn't hurt, when in reality, it had felt like my heart was ripped out of my chest and left beating on the sidewalk. That kind of pain didn't disappear just because I ignored it.

"So, like I mentioned at the start, he'd been writing to you for a couple of years by our senior year. I knew of it, but I hadn't paid attention. He was so consumed with his notebook, though, so I decided to look in it one day. I wanted a peek into his mind. We used to be so in sync, I knew everything he felt and thought before he even did, but back then, he'd become a separate entity apart from me. So, when he was gone one day, I found myself in his room, and I looked at his notebook. It had his drawings in there, and they did give me some insight into him. His talent had improved exponentially, and I was in awe. But at the back were your letters."

He stopped, watching me carefully. My eyes widened, and I had a feeling where this was headed, and I found myself believing Zane and Slade's version of things. Preparing myself, I swallowed, nodding for him to continue.

"I read them. I hadn't intended to, but you jumped off the page, and I felt your radiance in your words. Once I started, I couldn't stop. There were some from Fish too, but it was your letters that had me reading them late into the night. His letters weren't there, but I was jealous of how easy it seemed he shared with you, this person who was a complete stranger. I justified reading them as a way to verify you weren't taking advantage of him or something."

I rolled my eyes at his thought process but kept my words to myself. Zane saw me however, and chuckled. It brought attention to his hand that had started to rub back and forth on mine. Tingles spread up my arm, and I told myself to focus back on what he was admitting. He'd violated mine and Slade's trust. The breach of privacy stung, and I pulled my hand back. It had felt nice, but Zane didn't need comfort any longer, and I couldn't justify holding his hand any more either. Not to mention the sensations confused me, altering my feelings. His smile dropped at the edges, but he let go.

My hand instantly missed his touch, and I didn't like that.

"That's a pretty huge violation," I stated, the words finally finding an outlet.

"I'm afraid it gets worse." Sighing, I braced myself, ready to hear it. "At first, I only read your letters. I feel like such a stalker when I say it out loud," he admonished himself with a shake of his head. "But at the time, I didn't think about it that way. I didn't think I was doing anything bad."

"Oh, so invading privacy isn't bad?" I didn't know why I asked, but my heart was racing by then. I wanted to give him the benefit of the doubt, but nothing he said painted him in a good light, especially with everything I knew now with the mixup the night Slade and I were to meet. If he was Thane, had he done it? And if he was Thane, then who was the person I knew as Thane?

Neither scenario had a good outcome for me, and it was overwhelming to me to think about it.

"I know, I know. I realize that now. And while it doesn't excuse it, I really wanted to get to know my brother through you. Somewhere along the line, it became less about him and more about *you*."

"The night we met?" I asked, my voice in my throat. I didn't want one of the best memories to be tainted by secrecy.

"I had no idea who you were. I promise. It happened randomly. It was one of those lucky coincidences."

"Okay," I said, taking a deep breath. "You read my letters meant for your brother. Why do I have a feeling I'm not going to like the next part even more?" He cringed, and my stomach plummeted.

"When I discovered you guys were going to start emailing, I saw my chance. I could get to know you on a real level. So… I started writing to you."

"*You* wrote to me?"

"Yeah. I had to be careful and sneaky. Again, another clue I should've known it was wrong if I had to hide it, but I wasn't thinking straight. I only thought of my desires and what I wanted was to get to know you."

"I don't think that really makes it okay, dude."

"I know Lennox, and I am so sorry for it. Part of me wishes I could take it back, but I did get to know you, albeit in the wrong way, but I actually did. I don't know if I could ever regret that."

Darn it! Why did the creepy have to sound so logical and sweet?

"So, you like what, wrote to me as Blaze?"

"Yeah."

Something in my mind clicked, and I realized I'd kind of always known there was something different about some of the emails. I rationalized it as Blaze being more emotional or sweet at times versus the gruff and deep way he was at others. But now, knowing Slade was Blaze, it was easy to identify which letters were from him.

And not that Slade wasn't sweet, he was, but it was a different form of caring. His notes tended to be darker and emotionally driven. Slade and I had the creative aspect in common, and with that, we saw and felt things on levels others didn't.

But there had been some letters, I hadn't felt as deep of a bond in them. I'd enjoyed reading them because they were fun and encouraging. They made me laugh and smile. Sometimes, the letters made me think about important topics, asking probing questions. They always broadened my worldview, and if I had to guess, those were the ones from Zane.

"Does Slade know you impersonated him?"

"Yes, he knows. He discovered it one night, and we got into a huge fight over it. I stopped then, promising I wouldn't write to you anymore. I realized how much he cared for you, and I knew I could never be the one to take you away from him. He'd already lost so much, and I had violated his trust. It sucked losing the connection to you, but I couldn't lose my brother. I was so smitten by then, I knew if you ever found out the truth, it would ruin any chance I had, and there was no way I could keep writing to you and not fall head over heels. It killed me to stop, but I did. I knew it was the only recourse, and I hoped it would save my relationship with Slade. Besides, I knew you both deserved better, and I hoped with me stepping back, you'd get there."

I sat for a minute staring, not sure how I felt about his admittance. Zane was right in thinking if I'd known this as a teen before I met him, then I wouldn't have wanted anything to do with him. Adult Lennox knew differently, and how at the age of eighteen, I hadn't always made the best choices either. I also understood perception and emotion-filled decisions. Perhaps most importantly, I believed in second chances. This was a lot to overlook, but maybe that was when it mattered the most.

So many people discounted my mom because of the things that had occurred in our lives. They only ever saw her as a diagnosis and not the person she was, someone who struggled daily to be what she needed for her family or who had to live with the memories of the worst moments of her life. I hated the concept of evaluating a person based on one event. It dismissed the whole of their life and narrowed it down to things they deemed unforgivable. In my mom's case, she hadn't been well, and in perhaps Zane's case, he hadn't processed his grief. It was something I could relate to and understand now, and while it didn't excuse his actions, I knew one bad thing didn't cancel out a whole bunch of good things.

So I nodded, not ready to pass judgment on him. His smile lifted a little. "Okay, what's your next good thing/hard thing?"

"Ha, nice try. It's your turn now."

"Me?" I leaned back, shocked, suddenly uncomfortable. "I didn't agree to this."

"I think it's only fair, gorgeous."

His eyes were lit up, shining with glee, and I found myself matching it. Zane made me want to give in and just laugh with him. The endearment had me recalling the kind guy who'd helped me in the hallway that night, settling his deeds for good higher in my mind.

Blowing out of breath, I thought about something good in my life. "Well, I helped my brother with his school project. My life is kind of boring. Way to make me feel like I've not done anything good in my life," I joked, effortlessly pushing his leg.

"I would have to disagree with you there, Noxy girl. There are a lot of nice things that you've done." He lifted a finger and started to count them off. "All the ways you've helped your mom and practically raised Noah. You and Slade are similar in that sense, always willing to take care of everyone else, ignoring yourself." He gave me a narrowed look before continuing, lifting a second finger.

"Fighting against rumors and hypocrisy in your town. And third, choosing to stay close to monitor and take care of your family, putting your own dreams on hold. Those are just a few things I remember. I know there are plenty more in the years since we've spoken. You just don't see yourself or the things you do that way."

Shrugging, I hid my face, embarrassed at how perceptive he was. Even in a few small encounters, he knew me. I didn't acknowledge that he was right, either. I did struggle to see the good in myself, or thinking I did anything extraordinary. People always commented on the things I did naturally as being good, and it felt odd to be praised for it. I never thought twice about it and just did it. I never debated if I should do something, it was my natural instinct to step in. It felt weird when people made it out to be like I was an angel or should be given a reward for helping my mom. It felt ludicrous, honestly. She was my mom, of course I wanted to help her.

"Yeah, well. I guess we all have our demons." I picked at my pants, not able to look at him and his all-seeing eyes. It took me a few minutes to calm my racing heart before I could start again.

"The bad thing... I once put eyedrops into Shelley's drink, and I never told anyone, not even Simon. I was mad at her for what she said about my mom, and I reacted. She got really sick, and had to be hospitalized. I felt horrible about it. So much so, I volunteered to help her do her homework." My face heated at the memory of Si asking me why I was bothering with helping her, coming to the forefront.

Zane chuckled. "See? Even when you're bad, Noxy, you balance it out with some good. You really are one of a kind, Lennox."

His compliment made me feel warm inside, and I wanted to crawl into his arms. I knew it wasn't a good idea, so I shoved it away, focusing back on the conversation at hand.

"What's the other thing you wanted to tell me? Your other bad thing?"

"Well, this one... It's a little harder to explain."

Doubt and fear settled over me, and I found myself

wondering if I should've called someone. Looking at the clock, it was 3 am. Mother trucker. Maybe I needed to get my intuition checked out because I suddenly wondered if it had led me into a false sense of security, luring me into dropping my shields until he would really strike.

"It has to do with the night I learned your name, the night Duncan died."

Swallowing, I nodded, hoping I was ready to hear this.

"It's my fault you were taken. Slade and I were arguing and when we came back out, you were gone. I thought I saw you being led out, so I followed as best I could. I wasn't fast enough though when I saw him try to put you in a car. Before I could get to you, someone arrived, saving you. I was so relieved, I let you leave with him. I was half way home when I realized I should've checked on you. I decided to drive to your house to check you made it there. I'd known your address by heart for years from all your letters," he stopped, tears building in his eyes, and I held my breath for what was to come, the anxiety beating a rapid percussion in my chest.

"I never made it there because when I got halfway there, the road was closed. I left my car, and ran to the scene, praying it wasn't you. I... I saw them loading you into the ambulance, and I was relieved you were okay. I stood there for a while, just watching. I heard a car starting behind me, but I stayed where I was, assuming someone was just leaving. Everything that happened next felt like something in slow motion... I watched the car drive by me, I watched your eyes go wide and your attempt to yell at him, I watched as Duncan kept walking backward unaware, and I watched as the car struck him. All I did was *watch*. If I'd done something, *anything*, then maybe Duncan would still be alive. Don't you get it, Lennox? It was *my* fault. *I killed Duncan.*"

THANE TO NOX

From: blazetats@heartsemail.com
To: noxsmiles@heartsemail.com
Subject: It's time to go to war!

My Noxy girl,

I'm sorry that happened to you. I had to take some calming breaths when I read that to not demand you tell me her name so I could tell her just what I thought about her opinion. But I know that wouldn't do anything for you, so instead, I'm trying to be supportive. What do you need? An alibi? Prank ideas? A random package of shit to be delivered to her door? Or one of those glitter bombs? Or a candy penis? Please tell me we can do one of these. It must be done.

No? I'm very saddened by this.

I appreciate you thinking I'm brave, but really I'm scared out of my mind. The only thing that makes me feel excited about it is knowing I'm going to do something I love. I hope my mom would've been proud of me. Even when she was sick, she always told me to pursue my dreams, that she would get to live vicariously through me as long as I was happy and doing what I loved. When I was twelve that meant baseball and school.

Bringing home a good grade was the only way I knew how to make her smile back then. She had a bond with my brother I didn't have, but I worked hard not to be a nuisance, to be the easy child. In the end, it didn't matter. She still died, and I didn't get to say goodbye. I never did play baseball after that.

Imagining you driving and hitting a bush makes me chuckle. I'm sorry your friend is refusing to teach you now. Is there anyone else you can ask? My car is an automatic, so I'm no help.

I'm excited you chose dare first…

I dare you to sing in the talent show.

I know… it's probably mean of me, but I figured maybe I can be the push you need, to remind you that you *are* brave and strong. If anything, it will stick it to the mean girl since you won't let me prank her with a glitter bomb.

If you choose to skip the dare, then you have to wear a Ronald McDonald costume to school for the entire day. And I'll need picture proof that this occurred.

Better get to practicing those vocals, songbird.
I'll take a dare in return.

What do you call a pig that knows karate?
Pork Chop.

You're welcome.
Not a comedian Blaze

Chapter Nine

LENNOX

MY HEAD POUNDED from lack of sleep, and my eyes were barely staying open. I'd gotten to bed around 5 am after the last bomb Zane dropped on me. I'd only been awake an hour, enough time to shower and get dressed before I had to meet Simon and Slade. Crapola, that was a mouthful! Chuckling at my ill-mannered innuendo, I walked in and spotted the guys in a booth in a circular corner.

Slade stood when he noticed me and waited for me to travel the distance to him. When I was close, he pulled me into a hug, breathing in my hair. I was so tired, I didn't fight it and just accepted the comfort. After everything Zane had told me, I found myself not hating my bossnemy as much anyway, the Blaze I'd known rising to the surface.

"Peach, you look like hell, but I'm happy to see you."

Snuggling in close, I ignored his comment and found myself almost falling asleep against his chest despite still standing up. I nestled against him and hummed in contentment. I felt his chest rumble against my cheek, but I didn't hear what he said. His hands were resting on my lower back, and his thumb had found its way under my shirt, rubbing against my bare skin.

"Hmm?"

He pulled back, a look of concern on his face now, the worry lines appearing between his brows. Lifting up, I could only reach his chin, so I hopped once, attempting to get the spot to smooth it out. Unfortunately, I was still too short and only managed to boop his nose.

"What are you doing, Peach?" He asked, smiling down at me adoringly.

"Trying to smooth out your wrinkles."

He looked at me, a smile in his eyes. "Should I ask why?"

Before I could reply, his arms banded around me, and he lifted me up, bringing us face to face. Blinking, I lost my breath as I stared at him.

"Oh."

"Yes, Peach?" He waited, staring at me intently, and I found myself falling into his deep eyes.

Hot Fudge Sundae! A girl could get used to being stared at like that.

Moving my hand, I smoothed the skin between his eyes as he watched me, until his eyes fluttered closed. His eyelashes were so long against his face and I wanted to pet them. Simon cleared his throat, bringing me back to the present, dropping my hand. I expected Slade to set me down, but he didn't. Instead, he turned and placed my feet on the bench, pushing me in toward Simon. Sitting down. I suddenly found myself in the best type of sandwich—S&S. I think I was going to need to steal Bab's moniker for them so I didn't have a tongue twister every time I tried to say their names.

The only tongue twister I wanted was below. Giggles erupted out of me, my earlier dirty thoughts also rising to the surface. I wonder what I could make S&S stand for.

Slip & Slide
Salty & Sweet
Start & Stop
Sweet & Sour
Strip & Stare
Supply & Service
Short & Sweet

Though, there wasn't anything short either of them had. Hiding my reddening face, I turned and hugged Simon, needing his comfort after the emotional upheaval the night before. I still couldn't wrap my head around everything that had been spilled. When I pulled back, he looked at me oddly.

Sugar sticks! I wasn't supposed to be all handsy with them. *Friends, Lennox, Friends.*

"Don't take this the wrong way, but you look like shit, Lenn. Did you not sleep okay?"

"Thanks, Si." I rolled my eyes, thankful the waitress walked over to take our drink orders before I had to answer anything else. It also gave me time to put some boundaries in place since I seemed to be struggling with remembering they were friends only.

"How y'all doing today? What can I get you started with, suggas?"

"Water" was chorused out, and I found myself

giggling again. Slap-happy was a real thing, folks. She smiled, nodding, before turning to retrieve our drinks.

"Peach," he breathed into my neck, and I abruptly stopped the giggles as he trailed a finger down my arm. "Not that I don't love hearing the sound of your giggles, but what's going on?"

The low rumble of his words had my body freezing as tingles spread up along my arm and body. Simon moved in closer on the other side. And I found myself wishing we weren't in a restaurant. My lack of sleep clouded my judgment, deleted any hesitancy to give in, and allowed my hormones and arousal to take control.

Swallowing, I breathed through my mouth, attempting to give myself clean air, free of the intoxicating scents of Simon and Slade. Seriously, I needed a name. Two S's were going to become troublesome. S&S it was. I'd keep what it stood for to myself. Their smells together were a deadly combination I found hard to resist. Once I cleared my head of the desire, I was able to respond to their questions.

"Yeah, um. I don't know if everything's fine, per se. I didn't get much sleep last night because I was up till 5 am with Zane."

Of course, that was the wrong thing to say without context! A low growl emitted from Slade and had the opposite effect he intended. He was so close to my neck when he spoke that his lips brushed the sensitive area on my skin, hitting me straight on my lady bits below, revving me up more.

"Who the *fuck* is Zane?"

Even Simon tensed next to me, and I realized my mistake. "Oh, yeah, about *that*," I hedged, cringing.

Before I could finish my explanation, he announced himself.

"That would be me, Brother."

Slade whipped his head around abruptly, the hand I hadn't noticed tightened on my leg for a second before he released it, springing out of the booth to hug his brother.

"Thane! What the fuck, man? I've been trying to get a hold of you. Where the hell have you been?" He pulled back, checking Zane over for a second, calculating his appearance head to toe. I saw his actions now for what they were. Slade was checking him over for injuries or things that might've changed in his absence, his mother's illness and departure having created a desperate need to notice every detail. My tired brain fixated on it, and I slumped back into Simon's embrace, his arm pulling me close as we watched them.

When Slade was satisfied with his assessment, his look of joy dropped, and he glanced back to me and then to his brother, letting go of him as he stepped back, a look of hurt crossing his face.

"I can't believe it. Peach was *right*. You've been lying to me for months. You've been here this whole time, haven't you?"

Zane immediately began to shake his head in protest, his hands reaching out to pull his twin back. "No, I promise. I only got back last night. I went to the apartment—"

"And that's when he tried to snuggle me like a bear." I giggled, and my words had Slade relaxing before his face turned up again in question.

"If he's not *your* Thane…"

I brushed off his question, not ready to talk about that yet. "Thanks for asking if I'm okay when I found a stranger in my bed, by the way," I deflected.

Slade's face shifted, and he scooted back in toward me, crowding me against Simon. "I'm sorry, Peach. Do you need me to kiss it and make it better?"

My tongue froze to the roof of my mouth, and I almost nodded my head in an exuberant yes. *That would be great, thanks!* I felt a bit like I had whiplash or was on a carnival ride that was spinning out of control.

Something in my expression must've shone through because he pulled back, patting my leg, and dropped his intense questioning. His relief was evident though at the fact his brother hadn't been lying to him. It felt good I'd been able to give him that assurance, even if it meant the man I'd *known* was a liar.

"Mind if I join? Sorry if I didn't wait long enough Lennox."

"Uh, yeah, sure, man. I'm Simon."

My best friend offered his hand to Zane and scooted closer to me so he could join us. It was a snug fit, but I wasn't complaining. It was a hot guy booth buffet, and I wanted my fill.

"Hey, man, I'm Thane. It's nice to officially meet you," Zane greeted, offering his hand. Simon tilted his head in confusion at his statement.

"Officially?"

"Yeah, well…" Zane shrugged, looking toward me.

"He has to explain that too. Basically, does anybody want to play poker? Because our cards are growing on the table." I laughed, my joke amusing me.

"Peach. Start. Talking."

"Oh my goodness, Tatzilla," I cooed, turning to him. "Can you stop with the growls? It's not doing what you think it's doing. If you want me to share anything, I'm gonna need you not to be zinging my hoo-hah in a public place. You're making me tingle where the sun doesn't mingle."

He looked at me, not even blinking before he spoke. "I have no words, Peach."

"Good." I nodded in confirmation. "That's great because now I have some to share." Sitting up, I pulled out of Simon's hold. "Okay, class in session, everyone!" I clapped, bringing their attention to me.

Zane chuckled at my exuberance, perhaps also feeling the effects of the slap-happy. Grinning at him, I found myself trapped for a second in his blue eyes. Shaking myself loose, I tried to start again.

"So like I said, I came home, fell on the bed, then arms wrapped around me. I shrieked, tumbled out and tried to escape. When the lights came on, I realized it was Zack."

"Don't forget the part where you tried to attack me with your magic wand." We both broke out into hysterical laughter. The other two rolled their eyes, clearly not understanding the comical geniuses we were.

"Is that a name for your vagina, Peach? Wouldn't that be a better name for a cock?" Slade finally asked, stopping our laughter. He raised an eyebrow at me in question, and I shook my head at him. Clearly, he was a Slytherin.

"Wait!" Simon exclaimed, turning to his left. "You're the guy from the throwback party! I remember you now."

"Yep, that would be me. Hence the official part, I saw you, but we never spoke."

"What *party*?" Slade grumbled, and I found myself reaching over without any qualms to squish his lips between my fingers.

"Nope. Just nope, 'grouchy pants' Slade. This is Lennox time. Me speakey. Okay?" He couldn't respond since I held his lips, but I felt him try to smirk, his eyes saying everything, only heating me more. "Perfect, I'm glad we agree." Smirking, I let go and turned back to continue, but Slade groaned before a question left his lips for his brother.

"Did you give her alcohol or drugs?" Zane burst out laughing at the question, clearly knowing I was just hilarious.

"This is just my natural cuteness, Mister! Now, seriously, quiet." I waited, and when he mimed zipping his lips, I started again. "So I had a moment of glee at finding him, but then a moment of 'why is Zack from *Saved by the Bell* in my apartment?' And he was like, 'why is Kelly from *Saved by the Bell* in my brother's apartment?' And that's when I realized the whole brother, yada, yada thing. We talked, we shared some things, and I realized you were right, Slade, so here's me saying it. You. Were. Right."

I gave him a pointed stare. He didn't respond, but his lips tilted up in a crooked smile, and I knew he was gloating on the inside. Narrowing my eyes, I gave him the customary, 'I'm watching you' movement before I faced the table.

"I'm not in the mind-space today to think about the fact that the Thane I've known for months is an imposter. I worked out some other things with your brother. Which, by the way, his name is now Zane. It's easier to differentiate between the imposter Thane and real Thane because that's a lot of Thanes to say. And since he was Zack to me first, and he's Thane to you, viola Zane was born. Now, I just need to think of a name for you guys. Well, Babs gave me a name, S&S, so I need to figure out what it's going to stand for because Simon and Slade is a mouthful," I rushed out, laughing again. "Mouthful." Schooling my features, I took a breath. "Okay, okay."

"I only understood about a third of what she said," Simon mumbled, "but it sounds like you returned to the states, went to the apartment, you guys talked, and realized who each other were? Now, you're here?"

"Well, yeah," I interjected, rolling my eyes. "But there's also the whole matter of the fact he read and wrote to me for a couple of years as Blaze."

"What?" Simon asked, looking around at everyone. When it seemed to click, he nodded.

"That was the big fight you guys had?" Simon asked Slade. Part of me felt envious of the bond I could sense between them, but I couldn't do anything about it but increase my own. I watched Slade as he nodded, tense over the topic before he finally spoke.

"Yeah, when I discovered his betrayal, it took a while for me to trust him again. That's why I was so convinced whoever Peach was meeting with wasn't really Thane because we don't lie to each other anymore."

Zane nodded, a look of happiness on his face, and I realized he hadn't ever heard Slade say this in the past few years, still feeling uncertain of their bond. "No, we don't, Brother."

"Aww, look at you two. It's too cute. I wish I could reach both of your cheeks right at the same time, so I could squeeze them together."

Of course, this was when the waitress returned with our drinks. When she spotted Zane, her face lit up. A possessive streak rose up in me out of nowhere, and I had an urge to climb over the table and scratch out her eyes, all kittycat like. Two hands clamped down on my thighs, holding me in place, my intention apparently easy to read.

"Well, hey there, handsome. What can I get you to drink today?" Zane looked at her momentarily, and I watched him closely, memorizing each detail. I was happy to find he barely paid any attention to her while she was giving him bedroom eyes. Not that I had any claim on him, but the thought had jealousy roaring through me.

"I'll have a water, thanks."

She nodded, her face dropping a little at the dismissal. The waitress turned to me, and I expected the curve-lipped look of disgust or the double-take to check me over when none of the guys paid her any attention. However, I was pleasantly surprised when she gave me a huge grin, winking with a nod of approval. "Well done, girl! I'm impressed, and a tad bit jealous." My body relaxed, a blush rising to my cheeks, but I gave her a smug look back.

"Well, what can we get started with today? Our specials are… " I zoned out as she listed off the food, the tiredness hitting me fully from the highs and lows of the past few days and lack of sleep. When she got to me, I looked at her, blinking, unsure what to tell her. Thankfully, Simon took over, knowing what I liked. She nodded, giving me a soft smile. "I'll be right back with your appetizers, dolls."

Once she was gone, all the eyes turned to me. "So, what does this mean for the imposter Thane?" Simon asked.

Shrugging, I turned into his arms again. "I don't know yet. I've only had like four hours of sleep at this point, and I have to work later. So I'm going to leave the master plan to you guys. Think you can handle it?"

"Yeah, Peach. Close your eyes. We can handle it."

"Okay. Great idea. I'll just rest for a bit. Wake me when there's food."

Laying my head against Simon, I closed my eyes and was immediately out, the noise around me fading away.

Love Letter

From: emblazed_slade@heartsemail.com
To: emblazed_lennox@heartsemail.com
Subject: Are you swooning yet?

Dear Peach,

I hope by now you're starting to see I'm serious, that I care for you and I'm not trying to pull one over on you. I know my behavior in the past has made you doubt me, and I'm sorry for that. I've explained my reasoning for the choices I made. It doesn't excuse rudeness, and I would've been better off just staying out of your life. I mean that in the sense that if I wasn't in it, I couldn't hurt you.

But I couldn't let you go. Even with a broken heart, I wanted to be near your light, even if it hurt. Some days, it hurt so much, I could barely breathe. You were within my reach, and yet the furthest away you'd ever been. I think that's what led me to Simon.

When I met him the first night, I didn't make the connection, too consumed by my own grief and heartache to know Fish was standing two feet away from me. I should've, the connection and physical reaction almost instant like it had been with you. I was comfortable with my sexuality by that point, but I hadn't really branched out much, too scared to explore. I didn't fit into the "gay" stereotype and I couldn't ever find my place among them.

Once you started working at the shop, and Simon started to drop by every day, the connection finally clicked. I didn't say anything to him for over a year. And when I did, it was out of drunkenness and heartache.

Simon and I never wrote as often as you and I, but we did share letters and over the years, we both explored our fears and concerns around our evolving sexuality and it was a safe way to discuss things. Neither of us ever told you and for that I'm sorry. It wasn't meant to be a secret, but once we started down that path, it was easier to keep heading there. Somewhere along the way, I fell in love with him too, I just hadn't realized it at the time.

The night in question, we both ended up at Rookies, sitting at the bar drinking alone. Not that it makes it okay, but you were on a date with some guy, and despite me telling myself I was over you, that I hated you, it stung. Simon was feeling similarly and we both ended up drunk and commiserating our loneliness together.

Part of me wishes this wasn't true, but I pursued him in part to punish you. I had him keep it a secret to hurt you. I thought if I hurt you, then you'd look at me the way I deserved to be looked at for that night. I thought you'd be able to slice me open and cut me to my core, allowing me to bleed out my sorrow.

But instead, you smiled at me, you fought with me, and you made me fall in love with you even more. I don't deserve you, but I will.

Out of everything that's come to light and I know there's been a lot, don't hold it against Simon. I know he's his own person who can make his own decisions, but I convinced him it would be better because he'd already kept the secret from you for so many years. He's always been so scared of losing you, that it made him freeze in fear. You are the one thing that can break him, and that terrifies him. These past two months, he was half of the man you knew, half of the man he's been since just being back in your presence for two days.

That's how amazing you are, Peach. You light up everyone around you. We're all drawn to you because of the woman you are, and the men you make us want to be.

I enjoyed today, Peach. Having you in my arms for even a second was bliss.

I can't wait for more.

Your asshole

LENNOX

DISTANT LAUGHTER and the sound of a chainsaw had me waking, and I found myself being held down. Fear spiked in me for a second before I realized the chainsaw was coming from behind me, the noise sending vibrations through my body. Laughter sounded out again, and I recognized Simon's hyena chuckle, further calming me. I tried to peek over my shoulder at who had me snuggled close. I could feel their breath hitting my neck with each rumbly exhale. The grip was so tight, though, I couldn't even budge.

Glancing down at the arm, the tattoos gave me the answer I sought—my Tatzilla. Almost as if he could feel my intent to get up, he pulled me closer, his lips now on my neck, causing goosebumps to erupt. I didn't want to admit how nice it felt to be held by him. He smelled of pure masculine seduction, and it wafted around me in a cozy hug.

"Peach, go back to sleep. I'm not ready to let you go."

"But I gotta… you know," I whispered, unable to admit I needed to pee.

"You gotta what, *Peach*?" He whispered back sleepily, his lips caressing my sensitive skin as he pulled me impossibly closer. My body betrayed my heart, attempting to convince me to snuggle back into his embrace despite not being there mentally.

"Slade, *please*, I really need to drop the kids off at the pool!"

His hand let go of me instantly, and he lifted his head, looking down at me. "You need to take a *shit*, Peach?"

Horrified, I scrambled out of bed now that his arm was off me. "*That's* what that means? Holy Pajamas!" Too shocked to fix my blunder, I stumbled to a door I hoped was the bathroom and shut it behind me. Face flaming, I found a light switch as Slade's chuckles followed me in. I ignored them as I leaned back against the door, banging my head.

"I'm going to murder, Noah," I mumbled, finally opening my eyes. Thankfully, the room I found myself in *was* the bathroom, and I rushed over to relieve myself continuing to mutter about little brothers.

Feeling better, I tossed some water on my face and looked around the sink. A letter sat on the counter addressed to me. Sitting down, I opened it and found myself falling into a time warp where Blaze and Nox could share their feelings without recourse.

Wiping my eyes, I stood, trying to digest the letter. Going through the motions, I found a brush and picked it up to use, hoping it was Simon's, and not the owners. I managed to find mouthwash as well, and swished it around. Peering down at myself, I realized I was wearing different clothes than I'd been in yesterday. An oversized shirt fell off my shoulders that could only be Slade's, the size and color a dead giveaway. Not to mention the "I'm the tattoo artist you should've gone to" script on the front of it. I was thankful someone had changed me though because sleeping in jeans was miserable.

Shrugging, I figured it was probably Simon, not that it mattered since both of them had seen me naked, and I trusted them. The realization that I did trust them hit me. I was still upset with all the lies, but under the hurt was a solid foundation of trust and love. Slade's letter ran through my head as well, searing itself on my heart. At first, the realization I cared for them sat heavily on my chest, the need to deny it, to push it away, almost instinctive after years of doing it, of not even trusting my own heart.

I was tired of doing the same thing over and over, though.

My encounter with Babs filtered through my head, and I knew she was right. It was time I stopped blaming my curse and took ownership of my own choices. I'd had some misfortunes, but it didn't discount all the other wonderful things. Plus, I'd been in love with two guys for so long, no one else ever stood a chance. It wasn't a curse, just that my heart hadn't had room for anyone else. That was until Duncan. He'd been the exception... and possibly Zane.

They'd both been the only other two times I felt the same connection I felt to Simon and Slade. I could choose at this moment to keep lying to myself that I didn't care for S&S still, or I could embrace it and begin to live a life full of love. Duncan would want that, and I needed to live for him as well. If I was honest, I knew things still needed to be figured out between the three of them, even Zane. But none of that could happen in this bathroom.

Taking a deep breath, I stepped back into the bedroom and found Slade snuggled up to my pillow, snoring softly. I was jealous of his ability to fall back to sleep that quickly. Smiling at his peaceful form, I brushed his hair across his face and kissed his forehead before walking out into the other rooms. He only snored louder in response as I shut the door. It was nice to find the walking sex God had flaws. Of course, he'd been an Alpha-hole for years, so I guess he'd never been perfect. His hotness just distracted me at times.

I took in my surroundings as I made my way toward the laughter, and ended up in a kitchen. I found Zane and Simon laughing as they made breakfast. I stood watching them for a few minutes, enjoying the view. Neither had shirts on, only bottoms. Simon was in some low-slung grey sweatpants that I knew from previous experience were a walking thirst trap. Zane wore low-slung basketball shorts that were doing nice things for his backside.

He turned at one point, catching me checking out his butt, and his smile lit up his handsome face. Stalker Thane might've been one of the most attractive guys I'd ever met, but he had nothing on real Thane. You couldn't fake his cheerful nature or kind spirit, and that went a long way in the looks department for me.

"Good morning, sunshine."

I swear angels started singing at the radiant smile he beamed at me. His comment had Simon turning, a grin covering his face too. He immediately put down whatever he'd been working on and walked toward me.

"Lenn, how are you feeling this morning? You kind of passed out yesterday and slept for a whole day."

He naturally grabbed my arms as he spoke, our life-long friendship and comfortableness giving way to the behavior. I raised my brows when I realized what he said. "Really? Wow. I guess I needed it with everything that's been going on over the past few days. Fudge! What about work, though? I had appointments last night."

"Slade called Adam and had them rescheduled."

"Adam?" I mumbled but shook my head, not caring as long as it had been taken care of. "So, what?" I smiled. "Y'all decided to have a sleepover? Where are we exactly?"

"Yeah, well, we couldn't decide on who got to stay with you, so we decided to bring you to the place we're renting and then could take turns cuddling with you."

My face heated up at the thoughtfulness and the fact that three guys wanted to cuddle with me. "Oh, well, thanks."

"It's cute seeing you blush."

"I have to agree. Your blush is adorable," Zane piped in. I looked over Simon's shoulder and found him watching us, an easy smile on his face, though it was edged with some sadness. My stomach reminded me I hadn't eaten in a day, roaring its displeasure, so I decided to drop the heavy emotions for now.

"Well, hello, tum tum." I giggled, looking down at the offending noise. "So, what? Y'all are friends who make breakfast together?"

Simon turned and observed Zane before glancing

back at me, shrugging. "Yeah, I guess you could say we are, Lemon Drop."

His teasing didn't go unnoticed, but it helped break whatever sadness lingered around Zane as he sauntered over and leaned on Simon's shoulder.

"Ooo, Lemon Drop. I need a cutesy name for you. I can't be left out now. Hmm, what about pumpkin?"

Scrunching up my nose, I shook my head as Simon laughed. "Ew, no. My dad calls me that."

This, of course, started a rapid firing of ideas from the two of them.

"Sugar puss?"

"Skittles?"

"Berry sweet?"

"Oh, I know! Oranges! She's already peaches and lemons, might as well join the family with oranges!" Simon offered, barely able to get it out before he was bending over, laughing hysterically at himself.

Crossing my arms, I rolled my eyes as I walked over to the fridge, looking for something to drink. The cool air felt nice, helping to stop the blush from rising. Grabbing a soda can, I smiled inwardly that Si had gotten my favorite—Diet Sunkist. Popping the tab, I looked between the two, ignoring I was about to drink an orange soda after Simon's joke.

"I don't know how I feel about y'all becoming chummy."

"Too bad. You don't get a say Lemon Drop." Simon's arms wrapped around me, pulling me into him as I snuggled close.

"I don't think I'm supposed to be forgiving you yet."

"You can hate me all you want, babe, but you'll forgive me. I've missed you and don't want to lose any more time with you, so I'm not going anywhere."

"We need to talk about stuff, though, Si," I protested weakly.

"Okay, done. Let's go talk. Thane, you got the rest of breakfast?"

"Yeah, man. I'm good. It'll be ready in a little bit."

"All right, cool." Simon pulled me out of the room, directing me to a living room area. I started biting my lip, uncertainty coursing through me now we were here, about to have this conversation.

"Maybe we should wait."

"Nope, we're gonna do it now." He stopped once we were in the room, facing me. Simon gave me a serious look as he regarded me. "Tell me what's bothering you, Lenn. What's holding you up? Or maybe, holding you back?"

"I just... I guess, first I'm upset with you for keeping the fact you wrote to Blaze from me. And second, that you knew Slade was Blaze. On top of that, you then dated him behind my back." I paused, knowing I needed to get the rest out, but scared of what it might mean. Simon, being my best friend, waited, knowing I wasn't finished. "If I hadn't walked in when I did... what would've happened? Were you *cheating* on me? Do you want to be with him more than me? I mean, we hadn't had an exclusive conversation, but I thought it was understood, and—"

I'd started to ramble at the end, talking a mile a minute, needing to get the words out before I chickened out. Once they'd started, they kept coming, and it took

Simon grabbing me and leading me toward the couch before my word vomit stopped.

"Lenn, take a deep breath." Nodding, I breathed with Simon until my breaths slowed and my heart wasn't racing. He kept hold of my hands, squeezing them.

"I have nothing to say about my behavior and why I didn't tell you. Nothing at least that would make it okay," he sighed. "Believe it or not, I went to see a therapist when you left, and I realized I'm a sabotager. When things are good, I freak out and screw them up. Your friendship was the only relationship I hadn't managed to undermine. When I finally had everything I wanted… it scared me, and I couldn't admit there was a small part of me that couldn't let the idea of him go, either. I'm sorry it hurt you in the process. It took losing you to figure out my destructive patterns in relationships and how I didn't believe I deserved you for keeping so many things hidden."

"Why couldn't you just tell me, Si? I thought we told each other everything? I would've understood or helped you figure it out."

"I'm sorry, Lenn. I did everything wrong. I let fear consume me, and I thought having you as a friend was better than not having you at all, but it tore me up, and I became a version of myself I didn't recognize. I'm not proud to admit I kept writing to Blaze, and hid it, because I liked having something secret. He was a safe place to figure out my conflicting emotions. But one secret became two, and then more. I was carrying so many it was hard to look at you. After Duncan, I couldn't take the guilt of it all."

"What did you feel guilty about with Duncan? He was your friend too."

"Because maybe if I'd been honest with you, then we would've been together at the restaurant when you got the message. We could've commiserated together or just gone home, but my betrayal, on top of Blaze's words, sent you running away. If you weren't avoiding me, if I'd kept better watch over you, then maybe nothing else would've happened. You wouldn't have been drugged, and Duncan would still be alive."

Tears rolled down his face, and I found myself shaking my head violently to and fro, tears streaming down mine as well. "No, Simon. No. It's not your fault, just as it's not Slade's, or even mine. We all could've made better choices, but none of us are to blame for his death. Do you hear me? *You're not to blame for that.*"

He nodded, and we both moved at the same time, embracing one another as we cried. "He was your friend too, and he would never want you to carry around that guilt, Si. He wouldn't blame you, either."

"I failed him, though, and I failed *you*. I wasn't a good best friend. I didn't watch over you like I'd vowed to do. I let you down, I let your father down, but *especially* Dunc."

"No, Simon." I rubbed his back, my tears rolling down his bare chest as we clung to one another. This had been way overdue, and I registered now how much we'd needed this. Hiding hadn't brought me anything but more pain.

"I was stupid for running away from you, for drinking alone like I did. I was just so hurt, and I wasn't thinking. My whole world felt like it had been blown apart. I can own that now, that I didn't handle it the best, but I'm also not to blame for what occurred after." Pulling back, I held his face in my hands. "Neither of us are, only the person who killed Duncan. *Only them*, do you hear me, Simon Fisher?"

He nodded, bringing his hands to mine on his face. Leaning his forehead down, we stared at one another for a bit before I leaned back, wiping his tears away. "Wow, I hadn't expected this many tears before breakfast, but I oddly feel better," I admitted, chuckling through them.

"Me too. But I have some more things I need to say to you."

"Okay," I accepted, taking a deep breath as I took in his serious face.

"I'm sorry beyond words for destroying your trust and letting secrets build. When we were teens, I should've told you about my confusing feelings and writing to Blaze to talk about it. I should've told you about figuring out Slade was Blaze and that we'd been together. I wish I was perfect for you, but I'm not. I selfishly liked having him to myself. I'd always been jealous of your connection to one another, not wanting to be replaced. I also knew if I told you, it would end, and I didn't want to lose both of you. So, I settled for him in secret, but then it became too much to bear, and I stopped." He swallowed, his eyes searching mine. I held them, letting him see me to my core, nothing but vulnerability and acceptance staring back.

"I'll do whatever I need to do in order to gain your trust back. I'm done being a coward thinking I'm happy with just staying your friend. I want a chance to prove we can be great together, and perhaps, that includes all three of us. I think I knew we all needed to be together, but was too afraid to admit what I wanted wasn't normal... again. I got trapped thinking I needed to conform, to accept things could only be one way, but that's not you or me. Losing you taught me that no matter how hard the conversation or the consequences of the truth are, I have to speak up. Not having you in my life at all was the worst version of it. If you're mad at me, for months, a year, whatever it takes, it would be better than nothing. As long as I know you're still in my life, then I still have an opportunity and a chance to be a part of it. So, name your price for what it will take."

Simon's face was earnest, and I knew there weren't any more secrets hiding between us now. I hugged him briefly before withdrawing. Tapping my lips, I debated on what his 'price' would be. "Hmm, well, let me think about it. I need to be creative."

He smiled wide, his shoulders dropping. "As scared as that makes me, I'm ready, Lenn. I'll do it."

"Who wants to be the one to wake up grumpy pants?" Zane hollered. "French toast is done, so it's time to eat, folks."

"I'll do it," Simon offered, and I gave him a look. "Yeah, we'll make sure that's something *else* we talk about together."

"About you sleeping together?" I admitted.

"Yeah, and if it's going to be a possibility for all of us to be in a relationship. I want to be open with how I feel about you both," Simon admitted.

"Would you want to be with only him if I said no?"

"Never. I love you, Lenn, but I think I could love him too if I let myself."

I nodded, confessing as well. "I don't think I could choose between you two either, so I can't make you do it. I also think I have feelings for…"

"Thane?" He smiled in question.

"Yeah, Zane."

"So, are you really calling him that?"

"Most definitely. I can't call him that psycho's name, and stalker Thane, or imposter Thane, or whatever is just too long and confusing."

"Okay." He laughed at my reasoning, his eyes filled with humor. "How about we all talk about it over breakfast?"

"Sounds good."

He kissed me on the forehead and walked off towards the bedroom. I watched him go, his butt looking delicious, and for once I didn't feel guilty for lusting after him. Heading into the kitchen, I grabbed the dishes Zane had set out and placed them on the little breakfast table. He saw me and noticed my face, which had to be red and puffy.

"How are you feeling today after processing everything, gorgeous?"

"Not too bad." I shrugged, turning to look at him as he carried over the food. "I mean, the sleep helped. I'm just trying to figure out everything else, I guess, one step at a time. I keep thinking I need to be angrier and not give in to their cute smiles and touches. But in light of everything else, it doesn't seem as relevant anymore. It also makes me want to hold the people I care about closer, especially with everything I've lost." I looked up, holding his eyes. "That maybe this is how I can finally be with them, and I'd be stupid not to take it considering we all love each other."

His voice was quiet, but I heard it. "Does that include me?"

"I'd like it to."

"I'd like it to, too." He smiled, and I found myself reaching out for his hand.

"So, I guess *this* conversation is happening over breakfast," Simon said, announcing his presence.

"Mm, I'd much prefer other *things* to talking," a deep sexy voice rumbled from behind me. Before I knew it, I was turned around and dipped as Slade kissed me, and I mean *kissed* me. He didn't let it go too deep, and righted me. I was most stunned when Slade boinked my nose with a smile, and swayed his sexy rear over to the coffee pot. Filling up a mug, I watched, speechless as my fingers touched my lips, the kiss feeling imprinted there.

Slade turned, smirking as he caught me gaping after him. When he took a sip of his steaming mug, I think my ovaries wept. *Hubba hubba.*

"Damn. I wish I'd thought of saying good morning that way," his brother joked.

"You jealous I got the swagger skill, Brother?" Slade taunted, undressing me with his eyes.

"Yeah, I kinda am." Zane was watching me too, and the room became very heated for an entirely different reason than breakfast being ready as they both gazed at me.

"Okay, okay." I held my hands up, stepping back as Zane started to move in. "Y'all are crazy. Let's not go around kissing Lennox before we talk. I only have so much restraint, and I don't want my hormones to decide for me. Let's eat first. I'm starving and only a few seconds away from going hangry."

"You said we were gonna talk yesterday, and that didn't work out so well, now did it, Peach?"

Ignoring the impossibly attractive but stubborn man, I sat down and started to fill my plate with food. Once I'd taken a few bites, the stomach was appeased, and I could ask my own question, effectively dismissing Slade's jab.

"Speaking of, did you guys figure out a plan to deal with psycho Thane?"

"Do we really have to call him that? Because it's still my name, you know?"

"No, it's not," I protested, laughing. "You're Zane, get with it. I think we need to go down to the clerk's office and change it, make it all official." Smiling wide, I looked up at him, batting my eyelashes.

"Not going to happen, pretty girl."

"You can say no all you want, but I think you'll find it's gonna stick."

"Yeah, *Zane*," Slade agreed, winking at me for good measure. Why did he have to be so charming? Simon chuckled at my distress, and Zane only rolled his eyes, going back to his food. It felt nice sitting there with the three of them around the table. I loved how they got along with one another. I couldn't deny the chemistry between Slade and Simon either. Despite what Simon claimed about not being sure of his feelings, I couldn't deny they loved each other. It was obvious if you looked, the way they watched one another, and the casual touches I caught here and there. If I could love four people in my lifetime and want to be with three of them at the same time, then I couldn't deny them being together, too. If we could figure out a way to try this, they should also get a chance.

"Okay, I have an idea."

They all stopped eating and looked at me, the weight of their eyes on me was a heady feeling, and it felt nice being their center.

"Yes, Peach?" Slade asked, giving me a knowing grin when I didn't start right away, too caught up in their sexiness.

"Well, first, I think you should tell me the plan for psycho Thane." Zane grumbled under his breath at my comment, but it only made me smile wider. "Then, I think we should do something... together. That's if I can reschedule my clients again, boss?"

Slade traced his eyes over me slowly before returning to mine. "It depends on what we do if I'm going to let you off or not. I'm not line dancing again." He lifted the corner of his lips, the lip ring catching and I wanted to lick it. Slade's eyes held mine steady, daring me to say line dancing. Smiling, I almost said it, but I had a better idea instead.

"I think we should go to the go-cart and paintball fields first, and then I think a rematch of our truth or dare game is in order."

Slade held my eyes, his lips spreading wider as he remembered how the last one had ended with us naked. I'd gotten trapped in his eyes, so when Zane spoke up, I blinked, looking at him.

"Like we used to play in our letters." I nodded,

having to reconcile my brain again. He was part of Blaze too.

"Well, I don't know how this could go wrong at all," Simon joked.

"If it ends how the last one did, Si, there's only happy endings to be had."

Simon looked between Slade and me, a look of understanding appearing on his face. "That's when? You two? The night of the storm?" His words came out choppy as he looked back and forth, pointing between us.

"Yep, that's when Slade hit it and quit it."

"Oh, you pumped and dumped, Slade? That's so bad."

"Yep, he cum and go."

"Bust a load and hit the road."

Zane chimed into our game, and Slade couldn't get a word in as we carried on.

"Dicked and dashed."

"Ejaculate and evacuate."

"Ride and hide."

"Jizz n' jet."

"Nut n' bolt!"

"Wham, bam, thank you, ma'am." I managed to get out before Slade smacked his hands on the table causing the silverware to jump.

"Just because y'all think you're so funny, no day off, Peach!" He sat back, looking all smug, crossing his arms. "And not that it matters, but I still thought you were a liar at that point."

"Yeah, yeah." I rolled my eyes. "Well, I'm glad we

got that covered. Your request is denied. Try again! So, about this plan?"

Slade scowled, but at my last question they all turned, looking at each other. Almost all together, they looked at me, cringing a little.

"What did you do?"

NOX TO THANE

From: noxsmiles@heartsemail.com
To: blazetats@heartsemail.com
Subject: No pigs were hurt in that joke, right?

Dear Sweet Blaze,

I was entirely prepared to tell you how much I hate you and that you suck. But instead, I'm here to thank you.

Why, you might ask?

Because I did it. I completed your dare and I sang in the talent show. I didn't win, but I did come in 3rd, beating out stupid Shelley. I have to admit, that felt better than winning. Her face was so red when I walked up to collect my certificate for a free sundae. It was the best sundae I ever had. So thank you for pushing me to do it. I still was nervous as all get out, but I managed, showing myself I could do it.

Now I know I never want to do that again.

Laugh, but it was terrifying! So many people were

looking at me. No thank you. I'd have to be really wanting something to ever sing in public again.

My mom had a small incident this week. Fortunately, it wasn't out in public, but it was still scary for me. I worry about her and that one day I won't be there to help her. I'm teaching Noah how to draw, it's something fun we can do together. He seems to like it, so I'm going to keep doing it. Plus, it helps my mom out and lets her have some rest time. I know she's stressed being with him all day, her friends and colleagues abandoning her. I hope one day to have the best of friends who I never have to question.

Your joke was terrible by the way. But I did laugh, so I guess it worked. Here is my go to joke.

How do you make a tissue dance?

You put a little boogie in it.

Ha, ha. Lame, I know.

Your dare sir, is to do something fun with your brother like you used to. If you don't, then you must wear a chicken costume all day while asking people if they know why the chicken crossed the road. Picture proof must be sent.

Let's meet under the stars tonight, listening to track #3. Then it will feel like we're listening and watching together.

Nox

Chapter Eleven

LENNOX

MY QUESTION HUNG in the air as I waited for a response. The guys looked sheepishly at me as I glared daggers as I waited to be filled in. "This isn't the time to be keeping secrets, remember. Out. With. It."

Simon caved first as I knew he would. He blew out a breath, ruffling his hair. "It's not so much what we *did*, but what we *said*."

"Meaning?"

"Well, he texted while you were asleep, and…"

"And I told him where to go fuck himself," Slade grunted, going back to eating. Clearly, he didn't care about the privacy violation, feeling justified in his actions.

"How?" I managed to get out between my clenched teeth.

"You're really hot when you get all angry, Peach. You got some Scarlet Witch vibes going on there. You're not going to melt my brain or anything though, are you?"

His comment had me blinking as I tried to process. "What the what?" Slade smirked, taking a bite of his toast. My eyes grew as I tried to figure out what the h-e-double hockey sticks just occurred. Shaking my head, I returned my gaze back to Simon. He was the most likely to tell me without malfunctioning my brain in the process.

"*Explain*, please."

"Scarlett Witch is a character from Marvel, and she—"

"No, not that part! I've seen Wanda Vision, thank you very much. I'm talking about telling psycho Thane to, you know, eff himself." It didn't escape Slade's attention that I mumbled the last part, still not wanting to say the word out loud unless it called for it.

"*Fuck* himself?" he offered, tempting me with his raised eyebrow. "Just say fuck, Peach."

"Quit redirecting the conversation away from what *you* did."

"He uh, texted him on your phone," Zane offered, receiving a scowl from Slade. "What? She asked and deserves to know. *I'm* being open here."

Slade dropped his head, rolling it around dramatically before he looked at me. "Fine. *Zane's* right." He chuckled, apparently finding it amusing that I changed his brother's name. "Your phone vibrated when I was carrying you. It was a text from him asking why you hadn't called him back yet. So, I kindly told the psycho murder stalker to take his slimy fake self back to whatever hole he crawled out of and leave *my girlfriend* alone."

"Argh," I moaned, rubbing my temples. "So, you basically told the person who we think has been interfering with our lives for years you were on to him and then proceeded to insult him?"

When I opened my eyes, I found Slade looking contrite. "Well, when you put it like that... *yes*?"

"Awesome, so no plan other than to taunt psycho Thane. This is why I don't sleep, because *apparently*, the world falls apart around me when I do."

The guys all looked down, remorse heavy on their faces. My anger clouded the room, changing the mood and I didn't like it. Taking a few breaths to gather myself, I calmed my panic. Nothing I could do about it now, and berating them for something wasn't going to improve our relationships, either.

"I'm sorry, Lennox. I wasn't thinking clearly. I never do when it comes to you. I just reacted. I didn't mean to upset you, Peach. I just wanted him to leave you alone. But you're right. There I said it too," he sighed. "I probably only pissed him off more."

The bravado had fallen away, and I saw the guy he'd been the night of the storm, the guy I knew him to be as Blaze. Mostly, I saw the man I was beginning to find again through his love letters. I nodded, accepting his apology, and the way his face changed had my heart skipping a beat.

"I'm sorry for erupting at y'all. It wasn't helpful, either. I'm just furious I didn't know. I've been around him for *months*. I was the one to let him into my life. He even ate dinner with my family. Shit, I kissed him for crying out loud!"

My breathing came quickly, and I realized the problem. He'd taken away my sense of safety, perverting the things and people I loved with his deceit. The lines had been blurred between safety and danger. I didn't know how to trust myself, and if I didn't have that, what did I have? It was the problem I'd been having all along. Hands fell to my knees as my chair was spun around.

They squeezed a rhythm, and I found myself looking into the eyes of the owner.

"When I wake up in the morning, and the alarm gives out a warning, I don't think I'll ever make it on time," he sang, pulling a smile to my face.

"By the time I grab my books and I give myself a look, I'm at the corner just in time to see the bus fly by."

"It's alright 'coz I'm saved by the bell," we sang together.

"Thank you."

"No problem, butternut squash."

I screwed up my nose, shaking my head, but it had me laughing, and my panic receded.

"Not that I don't love some 90's Saturday morning nostalgia, but what the hell was *that*?" Slade moved his fork back and forth between us, utter confusion on his face.

"Don't be so dense, babe," Simon answered before I could. "It's clearly their nerdy way of saying they like each other. You're gonna have to get used to it."

Slade glanced at him, a look of shock on his face. "But, *no!*" I bristled, expecting him to say Zane and I couldn't like each other, but he surprised me when he grabbed Simon's arm, speaking to him. *"We're supposed to be the cute nerdy pair!"*

Simon chuckled, shrugging his shoulders. "There's room enough for us all to be nerds. But I don't think you're gonna convince anyone with all your tattoos that you're a nerd. Embrace your bad boy self, Slade. You got the whole resting asshole face down."

"I'm outraged you don't think I could pass as a nerd."

Zane leaned in, whispering, "I do like you, you know."

I met his eyes, nodding. "I like you too." His smile managed to grow wider. "Thanks for before. I started to think about it all, and it got overwhelming."

"No sweat." He winked, getting up and returning to his seat. Slade and Simon were still fake arguing about nerds and bad boys, and I laughed, realizing how much I liked their banter. Slade turned back to me, winking. He sobered, looking between me and Zane.

"Peach, I don't know how I feel about sharing you with my brother." My heart sank at his words, and I felt Zane stiffen.

"Babe—" Simon started before Slade hushed him with a look.

"*But,*" he emphasized, giving us all a look for jumping to conclusions, "it's not for me to tell you how to feel. I don't want to admit it to myself, but it's all been inevitable since the beginning anyway, the four of us. So… I'll figure out how to be okay with it. I can't guarantee I won't dick punch you, *Zane,*" he snorted, still finding it funny, "if I see you kiss her. Or that I won't start some arbitrary war of who can leave the best love bites. It's my nature," he shrugged, "but I'll try for you."

Zane and I looked at one another, smiling for a second. I looked back between the other two knuckle-heads at the table. "So, does that mean you two?"

He looked at Simon, his features softening, and I found Si, *blushing*. It was adorable, and I was surprised when I didn't feel jealous.

"We'd like to figure it out if you're good with it?"

Slade asked, looking back at me for an answer. I nodded, smiling. I felt contentment settle inside me, at such odds to how I'd been the past two days, months, years even. I liked it, and the anxiety of having to get it right fell away. It was time to just try.

"Yes, I'm good with it. But it's just us, right? We're exclusive otherwise? I didn't do this with Simon, and it led to a lot of hurt feelings, so I want the lines to be clear."

"Peach, I've been yours since I was sixteen. I told you I was all in, and I meant it. There's no one else besides this clown for me."

I bit my lip, moving uncomfortably in the chair at the heat in his words. Slade's eyes seared into me, promising me *all kinds* of things. I watched as he licked his lips, his tongue ring peeking out slightly. My breath hitched, raising for an entirely different reason this time. A throat cleared, bringing me out of the lust haze mere seconds before I launched myself across the table at my hunky Tatzilla.

"I don't want to date anyone else either, turnip. I haven't had feelings for you as long, but I haven't been able to stop thinking about you since the night we kissed. I'd like to see where our chemistry goes."

"Okay, well, I guess I have three boyfriends then."

"Now, who's cursed, Lenn?" Simon laughed, giving me a pointed look.

We finished breakfast, making plans for the rest of the day, ignoring Slade when he said I still had to work unless I wanted to work off my hours in other ways. I showered and wore my jeans with a borrowed shirt and boxers from Simon. We were going to stop by the shop to do a few quick reschedules and so I could change, then we'd head to the place. I found my phone in my pocket and pulled it out. I had a couple of messages from my family, and Darcie so I replied quickly to them. There was one from psycho Thane too, but I decided to ignore it, for now. I didn't want to ruin the day with his crazy threats, needing one day to escape everything he represented. I could see the start of a message, and it already gave me hives. I'd deal with him tomorrow.

Before shoving it in my pocket, I placed it on do-not-disturb and walked out with my three guys, a smile on my face. Slade was pacing outside, on the phone yelling at someone, but I ignored it, happy it wasn't me for once. When he caught up to us, I caught the tail end before he hung up.

"I don't *care*, Adam. You're the manager. Figure it out. Don't think I haven't noticed how absent you've been lately either. If you care about your job, then do this, or I'll find someone else."

He looked at me before he hung up, heat blazing down my spine. Slade Evans was a man full of possession and dominance, and I couldn't wait to be owned by him wholly—heart, body, and soul.

LAUGHING, I raced toward Equinox Ink, Simon hot on my tail as I attempted to make it to 'base' before he caught me. We'd decided to play tag the last block here after parking, and I'd barely tagged him before he was on me again. Slade ignored us, rolling his eyes, but I caught the smile playing on his lips as we laughed and ran around him.

I'd decided at the last minute to wear a dress again when we'd stopped at the apartment. The skull and rose material fluttered around my legs as I ran, reminding me how much I loved dresses. It had felt fitting for October, with it's gothic look and I found I felt more like myself wearing it, too, so that was a bonus.

It was something I hadn't realized until slipping it on. I'd taken some leggings and my chucks for 2 Good 2 Kart & Paint, not wanting to flash everyone while attempting to throw balls of paint. Thankfully, they'd given us jumpers to wear, protecting our clothes. Apparently, the setup was similar to a late 90's movie with Heath Ledger, but it was fun even if I hadn't been familiar with it. Zane had schooled us all at paintball, his natural athleticism giving him an edge. Though it had been Simon who won the go-cart races. It had been great to get away and laugh together. It was exactly what we'd all needed.

Some people had looked at us oddly when all the guys had taken turns holding my hand or sitting next to me, but I'd gotten used to shrugging off the judgmental stares long ago and just enjoyed being out with them. We'd dropped Zane off at the vet clinic on our way back after we'd eaten. He had to check in with his boss and do some paperwork after returning from Africa. I did get to hold a puppy for a few minutes as he gave us a tour.

In some ways, I wondered how I ever fell for the faker because the real Thane blew him out of the water.

The red flags I'd ignored seemed obvious now, but I couldn't beat myself up anymore over it. I had to choose to focus on us and move forward. I'd almost made it to the door, my victory in sight when arms wrapped around me, hauling me up over a shoulder, causing a squeak to leave me.

"Good gravy! I'm going to flash the entire street, Slade!"

"Fine," he bit out, moving me down into a bridal carry instead of the fireman hold he had me in. He looked down, daring me to say something now.

"Just put me down. I was almost winning. Besides, I'm heavy. I don't want you to carry me that far."

"Are you calling me weak, Peach? Because I know you're not calling yourself fat."

"No, I'm not. I'm fine with how I look, but I also know I'm not a skinny Minnie, size 2 either. Hell, I'm not even in the single digits. I'm not ashamed of my weight, but I'm *realistic* about my weight."

"All I heard was, 'Slade, please eat me out until I'm a quivering mess to show me how much you like my plump thighs wrapped around your head.' Did you hear anything different, Si?" He asked Simon, who grinned at me as he leaned against the door, having beaten me due to Slade's interference.

"You forgot the part where she said she would lick Simon like a lollipop."

Gasping, I looked around the street to see if anyone heard them. No one was around, and the two of them laughed at my outrage, finding it humorous to embarass me. Slade kept me in his arms, and to my dismay, showed no sign he was fatigued. Huffing, I crossed my arms, resigned to my fate of being carried, while inwardly loving every second of it.

"What's wrong, Lenn? Don't like being called out?" Simon teased, moving closer, crowding me in with Slade against the wall. Licking my lips, I shook my head.

"Pfft. I would never say lollipop, Si!"

He chuckled, and even Slade's chest rumbled with laughter. Simon looked down, then looked up through his eyelashes, and I swear every part of my body spasmed at the sexiness of that move.

"What *would* you say then, Lenn?"

"Um." I swallowed, finding my mouth suddenly dry. "An ice cream cone?"

He moved closer, effectively trapping Slade and me against the wall. "Hmm, is that so?"

I didn't know where this side of Simon had come from, but holy guacamole, it was hot. Slade shifted me, and my leg brushed against something hard, and I realized how turned on he was too.

"I uh, I think it's time to play truth or dare!" I shouted.

I wanted to slap myself but also knew I needed more time to process everything; even if it was only five more minutes, I needed to make sure I was ready for this step. Something in my voice must've conveyed it to Simon, and he nodded. "Okay, we can play, Lenn, if you really want to."

"Oh, yes, I do." I nodded, doing a great impression of a bobblehead. "I think it will be fun."

"*Fun*," Slade deadpanned. "You know we're just going to dare you to do sexy things, right?" His pierced eyebrow lifted at me, and I felt my face flush at the notion.

"Nope, I'm going to make a rule!" I proclaimed, deciding right then. "First, put me down, and we can walk up the stairs."

"Never, Peach."

He held me tight, walking up the single flight, and I held on, worried we'd fall, but he only smirked more at me triumphantly when we made it up the stairs, and he wasn't even a wheezing mess like I typically was.

"Show off," I mumbled, making him even more cocky. He bent down quickly, capturing my lips in a searing kiss before he pulled back and sat me down.

"Grab some stuff, and then we're heading back to the other place."

"Yes, sir!" I saluted, but it only had the opposite effect when his eyes heated more at the 'sir.' An idea struck me, and I spun, my skirt flaring out around me. Man, I'd missed that effect. "Actually, I think we should ask one question here before we go."

"Hmm," he assessed me. "What are you thinking, Peach?"

"You'll have to see. You going first?"

"Sure, if it means I get to ask you next."

"Nope, circle, otherwise it's not fair."

"Fine." He rolled his eyes. "Simon will ask the same thing, anyway."

"Speak for yourself, babe. I have my own plans!"

"I forgot how bratty you both can be together. Ugh, what am I getting myself into?" he fake groaned, rolling his head. Piercing me with his eyes, he locked them on me. "Fine. I'm going to need tequila, though. Do you have any?"

"Top cabinet, but it's old."

"Old works," he mumbled, heading there. I threw some clothes into a bag and grabbed my toiletries along with some other items I would want. I could always grab things if I needed them when I was at work. I had to be back tomorrow anyway, only able to push things off for so long. Dropping it by the door, I found the two guys sitting at the table, and I pulled up a chair.

"Okay, Slade, truth or dare?"

"Dare."

Smiling wide, I asked my question, hoping he'd give in this time. "I dare you to let me tattoo you."

He watched me with no emotion at first, and then grabbed the tequila, taking a shot causing my heart to sink. Slade slammed the shot glass down, doing a full-body shudder as the liquor coursed through him. "*God*, that's awful." He looked up, noticing my face.

"What's wrong, Peach?"

Shaking my head, I held back my disappointment. "It's your turn to ask, Simon." Realization appeared in his eyes before he was up, grabbing my hand and leading me downstairs. "I wasn't taking the shot to avoid the dare, Peach. I was taking it to prepare myself for the pain."

"*Oh*."

"Yeah, oh. But I have an amendment. I'll let you tattoo me if you let me tattoo you. Besides, I think you owe me, right?"

Nodding, I smiled, happiness filling my steps. Long ago, I'd agreed to let him give me my first tattoo. It had been a promise I made at eighteen when he'd started out at a shop. I'd held onto the promise, even when I thought he'd pretended the whole time, something telling me it was important I did.

"When you told me no last time, it was the first time I wondered if I had it wrong. Because if you'd known, I thought you would go for it, or if you didn't care about the promise, then you'd go for it or already have one. Either way, I was fully prepared to tattoo 'liar' on your ass or something. But when you declined, and said you had reasons, it made me stop and wonder."

"You're not going to still tattoo 'liar' on my butt, are you?" I asked, horrified.

"No, Peach. I have the perfect thing designed for you. We'll have to do it tomorrow as it will take too long tonight."

"Okay, I feel anxious all of a sudden." He ignored me, though, asking me a question instead.

"What are you going to give me? I'm sorry I never told you, but you're very talented, Peach. I've been tracking your designs on the feed, and I'm mad at myself for not giving in to you years ago. You're going to be so busy soon with requests you won't be able to do walk-ins."

"You really mean that?" I blushed, appreciating the recognition.

"Do I lie?"

"Well…"

"Fair, and that was more like keeping it to myself, but have I ever lied to your face?"

"Well…"

"Okay, I was an asshole in the past. But I'm not lying to you now. I promise."

"Thank you."

I moved him toward my chair and started pulling out items. There were a few other people in the shop, but they ignored us, and I got to work, blocking out the fact I was about to put something on Slade's beautiful inked skin. He didn't have very much free space, but I knew where I wanted it.

"Can you like, look at Simon. If you watch me, it will freak me out."

"I want to watch you work, Peach."

"Then you might end up with a dick on your finger."

Rolling his eyes dramatically, he turned his head away and began to talk with Simon, who had pulled up another stool and was looking around at everything. I grabbed Slade's hand and cleaned the area. Taking a deep breath, I sketched the design onto the inside of his ring finger. It only took a few seconds, the design was small, but once I had it, I went to work and inked him. He didn't budge as the tattoo gun started, and I laughed for a brief moment as I recalled my panic dream where I closed my eyes to pierce people.

Blowing out a breath, I filled in the design, carefully holding his hand steady as I did. Ten minutes later, I was done. I sat back, the cute little design a stark contrast to the rest of his skin, but somehow it also fit. Cleaning it, I wrapped it and covered it, not wanting him to see it.

"Done. But you have to wait to see it."

"Now I think you really did draw a dick on my finger."

"I was tempted, but I didn't, just look at it when I'm not around."

"I'll love whatever it is, Peach, because you drew it. Even if it is a dick. I happen to like dick, so it's all good."

Laughing, I felt better and quickly cleaned up before pulling them out of the shop. "Come on, it's your turn to ask Simon something."

We headed back upstairs, and my cheeks heated as I thought about the design and what it meant.

SLADE'S TATTOO

Love Letter

From: emblazed_slade@heartsemail.com
To: emblazed_lennox@heartsemail.com
Subject: My heart song

Dear Peach,

Each day I get to spend with you, I fall even more in love with you. I don't know if I believe in fate, but I know I believe in us. I think we're stronger than fate, finding our way to each other from across the country, through missed connections and lies, to a small town in Kentucky and the back of a tattoo shop. Maybe it's the destiny of the stars, or some cosmic plan. All I know is that I don't care about the reason, as long as it brings me to you.

Today I realized how much easier you make things. Thane and I are getting along better than ever, and I know that's because of you. In the last letter, I told you about Simon and me. So, this one, I'll share about my brother.

You know a lot of our history from our pen pal letters, but I kept a lot of it back too, not wanting to sully our relationship with it. Things started to change between us after the divorce. I'll admit I wasn't the easiest to get along with during that time, and I blamed myself for destroying our family. I was angry at my mom for a long time too, but when she got sick, I pushed it aside, wanting to be there for her. It was a lot of guilt and responsibility for a 12-year-old, and for the first time in my life, I felt alone.

Thane made friends easily and school came naturally to him. I was *jealous* of it and it started to come between us. I didn't know how to do those things on my own, and I blamed him. I know now that I should've never been put in that situation and that I was too young to understand everything, but it changed us. I started to resent him, and it put a wedge between us.

When Mom died, I raged out against him, wanting someone to blame. It was so scary being there by myself and not knowing what to do. To this day I can still hear her gasping for her last breath. It haunts me and for a while, I saw his face when I would hear it and how he wasn't there. I pulled away from him. I did. I was a mess and I didn't know how to handle my grief.

When I discovered he'd been writing to you, it was the ultimate betrayal. It took me a while to be able to forgive him for that. It wasn't until after we were both in Nashville that we'd started to work on things. The night everything went to shit, I thought he'd been lying to me again when I found him helping you. I pulled him into the bathroom, and that is something I regret because you were gone when we came out. I know I can't 'what if' it, but it's something I live with, and wonder.

I don't know why I told you that, perhaps to tell you that I wish I'd handled it differently, and even when I thought I hated you, I thought of you continuously. I have a lot of faults, Peach, but loving you was never one of them. I'm sorry I couldn't get my head out of my ass sooner and see how much I cared about you. But we're here now, and I don't want to waste a day where I don't tell you I love you.

I love you.

I'll meet you in the stars, under a million different galaxies until our song stops—may it never stop.

Your 'loveable' asshole.

Chapter Twelve
LENNOX

SIMON WALKED BACK to the table, grabbing the bottle when we entered the apartment again. He bypassed the chair and walked into the living room.

"So, are we staying here or heading out? I don't want to get comfortable if we're leaving soon," I asked, standing, shifting my weight.

"Let's just stay here, Slade. We can all fit on the bed, it will be fine. I'm sure there are some clothes for us around. If not, I'll run to the place in the morning and grab some."

Slade looked between us, nodding. "Yeah, okay. I might be able to do your tat before anyone else gets here in the morning too."

Gulping, I nodded, kicking off my shoes as I sat in the chair, pulling my legs under me. I didn't trust myself to sit next to them on the couch. I'd told myself earlier to let go of the fear, but it was hard to kick the habit. My heart raced, only emphasizing my nerves.

This was the first time we'd all three been alone since we admitted our feelings. I'd been dodging their advances as best I could all night, but it seemed my clock had run out, and I would have to face this. I didn't know why I was scared, Sawyer had seemed to like being with two guys at once in that series I'd read. Plus, it had been fine afterward. Some of my curse-filled doubt lingered, though, making me fearful.

"Fish, truth or dare?" Slade didn't waste any time, taking a seat on the floor, putting him between us both. To be fair, there wasn't much space in the room to begin with, but with his legs stretched out, he ate up the majority of the remaining area, and I found myself distracted by his long jean-clad legs.

"What the fuck, I'll do a dare."

Slade had a mischievous look on his face when he looked at me. "I dare you to let Lennox pierce *your* junk."

"Oh, fuck no. No offense, Lenn, I'm sure you're awesome, I just," he shivered, "*no*."

Laughing, I gave Slade a pointed look. "That's my dare. You dare stealer."

"All's fair in truth or dare, Peach. Your turn, Si. Now, Ms. Rule follower, can he ask you or me, or does he have to ask you? If that's the case, then we'll always be in the same order, and *that's* not fair." He pointed out, giving me a look. Visions of Slade as a hot teacher flashed through my head.

I nodded, pushing his authoritative look out and thought about a solution as I tapped my lips. "Hmm, yeah, I guess you're right. Okay, so new house rule. You can ask whoever, *however*, no ganging up, so you both can't only ask me. You have to trade off, no doubles!"

"Well, there goes my dare if we can't do any doubles."

I stared, not getting his meaning as he seared me with his heated gaze. "Um, okay."

"Oh, I think you can get her to do it," Simon offered.

His hand had dropped down and rubbed up and down Slade's neck subconsciously.

Narrowing my eyes at Simon, I gave him a pointed look. "Don't make me hurt you, Simon Fisher. I know *all* your weak spots."

He sat up, zipping his lips. "Okay, Lenn, truth or dare."

"Um, truth."

"Who's the better kisser?"

"Nope, not answering that one. Give me the tequila."

Laughing, Slade passed over the bottle, his fingers grazing mine slowly as he did. The tequila burned going down, and I stuck out my tongue at the bitter taste, my nostrils burning. "Oh geez, that is awful."

We managed a few rounds, sharing some truths, some dares, but they were mostly tame ones, and only a few shots were taken between us. The alcohol was doing enough of a job, though, and I felt confident to attempt the first sexual dare.

"I dare you to do a striptease, Peach."

Standing, I didn't hesitate as I watched the shock register a second later at my move before desire took over in his gaze. He licked his lips as I slowly started to move my hips, scrunching up my dress to the music in my head. Seductively, I unzipped it before pushing the sides off my shoulders. Simon turned on some music, and I found it easier to get into the feel of the dance. Their eyes tracked all my movements, making me feel even more seductive.

Pushing the dress off, I let it pool at my feet, standing in only my undergarments. I watched both of them gulp as I went to unhook my bra, feeling sexy under their gazes, my inhibitions lowered as I soaked it in. Letting the cups fall forward, I tossed it at Simon before I turned, mimicking a move I'd seen in the movies. Bending over, I slowly pulled my panties down, showing them all the goods.

I wanted to be embarrassed, but their groans as I pulled them off encouraged me to keep going. Standing back up, I found them laser-focused on me, and I tossed my underwear toward Slade. He caught it, tucking it in his pocket with a smug look. I could see both of their arousals tenting in their pants. Taking a bow, I walked over to Slade and held out my hand.

"I have nothing."

Shaking my head, I smiled. "No, you misunderstand. Give me your shirt."

"*Oh*, gladly."

He whipped it over his head and handed it to me. I pulled my head through the hole before threading my arms through the sleeves. Once I was covered, I sat back in my chair. Still feeling the seduction coursing through me from the dance, I placed my legs over the arm toward them, the shirt sliding forward, barely covering my love glove box.

"Okay, my turn."

"Holy fuck, Lenn. That was sexy as hell, but seeing you in his shirt right now is a close second."

"Good. Now, can I continue?"

"Sorry, please do."

"Simon, truth or dare?"

"Dare."

"I dare you to kiss Slade."

He bent down, not even hesitating, and I found myself shifting in my chair as I watched them. I'd wanted to know what it felt like to see them together but also to push their boundaries and what they were comfortable with. Clearly, it was only me because they kissed one another easily. It was *hot*. Slade had grabbed the back of Simon's head, the force more than he used with me, and I loved the power between them. It was aggressive, masculine, and sexy.

My pussy began to throb with need, and I tried to shift to relieve some of it. Slade caught my movement when he pulled back, giving me a mischievous look.

"I think Peach liked it, Si."

"I think she did too. Lemon Drop, truth or dare?"

"Nope, you just asked me. You can't double-dip!"

They laughed at me, and I still didn't understand what was so funny, so I ignored them, not wanting to admit my cluelessness. "Fine. Slade, truth or dare?"

"Dare."

Slade never took his eyes off me as he spoke, waiting for the dare. "Slade, I dare *you* to striptease."

He blinked, not expecting it before he looked up at Simon. "You're serious?"

"Yup." He nodded, grinning, then winking at me.

"Oh, I'm so ready for this dare! You going to chicken out?"

"Nope."

He stood up, the music was still playing, and he started to drop his hips dancing way better than he had the other night. Apparently, he couldn't line dance, but Magic Mike, he had that down pat. Fanning myself, my breath caught when he started to drop his jeans, and I realized he went commando.

"Holy guacamole!"

Smirking, he pushed them down, his cock springing free. I licked my lips at the beautiful thing, and I heard Simon moan in agreement. Lifting my eyes, I locked them with Simon's, and wowzer, I'd just been sold on the two guy hotness factor as I watched him rub his hard-on through his pants, his eyes heavy with arousal. Slade sat down, leaning back against the couch in all his naked ink glory. He stretched his legs back out, and his thingy waved at me like it wanted me to come play. He crossed his arms behind his head, showing even more of his inked body.

"Mother trucker, you're too hot for your own good." I wasn't confident the drool wasn't running down my face, as my eyes roamed his skin. "Like, how?" I waved my hands in the space, attempting to understand how *that* could exist. Slade stayed quiet, wearing his smug smile proudly as he watched me lose myself over him.

"Um, who's turn is it?" My brain had short-circuited, and if I had to keep staring at him on display like that, I wouldn't be able to keep my resolve. I knew I was kidding myself at this point, but my stubborn pride was holding on until the last minute.

"Truth or dare, Peach?"

Swallowing, I glanced between the two of them, both had hungry looks on their faces. Their taunts of daring me to do sexual things swirled in my head, and I knew this was it. I could choose truth and put an end to the sexual tension building in the room, or... I could take the plunge and erase the last step that was keeping me in the safe zone. Everything built inside of me, coming to a crescendo, and I felt the courage I needed to stop living in fear surge up. I wanted to take ownership of my choices, and quit being cursed.

Landing on Slade, his smile had dropped a little, worried he'd pushed me too far. The words in his letters, the ones he'd been sending me all day, branded on my heart, and I stepped into the truth, no longer wanting to hide in the shadows. Holding his eyes, I gave him the answer he wanted.

"Dare."

He gulped, his smile lifting, and I realized his body relaxed at my acceptance. Slade held eyes with me, not blinking either as he gave me a match, seeing if I would strike it.

"I dare you to spread your legs, and touch yourself for Simon and me, show us how turned on you are."

Gasping, I slowly opened my legs, the position I was in, the perfect view for them. I dropped one leg to the ground to give me better leverage. My hands smoothed over my thighs, and I held eyes with Slade, my Tatzilla, as I started to stroke myself. My breath caught at the first touch, and I knew I had to be soaking wet, glistening for them. Simon moved, grabbing my attention, and I realized he'd moved forward to get a better view.

Biting my lip, I started to swirl some of my juices around my finger and played with my clit first how I liked it. I watched them both, their intense gaze on me spurring on my arousal and comfortableness. Dipping one finger in, I watched as their breathing increased, Slade's chest rising faster as his eyes zeroed in on my digit.

Moving faster, I pushed it in and out, my thumb rubbing on my nub as I did. After a few times, I slid in two fingers and dragged them out slowly so they could witness how wet I was. Their groans of approval had me feeling powerful, and I reached up with my free hand and massaged my breast, pinching my nipple. I found a rhythm quickly, no longer feeling shy about the act, and gave in to the pleasure coursing through me. They never took their eyes off me; Slade didn't even move, outside his breathing. Simon rubbed his length through his jeans as he watched but made no other movement.

Slade's cock bobbed with each breath, and I watched, transfixed by it. I suddenly knew how Sawyer in my book felt when she said she'd been dicknotized because I became mesmerized by how it bobbed back and forth. Nothing could've made me look away. Building up speed, I plunged my fingers in and out, my palm now rubbing against my clit, and I wasn't far from my own orgasm. Knowing what I needed to topple over the edge, I pulled my fingers out and focused solely on my clit. Rubbing in circles, I pinched my nipple, a moan slipping out, and that was all it took as I increased speed.

Toes curling, I found myself clenching, wanting something thicker to squeeze around as my muscles trembled. My breath caught, and my back arched as I threw my head back, a long moan escaping me. When I opened my eyes, I found them watching me, enraptured still, and I licked my lips, loving how sexy it made me feel. Locking eyes with Simon, I gave him a wink.

"Simon, I dare you to do what you said earlier—"

"Fuck the game, Peach. If I'm not balls deep in you in the next ten seconds, I'm going to cum all over your tits instead."

He surged up, grabbing me and lifting me to his waist. My legs wrapped around him naturally, and he stalked off to the bedroom. "Simon, get your ass in here, *naked*, now."

Simon hopped up, and I saw the relief on his face. A moment of doubt had crossed it, and I reached out for him. His smile had me excited for what was to come, but I didn't get to lock fingers with him because Slade had me on my back, his lips on mine in the next moment.

He pulled the shirt off, breaking the kiss only to pull it over my head, and I felt him slam into me as he'd promised. Moaning, I wrapped my arms around his neck tightly as he breathed into mine, pumping into me in short quick bursts. I felt Simon move up next to us on the bed, smoothing my hair back as much as he could so he could see my face. Turning my head, I broke the kiss with Slade and pulled Simon down to me, kissing him with everything I had. Slade lifted up, pulling my hips closer to him as he started to roll his hips.

"Peach, feel like giving a 'double' a try?"

Breaking my kiss, I looked at him and Simon, and I knew I trusted them to take care of me. Nodding, I watched as his smile spread across his face. "I need your words, though, Peaches."

His voice always sounded deeper when he called me that, and I found myself moaning as he continued to slowly thrust in and out. "*Yes*."

Slade pulled me up off the bed, not even taking his cock out of me, and I felt Simon move to where I'd been lying. Slade kept us connected as he waited for Simon to get where he needed. Slowly, he laid me on Simon's chest, and I felt his arms wrap around me. Tilting my head, I found him staring down at me pulling a smile from me. "Hi."

"Hey, Lemon. I love you."

"I love you too, Si."

He kissed my nose, which felt so at odds in the sexual moment, making it mean even more. Slade started to withdraw, and I whimpered, instantly missing him inside me. Groaning, I looked up and found him smiling down at me. "I know, Peach. It will be quick."

S&S worked together, giving me that sandwich I joked about earlier with Babs. Slade lifted me up, sliding me down on Simon's dick. He watched us for a few moments, stroking himself from the view. Simon's hands were all over my body, and I kissed him, falling into the moment with him. When I felt pressure below, at first, I didn't know what was happening as it started to become tighter.

Was Simon's dick growing in size? Pulling away from his kiss, I looked down. Simon had my legs drawn in his arms, and Slade had the base of his cock in his hand, but the rest of it was already in me. Looking further down, I realized why it felt so tight.

H-E-Double Hockey Sticks! These fools were both spearing me with their cocks. I'd thought he meant double as in two guys at once, but apparently, the sly Alpha-hole had meant two dicks in my vagina. I wanted to curse at him, but as he pushed forward, I lost all my words and only moans sounded out. My eyes rolled back in my head, and I thought I might die right there.

"You're doing great, Peach. Fuck, you feel so tight. Rubbing up against Simon's dick feels perfect. It's like a dream, my favorite sandwich ever," Slade mumbled incoherently as he slid in.

Simon and I moaned together. He tilted my chin up and kissed me some more. Somehow they both managed to fit, and I felt so full, I didn't know if I'd make it if they started to move. They held the position for a few seconds, but then Slade began to rock his hips slowly. He leaned down, bracing his arms around us, bringing his face right next to ours.

He kissed me first, then Simon, and I knew this was the life I wanted. It felt right, and as they both took turns moving, my eyes rolled all the way back, the pleasure too intense, and I found myself falling over the edge as I came. It didn't take long for them to follow, and we all laid on the bed a sweaty mess, none of us wanting to move.

At some point, though, Slade did get up, bringing back a towel for Simon and me. He went out into the other room, picking up and turning off the lights. I heard him double-bolt the door before returning. He clicked off the lights in the bedroom and snuggled into me, kissing my cheek as he pulled me close. Simon had already passed out, his soft snores filling the room.

"Was that okay, Peach?"

Nodding, I looked up at him upside down. "Yeah, it

was amazing. Just don't leave in the morning. I don't think I could take it if you did."

"I'm not going anywhere, Peach. I promise. I love you."

My breath caught as I stared into his dark eyes, the gold shimmering around the edges more than ever. It was the first time he'd said it out loud. I'd read it in his letter earlier, but it was different hearing it aloud.

"I love you too."

His smile was radiant as he looked at me, and kissed me briefly before laying his head down. I fell asleep between the two of them, and I felt safe. But most of all, I felt happy and hopeful for my future.

THANE TO NOX

From: blazetats@heartsemail.com
To: noxsmiles@heartsemail.com
Subject: I'll meet you anywhere

Dear Noxy girl,

I'm glad you don't hate me. I honestly don't know what a world without Nox in it would be like. Even though we've never met, I feel your words on my heart, written in songs and letters between us in a language only we know. It sounds absurd when I say that out loud, for how can I know this person as well as I do? But somehow, I just know. It's been what, a few years now? That's practically a lifetime for most people our age. Hopefully, I don't scare you, but I hope to always have you in my life as a friend.

When I read you succeeded in your dare, it made me smile and I wished I'd been able to hear you sing. I'm sure it was beautiful and even better to win over your nemesis. I hope you don't stop singing though. It might have been scary, but in my experience, the more you do something, the easier it gets.

Which brings me to your dare. Oh, how I wanted to avoid this one. I even looked up where I could get a chicken suit online. But at the end of the day, your words sunk in, and I knew I couldn't "chicken out". Very clever if that was your intention.

So, I did it. I asked my brother to hang out. He said no the first time, but that was to be expected. I kept asking though. Getting the first one out of the way made it easier to keep hearing the rejection. I asked him to play a board game. I asked if he wanted to grab burgers. I even asked if he wanted to go to a baseball game. The one he finally said yes to? Going to our mother's grave.

I know it sounds weird, but it was good. I got to say goodbye and it felt like we were united again, even if only for the day.

It opened up the door though, and I'm asking him each week to do something small. So far he's gone with me to the grocery store, and then *he* asked me to give him a ride to a shop he wanted to apply at.

It's a start. So thank you for pushing me to do it.

Your dare this week... I dare you to let your brother pick out your outfit and wear it for a whole day, no matter what it is. (Assuming it's not anything that would get you arrested.) If you choose to pass on this, then you have to sing "I'm a little teapot" anytime someone asks you how you're doing for a day.

Your joke-
    What do you call a cow with no legs?
    Ground Beef.

Forever grateful for you. I'll be under the stars again. This week's music choice, track #9.
    Blaze

Chapter Thirteen
STALKER

THE MUG CRASHED against the wall, the liquid dripping down in brown streams against the white paint. I leaned over the desk, my breathing quick as I braced my arms on the surface and watched my princess sully herself with them.

At first, I'd been happy to see her in the apartment. She'd been avoiding my calls and hadn't returned the night before. I'd been worried they'd ultimately convinced her, destroying everything I'd built. When I'd woken up a few days ago and gotten the notification someone else had entered the apartment, I'd hoped she kicked his lying ass out the door, but after a brief standoff in the bedroom, I watched her slowly start to fall under *his* spell.

Thane didn't deserve her either. He'd always gotten everything he wanted in life, never even having to try. I wouldn't let him steal Lennox. He'd been easy to impersonate though, his relationship already strained with his brother. Add in our similar looks of blue eyes and blonde hair and it had been an easy choice. I'd hoped to cash in on his good fortune and get the girl for once. But now he threatened years of planning and waiting!

Knocking the cup of pens off my desk, I clenched

my fists as I debated punching something. Fuck! How did I spin *this*? What did I do now? They were ruining everything!

The knocking on the door made me scowl further, and I stalked over, yanking it open, the hinges whining in protest.

"What?" I barked, taking out my mood on my coworker.

"I just wanted to make sure you were okay, Mr. DeLuder. There's been a lot of crashing sounds."

"Mind your own business, Jolene. I'm fine."

I slammed the door before the busy body could ask anything else. I didn't need another person sticking their nose where it didn't belong when I already had three people to deal with. My threats had gone unnoticed so far. I would need to make myself known now. It was clear she'd already decided about me. I didn't need to lurk in the shadows any longer.

It was time to enact my bigger plan and remind her why she needed to be with me, her blue-eyed rescuer.

First, I needed to deal with the sexual arousal she'd built in me. Rewinding the feed backward, I put a piece of paper over the part of the screen where the two assholes were, and unzipped my pants, freeing my length. Watching Lennox, I stroked myself, trying to imagine it was just the two of us.

The knocking sounded at the door again, breaking me from the moment. Grunting, I turned to shout at whoever it was to go away, but the door opened before I could protest. The slutty new girl stood in the doorway, a look of shock on her face for a second when she saw I was beating myself off. I flicked off the screen, not wanting her to realize it was an actual video feed. I started to shove myself back into my pants, a scowl on my face at her interruption, when she smiled seductively and entered. She closed the door, locking it behind her, something I'd forgotten to do in my anger earlier.

"You know, I could help you with that. There's no need for you to stop or have to use porn."

I blinked, unsure what she was saying when it hit me. Thankfully, she'd assumed it was a video. I stood, staring at her as I debated. I didn't like to mix business and pleasure, but she had offered, and I could use the release. If anything, I could always use her as a warning to Lennox.

She sauntered forward, biting her lip as she began to undress. I didn't even know her name, not caring enough to learn it when she'd started. I'd heard the talk about her, though, and she'd been spreading her legs for all the guys on the floor. This wasn't the first time she'd flirted with me, hinting she wanted more. It was a hassle I had to deal with my whole life, my looks attracting people when I wasn't interested.

My silence and non-attempt to stop her, gave her the courage to continue forward. Her dress dropped to the ground, her fake tits on full display. I almost stopped her, but she grabbed my dick, her grip tight, and I groaned. Shutting my eyes, I pretended it was Lennox instead, remembering how she felt beneath me the one night I had with her. I berated myself for not taking things further then when she'd been open to it.

The blonde dropped to her knees, swirling her

tongue around my base. Threading my fingers in her hair, I pulled tight, causing her to gasp. "Fuck—"

I didn't let her finish, shoving my cock in her open mouth. Her eyes watered, but she began to suck, and I used her hair to pull her back and forth. After a few minutes, it wasn't cutting it, though, so I wrenched her off, her cry sounding out in the room as I yanked her up.

She smiled seductively, but I ignored it, turning her around and shoved her down on the desk. She faced away from the computer, and I debated if I could get away with it.

"Play with yourself like a good girl," I commanded.

"Yes, sir," she purred and began to do as I said. I rolled my eyes. She was too eager to please, offering no challenge. I picked up my earbud and put it in while she was distracted, and Lennox's moans filled my ear. My dick grew hard again at the sound of my princess. I focused on hers alone and ignored the others, pretending they were mine. I turned the screen on, and for a second, I had to breathe through what they were doing to my girl, the urge to smash things returning.

Instead, I slammed into the girl in front of me, taking her by surprise. I turned my head away from hers and focused on Lennox, her moans in my ear as I timed my thrusts with theirs. When I heard her cum, I was grateful, on the verge myself, and I slammed into the girl, grunting.

When I came back into focus, I quickly flicked off the screen, dropping the earbud as I pulled out. I didn't say anything, walking into the bathroom attached to my office. Jumping into the shower, I quickly rinsed myself, needing to clean the slut off me. When I felt her hands run up my back, I tensed, gritting my teeth.

"Baby, my turn now."

I twisted, grabbing her throat in a tight grip as I slammed her against the wall, the urge to squeeze tighter rose to the surface as I watched her eyes bulge slightly.

"I don't remember giving you permission to come in here."

"I just thought," she spluttered, unable to get out much more.

"Your first mistake is thinking. You were an available hole. Nothing else. This is your one chance to leave before I make you regret coming into my office without permission."

She nodded, her eyes wide. "If you tell anyone, then you'll regret it. Do I make myself clear?"

"Yes."

"Good. Now go. Be gone by the time I'm out."

I let go, not wanting to deal with the clean up of disposing of her body at work. I focused back on my shower, attempting to get my breathing back to normal after her invasion. Once I was calm, I shut off the water and dried off. Thankfully, the bitch was gone when I'd dressed and returned to my office. At least she was able to follow directions.

I gathered my stuff, not able to focus on any other work as it was. Besides, I needed to make a trip, and leave a few presents. Tomorrow, Lennox would know how much I cared about her, and how *angry* she'd made me tonight. If she didn't choose me, she'd regret it.

They all would.

Love Letter

From: emblazed_slade@heartsemail.com
To: emblazed_lennox@heartsemail.com
Subject: I need you

Dear Peach,

Sometimes I look at you, and I can't believe I get to touch you and kiss you. Those are the times you probably catch me staring at you. I hunger for your touch, for your kisses, for your everything, Peach.

I hunger for it all. The darkest parts and the sunshine you so effortlessly provide.

I never realized it, but I need your love.

Not that I'm not capable of living my life without you, but why would I want to? I need your love because you shine on the best parts of me and remind me who I am. I cover myself in darkness because it's easier to push people away than to risk being hurt. I know I've done that ever since my mom's death, and I only got more comfortable doing it the more I did.

Opening my heart up has shown me all these relationships I hadn't known were there. With you, Simon, and Thane especially. Your father is another. Even Bubba. I can see the people in my life that matter and I want to be better for them. I think you love so effortlessly, you don't even know you do it.

The first time I knew I was in love with you was when you said you were going on a date and I got so angry. I didn't write to you for a few days. Don't hate me for saying this, but I went out and hooked up with someone. I thought if I could get you out of my mind, then I'd be okay. It was screwed up and of course it didn't work.

I tried dating, but no one ever measured up.

After the night I almost lost you, I was so angry and hurt, but I couldn't lose you, either. I hate that someone interfered with our meeting, but I also wondered if I hadn't met you randomly, not knowing who you were, if I would've fallen so easily. That might sound weird, but I was already so in love with who you were on paper, I was guarded and protective of that. If you didn't match up, it would've been hard to reconcile that, so I think I went into the meeting with already a precon-ceived notion that it wouldn't be the same.

You'd told me you wanted to stop writing because you needed to move on. I couldn't let you go. But I already felt like I'd lost you. My destructive nature believed so easily the lie because it was what I believed I deserved.

If I had stopped for one second and thought about it, if I had let myself see things without my fear and hurt, then I would've never believed that girl.

But our story is what it is, and it can only change as we take steps each day to make it the story we want it to be.

Tonight was the most amazing experience of my life. Being with you fully, it felt as if the stars had aligned and created our own universe. You, me, and Simon. If you're my equinox, he's the solstice, and I'm the blaze melting us all together. I'm not an astronomer, so don't fixate too much on the terminology, just the words and how we all fit.

At the risk of sounding like a love sick fool, I love what we are together. I can't wait to see what we become, and I definitely want double-dips as much as I can.

Your innocence is so adorable, but I can't wait to dirty you up so much, James. Seeing my inked skin against your creamy bare skin gives me the shivers in all the best places. I can't wait to ink you and show the world where you belong. With me.

I want to say you're mine, but that's not entirely true and I would never want to own you.

So instead, I'll say you belong with me, and I'll grow to accept whoever else that might be as well, like my brother. If anything, it brings him into my life again, and for that I can't be mad.

You're my sun, moon, and stars, Peach.

Yours.

Chapter Fourteen

LENNOX

A PHONE RINGING had me waking too early, the sun wasn't even out yet based on the darkness in the room. I reached for the offending item but found myself trapped by bodies on both sides. Last night's activities had me blushing until I remembered the phone. Shoving the person closest to the direction of the noise, I hoped they'd be easy to wake because I really needed the noise to stop.

"Wake. Up."

"Hmm?"

"Phone."

"Fuck."

The body rolled out of bed, flipping on the bedside lamp. I shielded my eyes as they attempted to adjust to the bright invasion. Once I could see, I dropped my hand and found Slade returning to the room, the phone in the crook of his neck. He had one leg in his jeans, the other halfway in when he stopped. I wasn't afraid to admit I was more interested in the appendage between his legs anyway.

Licking my lips, I felt Simon pull me closer as he nestled into my neck.

"Whatcha looking at, Lenn?"

"Breakfast?"

Simon chuckled, licking my neck. "I like how you think. You both look good enough to eat."

I couldn't help the small moan that slipped as I felt his hand skirt around my body, his hardening erection digging into my backside. However, it didn't get to go much further as Slade began to cuss, yanking the rest of his jeans up and drawing our attention. Sitting up, I watched him, his face a mask of fury, and my heart began to race.

"I'm on my way."

He pulled the phone away from his ear, dropping his head as he took large inhales. Simon pushed me, motioning for me to go to him. Climbing out of bed, I grabbed a shirt off the floor and tip-toed to him.

"Tatzilla?"

He looked up at the name, a small smile on his lips. I wrapped my arms around him, still unsure if he wanted it but decided he needed it. A look of utter heartbreak was on his face, and I wanted to give him comfort. His arms wrapped around me, pulling me close to his chest, and I relaxed. Until I thought about what would make him look that way.

Pulling back, I gasped, "Your brother?"

Slade looked down at me, confused. "He's in the living room."

I sagged in relief, and he realized what I'd thought. "No one's hurt. That was your father, though."

"My dad?"

At this point, Simon had climbed out of bed and joined us in our little huddle. "Why's Eddy calling this early?" he yawned. His words were muffled as well as he pulled on a shirt. Slade blew out a breath, and I wanted to shake him to tell me already.

"It's the shop." His eyes moved to me and then back to Simon. "There's been a fire."

"What? How? Is everyone okay?"

The questions rushed out of me, Simon's almost echoing. Our shouts roused Zane, and he stumbled into the room, rubbing his eyes. "Everyone dressed?"

"Yeah, you can look. Sorry, we woke you."

"It's fine. What's going on?" He sleepily mumbled. I grabbed his hand, pulling him to our huddle. He belonged too.

"That's what we're trying to find out. There was a fire at the shop."

He instantly looked to his brother, concern weighing heavily on his brow. "Shit, man."

"Yeah, I don't know anything yet. Eddy called to let me know. I'm going to head there now. I'm sorry, Peach, but I'll have to do your tattoo another time."

"Of course. I'll come with you."

"No, stay. It's going to be a mess of things, and you have work that you've already had to reschedule. I'll be back tonight."

"Do you want me to go with you?" Simon asked. Slade thought about it, looking between the two of us, and I realized he didn't want it to seem like he wanted Simon to go when he'd told me no. I understood it wasn't about that though, so I saved him from having to worry.

"You should go. Is the salon okay?" I asked

"I don't know. Your dad didn't say."

"I didn't even think of the salon. Shit."

"Then you should definitely go. Grab some clothes while you're there, or whatever, if you guys plan to stay around longer."

"Shit, the rental. We need to clean and do all the close-down tasks."

"I can handle it. Just leave the keys," Zane offered. I squeezed his hand, happy he was here too. I hadn't had any of them in my life in the past few months, just psycho, and I realized how much I missed having people who cared about me. With psycho's identity still being unknown, it made me feel safer to have one of them with me.

"I can help, too. My first appointment isn't until noon."

"Perfect." He smiled and I suddenly found myself looking forward to cleaning if it meant I got some alone time.

"Thanks, that's… just thanks," said Slade. He pulled his brother into his arms, hugging him hard. He held on for a while, and it felt like the final piece of healing their relationship—being there for one another and leaving all the past mistakes behind them. Simon pulled me to him, and I wrapped my arms around his middle, laying my head on his chest, squeezing him.

"Be safe, Lenn. I can't lose you."

I looked up, the seriousness of his words surprising me. "I'm right here, Si. I'll be here when you get back tonight. We can order in and just chill. All of us."

"Sounds like the perfect evening."

He kissed my head, pulling me close again. A warm body covered my back, and for a second, I relished the feeling of being entirely surrounded by their safety.

Letting go of Si, I turned and hugged my former boss-nemy. He lifted me, his hands going to my lower half. Slade's eyes bugged out for a second when they touched bare skin.

"Shit, I forgot you were practically naked." He seared me with a kiss full of heat, leaving me breathless. Wrapping my legs around him, I deepened the kiss, our breathing becoming ragged as we lost ourselves in one another.

"Not that I don't love a show from you two, but Eddy called again."

My dad's name had me pulling back, but Slade didn't seem to care. He kept me lifted, his eyes on me. "Can I have a moment with Peach?"

He asked the other two, his eyes never leaving mine. I couldn't drop his either, too enamored with what I saw in them. The sound of the door closing was our only clue they'd honored his wishes.

"I really wish I had time to enjoy the morning after with you, Peach. I'd planned to wake you up with me between your legs and then fuck you in the shower with Simon." My breath hitched, and I found myself unconsciously rubbing against his chest. He groaned but didn't put me down.

"The only thing making me leave is the fire and what your dad told me."

His seriousness had my arousal decreasing, and I grasped his face, attempting to smooth out the worry lines. "What did he say?"

"He's not certain, but he expects arson. There was a broken window and a message, but he wouldn't tell me what it said over the phone."

"You think it's," my throat dried, the realization of what he meant hitting me. It had been funny to joke about it yesterday, easier for me to deal with. But facing the reality of the situation made me want to hide.

"Yes, it's the fucker who's been pretending to be my brother. He doesn't deserve to keep using his name. Promise me you'll stay with Thane until we're back. If he has to work, go and stay with your friend. Just don't be alone, Peach. *Promise me*."

"I promise."

His hands gripped my thighs, flexing as he tried to hold in his emotions. He kissed me softly at my words, dropping his head to my forehead. "I love you, Peach."

Smiling, I smoothed my hands over his face once more before kissing his nose. "I love you, Tatzilla."

He smiled, some of his fear receding as he placed me back on the ground. "Be prepared to be wooed tomorrow morning. I get a do-over. I can't have you thinking I ghost or scram each time we make love, Lennox."

"Love, huh?"

He arched an eyebrow, stopping with his hand on the doorknob. "Yes, Peach. *Love*. Even the first time. Sex that hot?" he smirked. "Definitely because I hated how much I loved you. Don't forget to check your email." He winked, walking out of the room.

Part of me wanted to rush to my phone and read it right then, but I exercised some self-control and followed him out into the other room. Zane was making coffee, filling some to-go mugs for the guys, and Simon popped some Pop Tarts into the toaster. He had them standing up, and I rolled my eyes as I walked over, grabbing the toaster tongs he always refused to use to change them to horizontal. We'd had this debate almost every morning when we lived together.

"Barbarian!"

Simon chuckled, used to our dispute on the proper way to put Pop Tarts in the toaster. I honestly think he did it the wrong way to get a rise out of me now. Slade walked in fully dressed a few minutes later, and I looked down at myself, finding I still wore his shirt. Guess he found something after all. He watched me curiously as I pulled out the Pop Tarts and handed them to him. He looked at me with an incredulous look as I held out the toasty treats.

"What the hell are those?"

"Um, Pop Tarts. It's not gourmet, but it will suffice. You have seen Pop Tarts before, right?"

"Not those, Peach, those." He pointed to the thin wooden tongs I held in my hand snapping them at him as I laughed. "Toaster tongs! Aren't they awesome?"

Simon ate his breakfast silently, watching in amusement. His silver-grey hair laid flat against his head, and I didn't miss the twinkle in his eyes as he watched us. Zane walked over, handing his brother some coffee. Slade still hadn't said anything, staring at me.

With the brothers next to one another, I could take them in fully. While they differed a lot, Slade with his darkness and Zane with his brightness, they matched the way they stood, their heights and build were almost the same. They even had similar facial features such as their eyes and nose, and as I watched, even some of the same expressions.

"I think she just realized we were twins," Zane

whispered, causing Slade to lift the corner of his mouth as he drank from the travel mug. He took a long drink before giving me a heated gaze.

"Your oversized chopsticks are ridiculous, Peach, but you're cute using them, so I guess I'll leave it. And don't get any ideas about twin sandwiches. I'm still getting used to the idea of you 'bumping uglies,' as you say with my brother. So for now, the only sandwich you're getting is the S&S special."

"Yes! Which one though, short and sweet?" I grinned.

"No, Peaches, the slip and slide." He kissed me quick, leaving me breathless with his words as he walked out. Simon almost choked before he walked over and gave me his own farewell. Pulling me close, he held me for a second and kissed me passionately.

"I'm partial to the service and supply myself." He grinned mischievously. "Love you, Lenn."

"Love you too, Si." I laughed back, unable to help myself. "Can you stop and check in on my mom and Noah while you're there?"

"Of course. Be good."

"Aren't I always?" Snickering, he nodded to Zane before heading after Slade.

"And then there were two," Zane spoke into the quiet room. Nodding, I placed my beloved kitchen utensil on the counter. I found myself nervous all of a sudden, not sure how to act now they were gone. "I uh, do you need more sleep? I'm not even sure what time it is or when you went to bed."

"It's just after 6 am. I got about 5 hrs. I'll take a nap later. It's fine. Do you want to head over there and get it out of the way, and then maybe we could have breakfast?"

"Yeah, I'd love that. I need a shower, though."

"You might want to wait until after. I'm not sure how much cleaning is needed."

"True. Okay, well, I at least need to put pants on."

He blinked, his eyes dropping and taking in my bare legs. I watched as his Adam's apple bobbed, his heated gaze lifting to me. "Uh, yeah, that'd be good." He pulled his collar, and inwardly, I relished the fact I affected him.

Winking, I found myself swaying my hips more than usual as I walked off to grab some clothes. I stopped in the doorframe, looking over my shoulder. Zane's eyes were glued to my butt, and when he noticed I'd stopped, he looked up, his cheeks heating. Smiling, I turned back but left the door open, feeling brave. I hadn't missed the erection he'd been sporting and knew I was playing with fire, but something in me delighted in it.

Maybe the sex last night had scrambled my brain, making me addicted to dick. Huh, aDICKted. Giggling, I grabbed some clothes, changing quickly, before pulling my hair back. When I exited the room, he'd finished getting dressed too and held out a mug for me. The thoughtfulness of the gesture had my cheeks blazing now.

When I took a sip, I was surprised when it tasted exactly how I liked it. Giving him a curious look, he smiled knowingly.

"Simon told me how to make it."

"Ah, still, thank you. I like that you're becoming friends, though."

"Me too. He's a good dude."

"Alright, are we ready to do this?"

"Yep."

We left the apartment and headed there together, walking down the block in the early morning light, and I felt hopeful things would be okay.

STRIPPING THE LAST BED, I huffed as I pulled the heavy comforter to the middle of it. I wadded all the bedding together and took it to the laundry room. Wiping sweat from my brow, I was glad Zane had suggested waiting to shower, considering I dripped sweat now. My face was beet red, and I was a dirty mess. Walking back out into the room, I found Zane gathering the last of the trash bags.

"I think that's all of the bedding and towels. Geez, I never knew it was so much work to stay at a place like this. Makes hotels seem more appealing."

"Possibly, but then you have to deal with all the other guests. Traveling a lot, you get sick of the same basic setup and the loud TVs that drone on when you want to sleep."

Grimacing, I'd forgotten they'd moved a lot. "Ah, yeah. I guess you're an old pro at this stuff, then. I'm ashamed to admit that Nashville is the furthest I've ever been."

"Nothing to be embarrassed by, Lennox. Your experience is yours, just as mine is mine. I wish I knew what it felt like to know someone as long as you have Simon. There's pros and cons to every situation."

Smiling, I nodded, feeling better. I'd forgotten how he'd easily done this before, making me feel comfortable and encouraged with his words. "You're right. I do want to travel someday. Are you sick of it? How long were you in Africa?"

"No, I love it. Maybe it's the constant newness of getting to experience things, but there's something about moving each time I like. Don't get me wrong, it gets old, and I always crave a place to come home to. I definitely don't want to travel or move as much as we did as kids, or like I have the past few years. It just seemed easier to not be close by even if I wasn't always here. Knowing you were only an hour's drive north, well, some days it was a comfort and others a temptation. I didn't want to be far from you though, even if I couldn't be in your life. It's stupid," he finished, blushing.

"No, it's sweet."

We smiled at one another, and I looked at the paper, the moment feeling too intense for 7 am. "Well, I guess we only have the final walk-through left. Want to do it together?"

"Absolutely."

We walked room by room, checking the list and making sure we had all of their belongings. When we got to the last room, I nodded, signing off at the bottom that all the tasks had been completed.

"Yes! Mama needs some pancakes! Feed me, Zane!"

"Your wish is my command," he joked. He held out

his hand, and I took it, the butterflies filling me at his touch.

"Anywhere in particular you'd like to go?"

"Oh, I know! Let's go to Pancake Palace! It's just up the street from my apartment."

"Lead the way, gorgeous."

Blushing, I took off, ensuring I latched the door and dropped the keys back through the mail slot. The birds were out now, chirping as we walked along. More pedestrians were out too, the streets beginning to liven as we walked. We didn't talk, just held hands as we walked, and it was nice. Zane had a lot of the qualities I'd liked about Duncan. He was solid and confident, giving me space to be myself without constantly wondering if what I said sounded dumb or if he thought my intensity on specific topics was too much.

Zane made it okay to simply be me, and I didn't have to make excuses for my behavior. Simon accepted me and knew me better than I knew myself. Slade challenged me and pushed me, which I loved and needed. All three of them added something different, and I'd started to see how we could work perfectly together.

"I have an idea. Since it's early, perhaps we could grab food first? Then shower? I'm starving."

I looked down at myself, checking for any holes or stains. I had on a good pair of leggings, and my shirt looked clean. I sniffed my armpit, and while it wasn't the freshest, I probably wouldn't be the worst smelling human either. Shrugging, I ignored the way he smiled at me for smelling myself.

"I guess if you don't care about being with sweaty me, then I'm all for getting some food first."

"Honestly, I find you sexy as hell right now, sweat and all."

Blushing, I ducked my head, not sure what to say back. We made it to the corner, and I pulled him in the direction of the pancakes, my stomach making a siren call for them. The early hour meant the place was only half full. I grabbed a booth in the corner, giving us a little more privacy from people. I was surprised when Zane slid in next to me instead of across.

"Well, hello."

"Figured I'd save the waitress from your stinky self."

Laughing, I shoved his arm in offense. "Hey, you said I was sexy."

"And you are, doesn't mean you don't smell, pome-granate."

"You're mean." I scrunched my nose at the nick-name, and Zane only smiled wider.

"Nah, I just really wanted to hide your awesome-ness from everyone else. Plus, this way, I can touch you more."

"That's a much better reason."

Opening our menus, I knew instantly what I wanted. The waitress dropped off a pot of coffee, indi-cating she'd be back in a second. Zane seemed to take longer, but when she returned, he was ready.

"I'll take the chocolate chip stack with a side of bacon."

"Sure thang, and for you, doll?" she asked, turning to me.

"The Elvis special."

She grinned before nodding. "Perfect. I'll get those

in for you." She walked off, and I realized she hadn't written it down.

"It always amazes me when people can remember things like that without making mistakes. I'd be a horrible waitress," I mused.

"Me too. I tried one summer, and I ended up being demoted to the dishwasher because I was so bad. They'd hoped my good looks and smile would bring in the customers, but I made more mistakes than I didn't. It was a disaster. Slade was happy he was finally better at something than me."

"I'm glad you guys seem to have made up."

"Yeah, me too."

We talked for a while about his trip, what he liked about Nashville, and what he planned to do next. Zane was still working part-time at the clinic, but he thought it was time to move on.

"What would you want to do if you weren't working there?"

"I have no clue. I stayed because it was easy, but I'm wondering if maybe there's something else out there waiting for me."

Sadness filled me at the possibility of him leaving. "Well, I'll miss you."

Zane smiled, tucking a piece of hair back. "Don't you get it, Lennox? I'm not going anywhere without you. I'm just not tied down to the job anymore."

"Oh." My cheeks heated at the implications of his statement.

Our food arrived, and it looked delicious, and I dug in, unable to stop myself. Zane turned his nose up at my food, but I didn't care. It was marvelous.

"Gross, how do you eat that?"

"Easy. You take a fork, you spear a piece of yummy goodness, and then you put it in your mouth."

"Ha, ha, smart ass. I mean, how do you eat that combination together?"

"It's wonderful. You should try it before you just assume it's horrible, food snob." Spearing him a banana pancake drizzled with peanut butter and chocolate chips, I held it out for him to try. Zane's nose turned up, but he took a teeny bit, and I watched as he chewed. His eyes widened in surprise, and he grabbed my fork, shoving the rest of it into his mouth.

Laughing, I pulled it back, not wanting to share anymore. "Nope, the rest are mine. It's not my fault you were too good for them earlier." He pouted, but I was strong against its power and resisted giving in. Food was a commodity I wouldn't share if I didn't have to.

Once we finished eating, he paid the bill, smirking at me as I tried to hand him some money, only taking it to leave as a tip when we left. I waved at the waitress as we exited out onto the busier streets. We were almost back to the apartment when Slade called. Slowing, I answered, not letting go of Zane's hand.

"Hey you, everything okay?"

"Peach, where are you?"

"Um, I'm outside. We just finished eating at the Pancake Palace and are headed up to take a shower. Why?"

As the words left my mouth, we came around the corner, and I spotted my car in the back alley parking lot. I almost didn't hear what Slade said as I gaped at the sight in front of me.

"Peach? *Peach*?"

"Yeah, I'm here. What did you say?"

Zane and I had stopped, and he looked at me in concern as he glanced back and forth between me and the once pristine car.

"I said whatever you do, don't go back to the apartment. Somehow… *he* knows things, Peach," he paused, his voice soft and worried. "The message, it wasn't for me… it was for *you*."

"What did it say?" my voice shook as I asked, tears starting to spring to my eyes.

"It says, '*I tried to warn you, princess, but you didn't listen. You sullied yourself with them, demeaning your pure nature, and falling into the traps of those vile books you read. Now I have to show you why—*' But it ends there, mid-sentence."

Squeezing Zane's hand, I looked into his eyes. "I think I know what it's supposed to say next."

"What's happening, Peach? Is there another message?"

"Yeah, there is. One second."

Swallowing, I took a picture of my car, my hands shaking so bad, it took a few attempts before it was visible, and I could send it to him.

Keyed into the side of my car were the words '*You're Mine.*'

Meeting Zane's eyes, I tried not to let the fear overtake me. "I really regret not taking that shower first."

NOX TO THANE

From: noxsmiles@heartsemail.com
To: blazetats@heartsemail.com
Subject: I'm going to name a hot sauce after you

Blazey Blaze, my sweet haze,

You always surprise me. Some days you're so sweet, you make me blush, and other days, you challenge me to step out of my comfort zone. Then there are times I feel a connection with you to my soul, a deep soul agonizing one. You comfort me and get me as I am. No matter the day though, you're always there, ready to listen and respond. That's become such a valuable thing to me.

You definitely didn't scare me, and I agree, our letters and words aren't typical of our generation. We far surpass them in emotional intelligence in my opinion. I never thought years ago when I signed up for a pen pal program that it would become so integral to who I am and my day. It's always the first thing I look for. The time difference between our coasts has me getting yours when I'm asleep most of the time. It's a nice way to start my day though.

Your words are ingrained in me as well, and I can often hear you in my head along with my best friend. It's pretty great having two people who I feel this close to, even if I never meet one.

I'm glad you and your brother are starting to heal. I'd hate for you guys to lose your unique bond. I can't wait to hear how you continue to repair your relationship.

Ugh, your dare. So I did it. It wasn't pretty. He's very much in a TMNT phase at the moment and so he decided to dress me like his favorite character-Donatello.

First, he picked out a pair of green pants that hadn't seen the light of day in years, so I had to convince him a girl turtle would wear a skirt. It wasn't the prettiest color of green, but at least it fit. Next, he picked out a purple shirt, which wouldn't be too bad, but the one he chose also said "I got crabs at Joe's Crab Shack." With the sweater he made me wear over it, it cut off the Joe's Crab Shack part, so I walked around all day with it only showing "I got crabs."

The sweater and socks, again, not hideous on their own, but he decided to include April since again I was a girl, so if you're thinking, "there's no way he made you wear yellow socks and a sweater, surely you don't own those." Well, you would be wrong. I do in fact own a bright yellow cardigan, and yellow striped socks that go to my knee. So, yeah, thanks for a fun day of getting weird looks.

The best part though was Noah loved it. He wants to dress together and get matching outfits, so that was fun. Especially after the incident this week at the bank with mom. One of her old friends refused to talk to her, and then a busybody at the grocery store kept making comments in the checkout line about how she shouldn't have been allowed to keep her kids, and "crazy people like her belong locked up."

My father was irate, but there was nothing he could do about it. It shook mom up though and she's been in her room for the past few days, sitting in the dark. She doesn't want to leave the house either unless it's necessary. I've had to drop off and pick up Noah from school all week. I'm hoping I can coax her out this weekend.

I dare you to eat lunch with someone at school that is seen as the weirdo or class outcast. I think most of the time, it's just a misperception and you might find a new friend. I know I would like it if someone as kind as you sat with me at lunch. If I didn't have my best friend, it would be so lonely at school.

If you don't choose to do it, then there's no consequence, only that you're not the person I thought you were.

I'll be waiting.

Nox

LENNOX

MY HEART THUMPED SO LOUD, I felt it in my head, and the world tilted a little. I remembered the phone and brought it back to my ear, hearing Slade's shout.

"Peach? James? *LENNOX*?"

"Yeah, sorry. I'm here." My voice was small, a whisper as I stared at my car. It had once brought me so much happiness, and now, it just represented something else he'd stolen from me.

"Peach, *fuck*," he breathed, his voice softening. "You worried me. Can you put my brother on the phone?"

Nodding, I gave it to Zane and then realized I hadn't answered Slade, but Zane was already talking to him. I walked over to my car, the beautiful paint now chipped. Running my fingers over the keyed part, I could almost hear the car protesting against the violence committed against it. I didn't know what to think or feel. This was so outside of anything I ever imagined happening to me. I felt someone come up behind me placing a hand on my shoulder, and I jumped, spinning as a sound of protest escaped me.

"Shit, sorry, Lennox. It's just me."

Nodding, I wrapped my arms around him, no longer wanting to look at the destruction. I knew it was just a car. But it had been *mine*, the one Simon had found for me.

"They're going to head back as soon as they can. Your father is helping him with the insurance claims and getting someone there to help clean up. We're to go into the apartment and grab a few things and then leave. I'm not sure where we're going yet, but we'll figure it out together. You're not in this alone, Lennox."

I snuggled close, needing his warmth to combat the cold chill I felt taking control of me. We stood there together, the wind blowing around us and the sounds of the city muted in the alley. His heartbeat was all I listened to, the soothing tones reassuring me it would be okay. Zane kissed the top of my head, and the last piece of my heart clicked into place, giving me the courage I needed.

Drawing back, I smiled softly at him, taking his hand. Together we walked up the stairs, the silence feeling ominous now. The shop opened in a few hours, so no one else was in the building. When I entered the place that had been my home for the past two months, a cold chill ran down my spine. Some of Slade's words began to penetrate the fog, and I began to put some pieces together from what he said without saying anything.

"Fake-you watched us, didn't he?" I looked up to Zane, and he nodded, apprehension creasing his brow.

"Yeah, Slade believes so. There was, um, video footage sent to your father once Slade arrived at Emblazed. It was of the three of you from last night."

"Son of a gun!" Covering my mouth, I prayed my father hadn't seen much of it, my cheeks flamed. "Oh geez, I really hope he didn't watch it. I don't know if I could take it if he did or thought less of me, now."

"Your dad loves you, Noxy girl. He's not going to think anything different. I bet he's just as embarrassed as you. I believe that was the stalker's intention. To put a wedge between either you and the guys or you and your parents. If he separates you, then you're easier to manipulate."

"That's not creepy or anything," I muttered, moving into the living room. The furniture was still in the same positions, the bottle of tequila open and on the floor where we'd left it. Everything looked the same but knowing he'd watched us made the moment between us have a film of degradation about it that hadn't been there before.

Walking into the bedroom, my mind was in a daze, and I almost felt light-headed as everything pressed down on me. Grabbing a bag, I started to toss some clothes, shoes, and underwear in, my sketchbook, and my electronics. I grabbed my makeup bag and pulled my toiletries out of the bathroom. By the time I entered the bedroom again, I felt dizzier. I stumbled as I made my way to the bed. Sitting down, I stuffed items in, but my hands didn't work as well. Tossing it over my shoulder, I stumbled toward the dresser to grab my jewelry. I didn't wear much, but I had two pieces that meant a lot to me. Blaze's necklace was one of them, and the other a bracelet Duncan had given me. I found the bracelet and slid it on, but my necklace was missing.

Opening the stand, I sorted through them as Zane came in, his voice a hollow sound.

"Lennox, something's wrong. We need to go."

I turned my head to him, and it felt like my head moved in slow motion, the world blurring as it went by. Attempting to form words, I opened my mouth, but nothing came out. Zane lifted me up, and he stumbled out of the room with me, making it to the stairs where the air was clearer. Once we were free of the apartment, he sat me down and motioned for me to take deep inhales with him. The clean oxygen started to filter in, and I realized it hadn't been panic or a haze causing me to feel dizzy, but something else entirely.

Zane started to pull me toward the back door, urgently wanting me to move faster. My legs cooperated for the most part, but whatever I'd been breathing in still affected me. His words infiltrated my consciousness just as we made it clear of the door.

"You okay? We should move further away, I think there's a—"

He didn't get to finish his words as a large boom sounded out, knocking us forward as debris began to fall around us. Zane managed to lift me up again, running away from the shop and barely made it away before a louder boom sounded, this one rattling cars and windows around us. We fell forward from the blast, the heat searing our skin, luckily we were far enough away we hadn't been hit with anything.

Turning over, I looked up at what had become my home, my sanctuary, the place I'd found *myself* again. Equinox Ink was a wall of flames, and I was suddenly grateful it was before opening. Zane pulled me to his chest, and I realized I was crying. He began to rock us back and forth, soothing us together as we sat in the middle of the road, chaos surrounding us.

"What just happened?" I croaked out, looking up at him with tear-stained eyes.

"I'm not 100% sure, but I think it was a gas leak, though I'm not sure what they used as an accelerant to start the explosion. I didn't smell the gas though… "

"You don't have to say that. You can say *my stalker*."

His smile was sad as he looked down at me, and he nodded, accepting I didn't want to deny the fact this could only be his handiwork. My phone beeped, and I managed to pull it out, amazed it only had a small scratch on the screen from the fall.

There was a message, and as I read it, anger covered the fear that had been there. Psycho Thane thought he was going up against the Lennox James of old, but I wasn't her anymore. Whether it was finally grieving Duncan, my lucky encounter with Babs, or the guys coming back into my life, I'd finally embraced who I could be. This Lennox James didn't hide, and she most certainly didn't bow to bullies or stalkers. I hadn't done it as a teen, and I wouldn't start now.

Psycho Thane thought he had me, that I would cave to his demands and fulfill his deluded fantasy.

The only thing he had was an expiration date. It was time I uncovered the imposter and took back my life.

Thane: We belong together. Don't you see that now? Do I need to keep sending you reminders, or have you gotten the message? You're mine.
ME: *Message failure gif*
ME: In case the GIF isn't clear, I'll never be yours. The only person I belong to is myself. How about you face the consequences of your

actions? That would get my attention. I'm not going to play your games.

Standing up, I wobbled for a second before I steadied myself, grabbing on to Zane in front of me. Reaching for his hand, I gave him my phone to read. He gave me a curious look once he read my message, but I could also see a look of pride. Ambulances and fire trucks arrived, rushing to check us over as they attempted to put out the fire.

"Call your brother and let him know another property is on fire."

"What are you going to do?" He asked, worried.

"I'm going to figure out a place for us to go."

Zane smiled, kissing me on the lips, surprising me. Something on my face had him smiling as he pulled away.

"You're too cute, sugar plum. Here, use my phone to find a place just in case."

"Why?" I asked, raising my eyebrows.

"I don't trust yours, and mine's less likely to have been tampered with considering I've been out of the country. He knows too much, and has had too much access to you. I wouldn't put it past him to have cloned your phone. He messed with your messages before when you were supposed to meet Blaze, so why wouldn't he now? It's the perfect way to get you alone by making you think you were meeting one of us."

I shuddered at the thought. Zane had a point. I took his phone, figuring he'd be vague when he talked to his brother on mine. As he took care of informing Slade everything he'd worked for over the past four years was destroyed, I took care of what I needed to do—find a freaking shower.

I texted Darcie and asked if we could use her place for a while, briefly explaining what happened just in case Zane's phone was bugged or even Darcie's for that matter. She responded back quickly saying it was cool, and to be safe. I was about to return Zane's phone when another message popped up.

Bro: I love you, Peach. I don't know what I would've done if I lost you. We'll figure this out together. We're on our way back now. Your father is coming too. Don't do anything stupid until we get there. This isn't the time to run off being stubborn. Besides, no one really likes a hero. It's the anti-heros that are all the rage.

ME: I love you too, bro, but I don't think you should call me Peach. Kind of weird, don't you think? It's cute you think you're some form of hero, bro.

Bro: Haha, *funny*, Peach. Your dad is talking to Thane, so I know it's you. At least I know you're okay if you're making jokes.

ME: Honestly? I'm scared. But I'll be okay. Be safe driving back. I don't want to lose you either. We're headed somewhere safe for now. I need a shower and maybe a nap.

Bro: We'll meet you there or call you to meet back at the shop if your father wants to go there first. Do all those things. If you're sleeping, then

I'll let you be because I really want to text you every minute to ensure you're okay.

ME: I like when you wake me up.

Bro: It's weird enough writing to my brother how much I love him, but I don't think I can sext him, Peach. You'll have to use your imagination. I'll see you in a few hours.

ME: You're no fun.

Bro: I'll show you tonight how much fun I am

ME: Promise? *Winking emoji*

Bro: I promise you everything, Peach

Bro: Oh, and Peach?

ME: Yes?

Bro: I accept.

Smiling, I clutched the phone to my chest, as I whirled around. *He looked at his tattoo.* Warm butterflies fluttered to the surface at his answer. I'd basically asked him to be the music on my heart for infinity.

And he'd said yes. Slade 'Tatzilla Alpha-hole' Evans wanted to make music with me. Grinning wide, I looked through the gathered crowd and found Zane talking to a police officer. I walked over when I realized who it was, a smile on my face.

"Chief James from the Bowling Green Police Department has asked to be looped in. He believes this is connected to a fire that occurred there this morning. He'll be taking point from their end and will be in touch. He knows where we will be staying, and due to the circumstances, we're keeping it tight-lipped."

"Understood. I'll give him a call. He's an old buddy of mine. He called when this one moved down here."

"Hey, Officer Friendly." I hugged him and grimaced, remembering my injuries. "Ouch, sorry. I forgot I was injured."

"You okay, kiddo? No offense, but you look like shit."

"Ha! Thanks so much. Why do people think it's okay to say that if they put 'no offense' in front of it?" When he only held his hands up in surrender, I dropped it. "I've had better days, but I'll be okay. Dad knows where I'll be, so just call him if you have any more questions."

"Will do, kiddo. Be safe. We're all on the lookout for this psycho."

"Thanks."

Grabbing Zane's hand, I pulled him with me, ready to be away from the mess. "You're surprisingly calm."

"I trust the police to take care of it. Nothing I can do at the moment, and if I don't take a shower in the next thirty minutes, I might peel my skin off."

"Okay, okay, let's get you that shower. I don't want to be responsible for a skinless Lennox."

Doing a body shudder, I narrowed my eyes toward him. "Why would you even put that image in my mind?"

Laughing, Zane squeezed my hand as I led him over a few streets. Thankfully, Darcie lived close by, so it was only a fifteen mintue walk to her place. She was at work, so I let myself in using the key she'd given me.

"Wow, your friend is trusting."

"That's right, you haven't met Darce yet."

"No."

"She's the best. She'll be back later. You'll like her."

Dropping my stuff on the table, I realized the problem. "Well, crap. We need to wash all of this before we can wear it. I don't think I can wear any of Darcie's clothes either. Fudge."

"Here, I'll start a load. You take a shower or bath, and we'll figure it out." Zane had Slade and Simon's bags from their place, and grabbed mine as he waited for me to show him to the washing machine.

"Thank you. Gas leak I can handle, not having clean clothes, that's the last straw for me apparently."

"Don't go to Africa then, I was only able to wash my clothes sporadically there. Between the dust and sweat, it's not pretty."

Scrunching up my nose, I helped him sort things and we got the first load in. I tossed the clothes I'd been wearing into the pile, not thinking until I caught his hungry gaze. I stood in nothing but my underwear, a feeling of empowerment surging through me. Grabbing the bottom of his shirt, I lifted it. He quickly pulled it the rest of the way off, and I bit my lip as I took in his body. Cheese on toast, he was sexy.

"Want to take a shower with me?"

"Are you sure you're ready for that?"

"Yep, now toss your bottoms in as well so I can start it."

He did as I asked, leaving him in very tight boxer briefs, the outline of his dick clear as day. When I'd been staring at it for a while, I jerked back, realizing. Glancing up, Zane had a smug look on his face as he watched me. Turning my back, I hid my cheeks as I finished setting the dials, starting the wash.

Leading the way to the bathroom, I didn't face him

again until we were in the enclosed space. Slowly, I lowered the straps of my bra, releasing the cups as I pushed it off, following it up with my panties. Zane sucked in a breath, and the sound did something for me. His blue eyes were hungry as they dragged over my skin.

Carefully, he shoved down the last bit of his clothing, his cock springing free. I didn't feel bad for staring this time, considering he looked at me in the same way. Reaching in, I turned the dial, the water sputtering out as it began to heat up the small room. Once it felt warm, I stepped in and beckoned him to follow. The shower was small, so we didn't have much space to do anything other than stand under the stream.

"I think this might be the smallest shower I've ever been in."

Chuckling, I nodded. "Or it could be you're just tall, and I'm me."

"That's not a self-deprecating comment, is it?"

Shaking my head, I smiled. "No, I happen to like being me. I'm just saying I'm short and a little round, and you're tall and trim. That's a lot of mass density to ratio or something. It's math, so it can't be bad."

"I have no clue what you just said, but you sound cute doing it, so I'll let it slide." His hands slid onto my hips, and he bent down. "You have no idea how hard it is not to turn you around and slip inside of you right now."

Biting my lip, I found myself really wanting that but doing it in the shower spelled disaster. I didn't care what all my books told me. Shower sex, especially in

Darcie's shower, just wasn't possible for a short, curvy girl without killing me.

I grabbed some shampoo and rubbed it in, then motioned for Zane to bend down so I could wash his hair. His eyes closed when I started to massage it, and I found the experience both erotic and intimate in nature. We took turns rinsing, holding on tight to one another as we rotated places so we wouldn't fall.

Zane grabbed the loofah I'd set out and squirted body wash on it. He moved toward me and began to wash me. His gentle touch was soothing to my heart as he carefully lifted my arms and thoroughly washed around my breasts. Though, that might've been because he'd become distracted by them. When he was dipping lower, I found myself sucking in a breath as he briefly washed over my mound and then down my legs.

He squatted, lifting my leg gingerly as he washed my calf and foot. Zane looked up at me as he raised the other, his motions caring, his eyes hooded.

"I think I need to clean one area a little more thoroughly."

His words didn't make sense until he sucked my clit into his mouth. Leaning against the wall, I braced myself as best as possible as he placed one leg over his shoulder, his hands resting on my butt cheeks as he dove in.

It felt so good; I found myself falling into the pleasure, everything else from the day escaping me. The water continued to beat down on his back as he plunged his tongue into my core. Zane pulled back, a smile on his face as he started to pump his fingers into me.

"You're so wet, Lennox. I'm glad I affect you as much as you do me. I want to fuck you so bad, but I want to make sure you're okay with that. That you're ready, and it's not a reaction to what happened today."

He continued to plunge his digits deep, and I wanted to shake him for trying to have a conversation while he delivered mind-blowing pleasure. I nodded, hoping he got what I meant. My legs were shaking, and I knew I needed more. Quickly, I pulled him up, and I ran the discarded loofah over his skin, hoping it had enough soap on it.

Turning off the water, I pushed the curtain aside and shoved a towel at him. Drying off quickly, I wrapped my hair up in the towel and pulled him out into the room with me. Zane went along with my actions, a curious look on his face.

Shoving him on the bed, I crawled up and took what I wanted. Because he was wrong about one thing. This was about him and me, and while it might also be about what happened earlier, it in no way diminished it. I wasn't sleeping with him because I was scared. Far from it, in fact. Being in the driver's seat meant I saw both the current route I was on and the final destination of where I wanted to be.

The explosions and messages only reminded me of what I wanted in my life. I wasn't his. I was my own damn person, and I wanted to be with Zane. He was just as much a part of my future as Simon and Slade. Our history wasn't as rich, but it was there, smudged between layers of trust and friendship, of lousy karaoke and 90's pop references. Zane wasn't perfect like Slade had thought, and it made me like him better because of it.

He'd made mistakes, but when it came down to it in the end, he'd been willing to sacrifice his own happiness if it meant his brother got the girl. Some people might consider that weak, his unwillingness to fight for what he wanted, but I saw it as his compassion and self-lessness. He loved his brother in a way only a truly good person could—with his whole heart.

I wanted to be part of that.

I wasn't in love with Zane yet, but I knew I could be, and I would fight for us to get a chance.

My thighs bracketed his, and I watched him as I grabbed his length, stroking him. His breath hitched, and his eyes grew large, begging me not to stop. Lifting up, I positioned myself over him and slowly sank down onto him. We both moaned, my own breath catching at the sensation.

Falling forward, I began to move slowly, getting used to his size. My breasts swayed with each movement, my wetness guiding me easily over him. Zane let me have control, our tempo slow as we got acquainted with one another. He shoved the towel off my head, my wet hair falling around me. Cupping my cheek, he stared into my eyes as I moved.

"I never thought I could have you *and* my brother in my life. Being here with you, without hurting him, is the future I never could've imagined for myself. Especially after how everything went down. And yet, here you are, giving it to me, taking a chance to trust me, and letting me love you. You're so brave and beautiful, Lennox. You wear your heart on the outside, allowing all of us to tattoo our names there, permanently sealing us to you. While I hate that you have this crazy imposter after you, I understand how he could fall madly in love with you and want to do whatever it takes to have you."

Leaning forward, I kissed his lips, our breaths mixing. "There's a big difference between you and the stalker, Zane. You knew it was wrong and stopped. You admitted it and feel remorse. You're also not responsible for what happened to Duncan. Whoever was driving the car is. You've never tried to manipulate me or play on my emotions, like he has. You pretended to be your brother, but you never lied about who you were. And when it came down to it, you didn't try to steal me away. Intentions matter, and from my standpoint, yours were out of love, and his are out of lust or control. He doesn't know me, truly, or want me for who I am. Just the version of me he's created in his twisted mind. I'm not that girl. I won't *ever* be that girl."

He rolled us over, placing me under him on my back in one motion. The movement had him thrusting deeper, as I gasped, a moan leaving my mouth. Zane held one leg as he started to pull out and move back in, never taking his eyes from mine as he did, cementing our souls together as well. When he pushed forward once more, he kissed me passionately, and I fell over the edge as his pelvic bone rubbed against my clit, a long moan echoing around us.

Zane held me close as he filled me, and I realized we'd forgotten to use a condom again. Thankfully, I was on birth control, but we would all need to discuss it to make sure we agreed and were clean. I didn't doubt for one second any of them would've intentionally had sex if they knew. It was just one of those things I felt was important to talk about if you were in a relationship. The thought of being in a relationship with the three of them had me smiling wide, the reality of it sinking in.

"What has you smiling so wide, Noxy girl?"

"Just that I like the idea of being with you."

Zane smiled wider, dropping a kiss on my lips. He went to respond but was interrupted by a loud shrieking hyena.

"Lennox James! I know y'all ain't fucking in my bed?"

Turning my head, I took in my new bestie, standing in the doorway, hands on her hips as she attempted to scowl at me. Zane swore under his breath and tried to use the towel to cover his backside considering he was still inside me. The intrusion had him slipping out, though, and the emotional buildup of everything had me in hysterics. Laughing, I shielded myself as I looked at the blonde cowgirl. "Like you didn't screw that one guy in my bed while I worked last week."

Her scowl cracked, and she laughed while nodding. "Oh, yes. I climbed him like a beanstalk. Put some clothes on and throw those in the wash, will ya?" She asked, pointing at the sheets. She turned, waving over her shoulder, and I found Zane gaping after her.

"That's the one and only Darcie."

"She's something."

"You have no idea."

Laughing, we climbed off, rinsing ourselves again and managing to find enough garments to cover ourselves until the laundry was done. While we waited,

I introduced them to one another and filled Darce in on the whole tale. The more I said it out loud, the crazier it sounded. I didn't think it could get any weirder from there. I should've known better.

Looked like I still hadn't learned my lesson on shoulding.

Love Letter

From: emblazed_slade@heartsemail.com
To: emblazed_lennox@heartsemail.com
Subject: Written in the stars

Peach,

There was a moment today I thought I'd lost you. A deep wrenching pain hit me in my gut, and I felt like I couldn't breathe. Knowing you felt like that before, that you never got the rush of relief I did when I heard your voice, broke something inside me for you. The fact you kept living your life, kept trying each day, proves to me even more how strong of a person you are. I don't know if I could say the same of me.

I'd like to think I could, but even when I only thought you'd broken my heart, I couldn't leave you. I hate that I punished you for loving him, for being angry at you when your grief shielded you from seeing me.

Yet again, you remind me why I love you. Because I know you don't hold any of that against me. Your love and heart are pure. I'm not saying you're perfect Peach, there are a lot of things that drive me crazy, so don't let it go to your head. For instance, the way you open the store. You always blare the music while you sing and dance. Actually, I just hate how much it made me want you.

Okay, how about this one? I hate how you can't say a fucking cuss word to save your life, how you bite your lip when you're nervous, or hum when you're drawing. Shit, yeah, I love those things too. Well, James, you're not perfect, but it turns out you're perfect for me.

You know in those books you read how you sometimes like the grumpy one? (And before you ask, yes, I read your blog over the years and in my spare time, I would read some of the books you mentioned. Don't make a big deal out of it.) Well, that's me. Most people get on my damn nerves, and I have the patience of an ant. You're the exception. You've always been the exception. My circle is small, and you're the center of it. If anyone tried to take you from me, I'd burn down the whole damn world to get to you. I called myself Blaze for a reason, after all.

Your tattoo is perfection and my favorite one. Of course I'll be the music in your heart, you're already mine. I need you to do a bigger one for me too. I need your ink on me, Peach. I have the spot saved for you. I never forgot our promise either.

Love you to the moon, the stars, and the whole
damn universe.
My heart beats a rhythm only you can hear.

Our love song has always been written in the stars.
Yours forever

Chapter Sixteen
LENNOX

FORTUNATELY, our clothes were ready for us before my father and S&S arrived. Simon called Zane and asked us to meet them back at the shop. It was lunchtime by then, so we stopped and grabbed burgers on our walk over. I was grateful we were close enough to walk, but the pang of losing my beautiful Sunny still stung. I hadn't even checked after the fire. I was scared to find out the fate of my girl.

We rounded the corner, almost back to the shop, when I realized that despite the events of the day, I found myself laughing at something Zane said. It reminded me I hadn't checked with him on his name, either. As much as I didn't think I could call him Thane at the moment, I didn't want to steal his identity either.

"You're okay with me calling you Zane, right? I kind of realized I stole your choice. That wasn't my intention. I just don't think I can call you that name for a while, but I can make a cutesy nickname for the in-between time if you like. Oh, what about, hot doc? Or even better, hot diggity dog? Or even Zany Thane instead of Psycho?" I giggled, wiggling my eyebrows.

We were walking hand in hand again. Apparently, it was our thing, and I was A-o-kay with it. We'd been swinging them between us, the bag of burgers clutched in his other hand. My question had us stopping, though, as he looked at me.

"I love *you* calling me Zane, or whatever you want, Noxy girl. It makes me feel special to have my own Lennox-made nickname. Though, hot doc wouldn't be bad."

Laughing, I grinned, leaning up on my tiptoes to kiss him briefly. "I might still call you hot doc in the bedroom then."

Winking, I caught him off guard as I pulled him to keep walking. When we were within a few stores of the place, a hush fell over us. There was still a fire truck and police cruiser. The rest of the emergency personnel had left, though. People gawked and stared along the street, and I saw a news crew interviewing a few of the other shop owners a few feet away.

The air smelled of burnt plastic and chemicals, and as we came upon the destruction, a heaviness punctured my chest. Seeing the charred remains of my home and workplace felt like I'd been punched in the gut. I was so caught up in looking at it, I didn't expect the sudden hug from behind. Arms wrapped around me tightly before twisting me and swinging me up into their arms. Slade nuzzled my neck, his arms banded tight around me, and I held him back, knowing he needed this. I felt a warm body pressed into my back. I managed to move my head enough to spot Simon.

Zane nodded, and I assumed he meant he'd give us a minute, and I watched him walk over to the cop car, introducing himself to my dad. Eddie James looked up at me briefly, and I waited for the disgust to flash across his face. Thankfully, I only saw love and relief at seeing me. He smiled when he caught my eyes before turning back to Zane.

"I don't think I can ever leave you again."

"I'm okay, Slade."

"Just barely, oh shit." Instantly he dropped me, and if Simon hadn't been behind me, I would've fallen on my butt. Shrieking a little at the instant change, I glared up at him as Simon steadied me.

"Sorry, Peach." He grimaced, his hands hovering in the air. The unsure nature of him had me softening, not used to seeing him out of sorts.

"I'm fine, but why did you drop me?" I didn't want to ask what I was really thinking, afraid he'd hurt my feelings if it was true.

"I remembered you had injuries and worried I was hurting you, so I instantly dropped you, but shit, that wasn't smart either. I'm sorry, Lennox. I'm such a mess."

Simon had pulled me back into his embrace, his head practically in my hair, and I was grateful I'd been able to shower. At Slade's words, he chuckled into it, making the pieces flutter with each word.

"He really is. I had to drive because he kept wanting to pull over to call you every five minutes. It's like when the Grinch's heart grew three times its size, and now he doesn't know what to do about it," he said, laughing.

Slade pouted across from us, but it was too cute, and I reached out, pulling him back into our hug. "None of that now. I'm fine. See? Come on, let's go talk to my dad and save your brother from the third degree."

Slade sniffed me, giving me an odd look when he pulled back. "You slept with him, didn't you?"

I stopped, mouth opened, staring at him. Sputtering,

"What? How?" He gave me a knowing look, and I slapped his chest playfully once I regained my composure. Planting my hands on my hips, I gave him one of his very own cocksure smiles. "Yeah, I did, and it was great. What are you going to do about it? Hmm?"

It took him a few seconds to recover and I used it to my advantage, walking off toward my dad before my composure fell. Simon had bent over, laughing his head off at the exchange, but I paid no attention to him either, and hugged my dad when I got close.

"Hey, Dad."

"Hey, pumpkin."

He pulled me close, and I relaxed in his hold. My dad was the best, and no matter what, he always made me feel okay when he was near. When we pulled back, I noticed his eyes were a little misty, and I ignored them so he wouldn't get embarrassed. He kissed my temple before letting me go, his composure back in place.

"Seems like you got yourself into a pickle."

Snorting, I grabbed a hamburger out of the bag and handed it to him. "Speaking of pickles." He laughed at my ill-timed joke, but accepted the burger. The guys grabbed some too, and we all leaned against the cars as we ate them, filling one another in on the information we knew.

"It seems this fire was set by a timer. They found two mechanisms attached to the stove and the microwave. Did you notice anything before y'all left?"

Shaking my head, I bit my lip in thought. "No, it was early, and we were in a rush to get them out the door. Zane made coffee and Simon Pop Tarts, but both are on the other side of the counter. I haven't even used the stove, to be honest."

I shrugged, looking at the guys, and they had similar expressions on their faces. "So it's hard to determine if this was set before or after the other one?"

"Yeah. The security feed was disabled, so we have that as a guide to when your car was scratched, but there's no way to say if it was when he also set the timers. If so, he would've been in the apartment when y'all were asleep. I find it highly unlikely you all slept through it in that space. As whack-a-mole as it sounds, I believe he set the fire at Emblaze first, then high-tailed it back here. He either thought you'd all go or wanted to separate you. I'm unsure if he intended for you to be inside or not at Equinox when it exploded."

Thoughts rolled around my head, and I couldn't make sense of it either. I hated that I had no clue who this was, to begin with. Not knowing their intention made it feel insurmountable. I didn't want to think about whether or not he wanted me dead.

"So, what now? Are we just sitting ducks waiting for this faker to make another move? I don't know if I can live like that," I admitted. I was surprised when it was Slade who tugged my hand, bracing his body around me.

"We'll figure it out, Peach. We just have to stay strong. Did the fire marshall give the all-clear for Equinox?"

I looked up and saw my dad's features softened at me in Slade's arms. I knew I would need to talk to him to explain my unconventional relationship, but at least he appeared accepting of it for now.

"Yeah, he said to not go upstairs, but the lower half was okay. There's not as much damage since the fire started above, but you'll have to tear down to start over. If there's anything you can salvage, now is the time to grab it."

Slade nodded, his head bobbing on mine as he did. His whole body was draped over me like an extra-large koala, and I didn't hate it. In fact, I think Slade was my new favorite accessory. A tattooed Alpha-hole blanket?

"Come on, Peach. Let's see if we can save anything."

We all walked toward the building, silence descending on us as we approached the shop. The sign hung crookedly, one hinge hanging on for dear life as it swayed in the wind. The glass front window had blown out from the force, the crunch of it under our shoes loud as we entered. The door still chimed, the sound a waning sad sound as we entered. We all looked around, none of us knowing what to do or where to start.

"I'll grab some bags and gloves, and we can start sorting stuff. Simon, you take the first two stations. Zane, can you get the front? Slade, you and I will cover the back section."

They all nodded, and I walked to the storage closet, hoping the items were still intact. They were on the opposite wall, and from my quick glance, it seemed things on the left side of the building had fared better. The door was slightly jammed, the wood warping in the heat, but I managed to yank it open, the wood creaking at my intrusion. The motion sensor light still worked when I waved my hand under it, allowing me to find the items I needed. I also grabbed a broom and headed back to the front.

Handing out gloves to everyone, I placed some garbage cans around, pulling the large can to the center. We all got to work, the sound of items being tossed into the trash echoing around us as we worked. At some point, someone got sick of it and turned some music on from their phone. It felt weird singing as I swept off the remains of my job, but it did help.

Sweeping along the back wall, I came to a row of pictures that had fallen off, the glass shattering everywhere. One by one, I dumped the shards into my bag, sweeping up the tiny slivers as I put the frames that were worth saving in a pile. Singing along to the music, I dumped the last picture and moved it over to the pile. Something stopped me, though, a familiar face peering back, catching my notice.

The music swelled around me, and as I stood with the photo in my hand, the chorus of the song built up. Peering up, I locked eyes with Slade just as the words *"This is a revolution, we are rising up"* played, and I felt it all the way in my bones. The violin played around me, spurring me on, and I strengthened my features, pushing the fear away once and for all. Immediately, Slade was by my side, the emotions dancing across my face bringing him to me.

Turning the frame toward him, I pointed to the blonde man next to him in the shot, my words frozen on my tongue until I knew. *I had to know.* He looked up at me, his brow creased, not understanding. "It's a picture from the first-year celebration. What's it have to do with anything, Peach?"

"Who," I started, swallowing. "Who is this?"

"That's Adam. The one who hired you."

I shook my head violently. "No," I croaked out, pushing the tears back.

All the times over the week he'd mention the name, it had niggled at the back of my head, wondering who it was, but I'd ignored it. Slade's face scrunched up, still not understanding the importance of this discovery.

"*He* didn't hire me. Ethan did."

"Ethan? But why? He's just an apprentice. He's only been here a few months."

Now, it was my turn to look confused. "No, I'm positive. Ethan interviewed me, offered me the job after he caught me peeking around. He's been the one making my schedule, telling me when my appointments were. He was the male version of me!" My voice raised an octave toward the end, the panic beginning to creep up my throat. I needed him to understand.

"Okay, Peach. I believe you. So, you've never met Adam?"

"Oh, I've met him. Just not as *Adam*." The one percent of doubt I had that he'd known the whole time vanished.

Swallowing, I squared my shoulders, filling myself with courage as I gave him a pointed look. Finally, it began to click in place for him. Slade clenched his jaw, the muscles moving as he attempted to contain the rage I saw bubbling up in his eyes. My own never left his as I tried to search them for something. Simon and Zane walked over, noticing our weird standoff.

"What's up? Did you find something?" Zane asked before noticing the picture in my hand. He smiled, taking it from Slade.

"Oh wow, I haven't looked at that picture in a while.

That was after Adam had finished his apprenticeship, right? You'd been opened a year if I remember correctly. You never liked that guy, though, did you?" Zane chuckled as he recalled something, and I felt my shoulders relax even more. Slade noticed, and he closed his eyes for a brief second, breathing in.

When he opened them, he nodded, accepting my one percent doubt that had flared. Simon noticed where we were all looking and turned to look at the picture. His eyes jumped to mine once he recognized who it was.

"Holy shit, it's *Thane*. Psycho Thane, I mean."

"He's a fucking dead man."

"Wait, what?" Zane asked, catching on we weren't reminiscing. "*This* is who has been pretending to be me?"

I nodded, not able to say more. "Shit. I guess that explains how he knew so much about us at least."

"What do you mean?"

"Slade roomed with him when he first moved to the city. He bugged him for months until, eventually, he let him apply for the job. He had skills, so he couldn't deny him the opportunity. Slade never liked him, though, but he couldn't find a reason not to hire him when he had talent. You met him off one of those roommate apps, right?"

Slade nodded, his whole body tensed, and I worried he might crack a tooth he was grinding them so hard. "He's been working here for *years*. Became the manager when I went to set up the Kentucky store. He's had access to my schedule, emails, and *everything*, basically if he wanted to... Fuck."

Slade looked at his brother, his eyes full of emotion, before looking at me again. He didn't want to tell me whatever it was. "Just go ahead. I need to know."

"He was a bartender at the bar where...." Zane started.

"Where I was drugged and almost kidnapped," I finished for him. The memory rushed back, practically slapping me across the face. But I didn't push it away this time, finally ready to face it.

THE REST OF THAT NIGHT PT 2

My cheek rested on the sticky floor, the bass from the music reverberating it. The tattooed angel had been hot but angry when he'd been here a minute ago. I wondered where he went. Smacking my lips, I attempted to gather some saliva, my mouth impossibly dry. My eyes began to close as the sound drowned out behind me. My whole body felt heavy, and I gave into the haze, unable to move.

Blinking open my eyes, I found myself being lifted up. The person wore a hoodie, their face hidden in the dark recesses of the fabric. "Are you here to help me?"

"Of course, princess. I'll always rescue you."

"I'm no princess," I muttered, not liking the word. I didn't want to be a princess. I wanted to be my own knight, not in need of rescuing. I always hated when the girl had to be saved by the guy. Why couldn't the girl save the guy for once?

"You're my princess, and it's my job to make sure you know that. Come on. We don't have much time."

We started to move through the bar. The crowded

area was hard to maneuver with how my legs barely seemed to work. The hooded figure next to me was practically dragging me at this point. "I'm drunk," I slurred. "I need Duncan."

"No. You don't. You only need me. You'll see."

"I don't even know you." I had to be dreaming. No way this dude was for real.

"Yes, you do. I'm Blaze, Nox."

The name had me stopping as I looked at him. "If you're Blaze, then I really want nothing to do with you. You're a liar and a big meanie head."

"Yeah, sorry about earlier. Someone stole my phone, can you believe it? I got to the restaurant, and the hostess said, you'd left, crying. I've been trying to find you ever since."

"I don't believe," I mumbled, the alcohol making it difficult to judge him. We made it to the door, and he dragged me through it. The air stuck to my skin when we made it outside. He kept dragging me down the sidewalk, and I realized I didn't want to go with him. I didn't care who he was.

In an attempt to fight, I tried to wrench myself out of his hold, but I stumbled, almost falling to my knees in the process.

"Don't be a little bitch. I had to work hard to get you here, don't go and ruin it now."

"I don't understand."

"I know, and I'm sorry about that, princess. But you will once we get to where we'll be staying."

"But I don't want to go anywhere with you. I just want Duncan," I wailed.

I began to cry, the thought of being alone with this

stranger the last straw. Tears ran down my face, and I started to hiccup, the alcohol and tears making my esophagus spasm.

"Well, too bad. You get me. You'll love me. You'll see. I just know we're destined to be together."

He opened the door to a car and began to push me in. I braced my arms on the roof, bracing my body so he couldn't, and locked my legs. He stumbled when I didn't go in willingly. My father had told me the statistics of kidnap victims, and I didn't want to be one.

"No. I said I don't want to go."

Somehow in my drunken state, I managed to lift my leg, kneeing him in the groin. He buckled over, curses falling from his lips, and I took my chance. Spinning, I wobbled on my heels, but only made it a few steps before he was on me. Grabbing my leg, he yanked me down hard, my balance going off-kilter. I barely had my hands out in front of me before I was bracing myself against the concrete.

Realizing I needed to scream, I opened my mouth to belt one out when he climbed up my body, sitting on my back. Thrashing, I tried to knock him off me to no avail. Until my real knight showed, stopping him from taking me. The weight lifted off me, and I scrambled away, rolling over. When I realized who it was, I quit fighting, my body even more tired now after the exertion.

"Oh, Dunc," I cried. "I was so scared."

"Ssh, LJ. I got you."

He helped me up, checking me over quickly for injuries. "Come on, babe. Let's get you home. I'm sorry it took me so long to get here."

"You're here. That's all that matters." I kissed him, happy to be safe in his arms.

PRESENT

Blinking, I came back to the present, finding Simon's hands on my face as he watched me. "Back with us, Lenn?"

Nodding, I licked my lips, swallowing back the tears that wanted to emerge. "Yeah, I'm here. I remembered something."

Twisting, I looked at the twins, matching expressions of concern and devastation on their faces.

"Your recollections triggered my own memory. I remember you guys in the hallway. You were there one second and then gone. When I woke up again, he was there, walking me out. He kept saying I was his princess, that he was Blaze, and we belonged together. I... I think he'd planned to kidnap me that night. If you say he was the bartender there, then that's how I must've been drugged. He slipped it in one of the drinks you guys might have given me."

Simon and Slade looked to another, guilt on their faces. I shook my head, trying to stop them from taking that on. "It's not your fault. For all we know, he spiked multiple, hoping I'd get one of them. When he tried to push me into a car, Duncan showed up and stopped it. But he..." I stopped, the words becoming thick in my throat.

"He must've followed you and chased you off the road. He was there, watching, and when he saw you were okay, and Duncan had survived," he swallowed, never dropping my eyes. "He must've improvised, stolen that car and made sure to finish the job that time," Zane relayed, finishing where I couldn't. The guilt sat heavy on his face from his earlier confession.

"It's still not your fault, Zane."

He nodded, but I saw his struggle to accept it. "I can't believe Adam's your stalker, and he killed Duncan. Holy shit." Zane stated, dropping the picture to the ground. I reached out and squeezed his hand, hoping he got my message. I locked eyes with Slade next, the torment there mirroring my own. Reaching out, I grabbed his hand too with my other, threading our fingers. I stood between the twins, as we processed the new information.

"It's not your fault. It's not my fault. It's his, and I think it's time we show him how strong we are as a foursome. We know who he is now. I say we use that to our advantage."

Slade pulled me close, wrapping me up tight, not caring that my hand remained in Zane's. I knew I'd never get tired of being in his arms. He had a way of hugging you with his whole body, making you feel cherished and safe.

"Let's go tell your father. Looks like I have an employee to fire."

Call it the gas, or even the realization that four years ago had all been orchestrated, but whatever it was, Slade saying he had someone to fire had us all bending over in laughter.

It felt nice to laugh for a second. We made our way through the door when I realized something. Crying out, I stopped dramatically, a tear falling down my cheek as I stared up at the charred remains.

"What's wrong, Peach? We'll get this guy. I promise."

Shaking my head, I wiped a tear. "It's not that."

"Then what is it? Tell me."

"It's my toaster tongs," I wailed.

Slade looked at me, rolled his eyes, and then threw me over his shoulder, playfully swatting my behind.

"Peach, I'll buy you a dozen toaster tongs. We've just got to survive your stalker first, okay?"

"Okay," I mumbled, but decided I was holding him to that. He carried me the rest of the way, and I smiled considering his words. In Sladeland, that was practically a proposal.

THANE TO NOX

From: blazetats@heartsemail.com
To: noxsmiles@heartsemail.com
Subject: I'll always be waiting

Dear Noxy girl,

I've done something bad that I worry is unfor-givable. Writing to you has shown me I can change, and that the most important thing is trying. I admit that is something I've struggled with. But you, you've shown me I can be better, do better.

I did ask someone to sit with me, and you were right. It was one of the best decisions I've made. I think I made a real friend and not someone who likes me just because of my looks or what I can do for them. I know that might not make sense, but one day I think it will.

If my letters change, it's because I'm changing, and I don't want you to worry. No matter what happens from this point forward, I want you to know I'm better for it. You've imprinted yourself on me, Noxy girl, and I'll never let you go.

Thank you for listening and pushing me to step outside myself and be a better person.

No more dares. You don't need them. You're brave. The bravest person I know. I hope you one day realize it and know how many people you've changed with your kindness and light. I don't deserve your friendship, but I will, one day.

I'll always be waiting under the stars, hoping for a world where there are a million of you to spend all my minutes with.

Blaze

Chapter Seventeen
LENNOX

SLADE SET me down on my feet, brushing my hair back. His eyes were intense as he looked down at me. My eyelashes fluttered closed at his gentle touch. Seeing this Alpha-hole be so sweet had me turning to goo inside.

"Come on, Peach. Let's figure out a plan."

Nodding, I linked our hands, and we joined my other two guys and my dad. My dad appeared deep in thought, his hand covering his chin as he stared at the ground. It looked like Zane and Simon had filled him in as we approached. The sound of our steps drew his focus, and he lifted his eyes, meeting mine, before flicking to Slade.

"You're sure this is the guy?" I handed him the picture, and he nodded, recognizing 'Thane' as well.

"Alright, I'll send this over. At least now we have a photo. It should help. I'm gonna head back home. You going to be alright, pumpkin?"

"Yeah, Dad. I will be." I nodded, hugging him.

"You guys look after her, you hear? I'm trusting you to keep my daughter safe."

"Yes, sir," they chorused. But of course, Slade had to have the last word. "But in all fairness, Eddy, Lennox can do that all on her own."

My dad smiled, pleased with his response, and I rolled my eyes despite being happy as well. I wrapped my arm around my Tatzilla, pulling him close to my side. "Good answer. Simon, you might be getting replaced as my favorite if you're not careful."

"What? Hey!" Simon yelped, turning to punch Slade in the arm, but in the end, it was Si who was shaking his hand out after coming into contact with the hard muscle. Laughing, we waved my dad off as he got into his police cruiser and drove away. We were left standing on the sidewalk, the sounds of the city beginning to filter back in.

"So, what now?" I asked, looking at them.

Zane walked forward but stopped when Slade growled. Smacking his stomach, I dropped my arm and grabbed Zane's hand. He squeezed it before continuing. "Now, we try to live our lives and figure out a way to draw Adam out."

"Assuming he doesn't come out himself," I muttered.

"Yeah, but we can't live our lives waiting for him to act. He's gonna lay low I bet after the two explosions, or maybe he'll show his hand. Who knows? He seems to be becoming more and more unhinged. I think we should finish up here, figure out where we're all staying, and then watch a stupid movie that makes us all laugh until we can't breathe."

"Excellent plan."

Even Slade couldn't find fault. Rolling his eyes, he sighed, giving in. "Fine, but I refuse to watch that reality show you both are obsessed with."

"Real Housewives? Say it ain't so!"

Naturally, Simon and I had to poke at Slade the rest of the time we cleaned the shop. His constant muttering under his breath about dealing with the two of us only spurred us on. Despite picking up the destroyed remains of the shop and my home, the next hour went by quickly. We converged on Darcie's place, figuring it was the best bet for the night, and we all pigged out on junk food before having a sleepover. It was nice remembering there was more to life than stalkers and lies.

A WEEK HAD PASSED, and we still hadn't heard anything from Adam. I was beginning to wonder if he'd given up, or maybe he'd been hit by a bus, his body so mutilated no one could identify him. The police had his picture, and as things unfolded, it became clear he was a psychopath. The place he'd been staying had a wall of pictures of me from over the years and countless emails printed out with things highlighted and circled. He'd been planning this for so long, becoming the perfect version of who he thought I wanted.

The creepiest thing they found…. His journal.

Adam had been meticulous. He wrote down every encounter he ever had with me from online to in person, including the first when he'd saved Noah. To discover that was where it all began had me puking in the closest trash can for a solid ten minutes. He'd been my hero then, but became my nightmare.

It made sense he was also the blog harasser, something I'd never told the guys about. Slade had grumbled for a good while, but eventually let it go saying he'd punish me later. It sounded more exciting than terrifying, but I wasn't going to let him know that.

All of his deluded fantasies, what he wanted our lives to be, and how he planned to make it happen were too scary to be real. At least that was how I had to look at them or I'd go and hide behind my rock forever. My father asked me if I wanted to read it, but after the first couple of pages, I decided I didn't need that information in my brain. They'd found my necklace from Blaze as well. I chose not to ask where or what condition it'd been found in, just happy it was returned.

With all the evidence in his place they were able to tie him to Duncan's murder and even had suspicion of another unsolved case from years before. I couldn't believe I'd almost fallen for him, letting him in my life so easily. Fortunately, the three men in my life wouldn't let me hide from it, and helped remind me of all the good things life had to offer, like tacos and orgasms. They reiterated that Adam had an agenda all along, and I couldn't go through life distrusting everyone's intentions. It just wasn't me, and I didn't want to live life that way. With the amount of orgasms they kept giving me, I didn't have any fear I would.

We'd all returned to Bowling Green, nothing in Nashville for us at the moment. Though the shop was just as destroyed here, at least my family was nearby, and we had a place to stay. Zane took a leave of absence from his job, cashing in years of vacation hours while we figured things out.

We'd all ended up at Slade's house, Simon and I's apartment not feeling safe enough. Though my dad did have the Fire Marshall check it out, it still felt too vulnerable. I'd always known where Slade lived, but I hadn't spent much time there. I'd only ever dropped something off on his porch once, never stepping into it. So, when I discovered the remodeled farmhouse, I almost had another spontaneous orgasm.

"Wow, this place is beautiful. I can't believe you live here. It's the type of house I've always dreamed about," I admitted.

"I know, Peach." He wrapped his arms around me, pulling me back into him. I melted, the feel of his body welcoming.

"What do you mean, you know?"

I looked up at him, and his smirk was too cute. "You drew it once, and I saved it. I started working on it, telling myself it was out of spite, but really, it was because I wanted to create your dream."

"You did this for me?"

"I did it for *us*."

"I don't know what to say."

"You don't have to say anything, just agree to move in, and we can move on."

"You want me to move in?"

"No." Disappointment hit me, and I lowered my head. His finger lifted my chin, his eyes blazing as he stared at me. "No, I don't want just *you* to move in. I want you, Simon, and even Thane to move in."

"You've forgiven him, haven't you?"

"Yeah, well, I love the fucker even if he is annoying at times. Besides, we could both use a clean slate and all."

"Good. I'm glad." I started to walk away, and he

pulled me back into his arms. I smiled up at him mischievously. "Fine. I accept."

"Like you had a choice, but I'm happy to hear it." Stretching, I kissed his lips, realizing I was happy. It was something I hadn't truly felt in a long time. I'd had moments of it, but there was the underlying grief and anxiety reminding me I couldn't trust it. Today, though, I could relax into this and trust I could handle whatever life threw at me.

"Hey, do we have anything going on tonight?" I asked, a plan forming in my head.

"I don't think so. Why?"

"There's a corn maze and haunted house out at Lost River. I promised Noah I would take him. Y'all want to go with me?"

"Yes, we can get dressed up and everything," Simon chimed in. "Plus, Lenn, I'm dying to get my hands on your hair."

"Oh, thank goodness," I sighed with a laugh.

Slade showed us all to the rooms we could use, and Simon and I got to work on going through the clothes we had on hand for ideas. When we figured it out, we put them into piles for each of us before he started on my hair.

"Simon, you're happy, right?"

"The most, why, aren't you?"

"No, I am. I just wanted to make sure you were too."

"Lenn, I get to be with the two people I care about. It's the life I've always wanted."

"I just don't want to lose us, I guess."

"How can we lose us?"

"I guess I'm just worried with Slade and Zane in the mix that you could feel left out."

"Nah, don't you see, it's perfect. When you're with Thane, I can hang with Slade, and when you're with him, I can have alone time or get to know Thane better. The pressure to be perfect is removed, and I can develop other deep relationships simultaneously. I'm not losing anything. In fact, I'm gaining so much more."

"I like the way you think about it."

"Good. Now, hold still, and lean forward."

Following the familiar routine, I gave in to his ministrations as he tilted my head, cutting the ends. A few hours later, I found myself with a kaleidoscope of colors, my hair looking like an ombre rainbow peacock.

"Wow! That's amazing, Si. I love it!"

"I figured you could use a change. Liven it up a bit. Plus, I've been dying to try out this new technique."

"Well, it will be perfect for my costume too. Speaking of, we should gather the others and get dressed. I'll tell Noah to be ready as well."

Texting my brother, I was glad I didn't have to worry about any of my messages being received by Adam. We'd all gotten new phones and changed all of our passwords, hoping to keep him out of our business.

Picking up the pile of clothes, I quickly changed and then walked into the room to give the twins theirs.

"No." Slade shook his head, not even willing to hear me out as I showed him the costume.

"Come on, please."

"I'll wear it," Zane agreed, walking over to take the one I had for him.

Simon walked in wearing his, a smile on his face. "I

knew he wouldn't go for it," he teased, kissing Slade on the cheek before he whispered something in his ear. Slade's eyes heated as he shifted on his feet, dropping his arms and defensive position.

"Fine. One hour, no pictures."

Squealing, I jumped up and handed him the costume. The twins were changed a few minutes later, and we headed out together.

"THIS COSTUME IS RIDICULOUS."

"Oh hush, you're a great Buddy Blue."

Noah laughed as we walked toward the maze, finding our interactions hilarious. He'd gone as Captain America, his shield in one hand and his bucket for candy in the other. The smile on his face as we approached was worth it.

"What are you guys, again?" he asked. Noah had been quiet on the drive, still not used to Zane. Dad had talked with him about how the guy he met as Thane wasn't the real one, but it seemed to make him extra cautious toward Zane now.

"*Whipped*, that's what," mumbled Slade as he adjusted his blue pants. Since we hadn't had much time to prepare, Simon and I had kept it simple and color-coded our outfits, allowing us to go as characters from Rainbow Brite, one of my favorite classic cartoons. Slade was Buddy Blue, Simon was Canary Yellow, and Zane was Red Butler. They were dressed head to toe in their respective colors, and I was Rainbow Brite. It was no surprise I had a rainbow skirt or Rainbow Brite t-shirt, so mine had been simple. I was good to go by adding some old snow boots, colorful tights, and a ponytail on top of my new rainbow hair.

"Rainbow Brite, bud."

"Ah," he shook his head, smiling at me. "Still, no clue."

"You hurt me with your words."

My joke thankfully had Slade smiling, his scowl leaving temporarily. Seeing him in a color that wasn't black was disorienting, but I didn't dislike it. My eyes must've been giving off heated vibes because I found him looking at me a second later. Licking his lips, his tongue ring poked out, and I found myself moving toward him instinctively.

Zane grabbed my hand, though, pulling my attention. "Can I go with you and Noah? It might help to make him more comfortable. I want him to like me."

"Yeah, of course." The crease in his brow lifted some, and I focused back on what my priority was for the evening. *Noah and fun.*

No sexy times till later, you got that va-jay-jay.

"Noah, how about we form teams and see who can get out of the maze the fastest? You, me, and Zane against Simon and Slade?"

He'd looked excited until I said Zane, but he nodded. "Yeah, sure."

We paid for our tickets and entered the maze, kids and adults screaming around us as we started our way in. The maze was a mix of corn stalks and hay bales, and there was a haunted house and spooky village when you exited it, but first, you had to finish the maze.

Noah, Simon, and I did this every year, and the farm made it different each time.

"On your mark," I cheered, "go." We took off, going to our right as we began to twist and turn. When we got to a fork, we looked, debating. "Which way, Noah?"

"Hmm, um, how about this way?"

"Let's do it."

A few turns later, and we were stuck at a dead end. "Okay, let's backtrack."

"Sorry, Lennox," Noah said, hanging his head.

"Nothing to be sorry about, little man. It's how mazes work. We just have to keep trying until we find our way out."

"How about I go one way, and you the other for a minute, and then we return to see which one was the right way?" Zane offered.

"Uh, sure." I hedged, but Noah nodded eagerly, and I gave in. He really wanted to get it right. Zane went left, so we went right, and I set a timer on my watch so we'd know when to go back. When we came around a corner, though, it was another dead end.

"Well, I guess this means we turn back."

"Yeah," he sighed, agreeing.

Pivoting, we found our path blocked by someone wearing all black. "Excuse us," I tried, attempting to skirt past them.

The figure reached out, grabbing Noah, pushing me down as they took off running.

"No!" Clambering up, I raced after them, smacking into a chest.

"Lenn? What's wrong?"

"Si, someone took, Noah! We have to go! Now!"

I kept trying to move him out of the way, but he held on tight. "Stop, Lenn. Let's think this through, okay? Call your Dad. I'll call Slade."

"Where is he? Why aren't you together?"

"We got to the end, and when you didn't show, I came back to find you. He's waiting at the exit, so they won't pass him."

Nodding, some of the fear left me as I dialed my father. Explaining what happened, he said he was on his way and would send whoever was close to the farm. I felt calmer, knowing we had people on the way. A message came through when I went to put my phone away.

Unknown: I saved him once, and I'll save him again. Then you'll remember we belong together.
ME: Where is he? What did you do?
Unknown: I didn't do anything, princess. Don't you get it? I'm always *helping*.

"Ugh!" I screamed, shoving my phone into the pocket on my skirt. I took off in a direction, ignoring Simon as I went, who was still on the phone. Adam had pissed off the mama bear in me. Whether he was the hooded figure or had just staged this, I wouldn't let him get away with it. When I found a hole in the maze a few feet ahead, I knew it was the direction I needed to go. He was smart and wouldn't have put himself in a situation without a way out. We were the dumb ones thinking otherwise.

Stepping over the broken stalks, I focused on where I was walking as I entered a part of the field that hadn't been transformed into the maze. The lights faded the further I went, but I knew I was on the right path. I could hear shuffling and a muffled sound ahead. When I heard voices, I slowed to listen, creepingly along slowly.

"You moron! You were supposed to wait until they were in the haunted house. You exposed yourself too soon. This is why I can't trust anyone to do anything for me."

"Listen, man. I grabbed the kid. Does it matter where?"

"Of course it matters!" Adam roared. "I can't save him if she thinks *I* took him, idiot. Just give him to me."

"When will I get paid?"

"When I get the girl."

"That wasn't what we agreed upon."

Hearing enough, I jumped in, hoping to use their distraction. "Thane, you found him! Oh, thank God."

My cry surprised them both, my use of his fake name doing as I hoped. They turned to look at me with shock on their faces. Rushing forward, I used their distraction and snatched Noah, pushing him behind me. We slowly began to back away from the crazy dudes, Noah clinging to me.

"Princess," he finally stated, the shock of me finding him fading. "You see, I'm the hero here. *This* man is the bad guy." Adam grabbed the man, putting him in a headlock. I watched in slow motion as he lifted a gun, placing it against his head. The hooded guy immediately began to backpedal when he felt the cold steel.

"He's crazy. He paid me to do it. I'm innocent here."

I ignored him, keeping my eyes on the real danger

as I kept backing away, pushing Noah back with each step.

"Princess, why are you leaving?" His face was twisted up, the once beautiful facade, now a hideous disguise full of lies and betrayal. He took a step forward to come for me, but the guy he was holding took the opportunity to punch him in the gut. The gun fell, and I gasped as a shot went wide, ringing out into the night. I froze in fear at the sound, my eyes locked on the weapon and I debated if it was worth moving forward to grab it or just to run.

Adam bent over, the air knocked out of him as the hooded guy took off, drawing my attention. He was so focused on watching Adam, he hadn't taken his surroundings into account. The area they'd stopped in had hay bales built around, and a tractor-trailer parked that was packed to the brim. It must've been a staging area or storage for them to use.

The rake used to gather the hay from the truck laid on the ground, and the hooded man stepped on it. His foot went right through the spikes, and he cried out in pain. It was soon followed by the handle coming up and smacking him in the forehead. He stumbled back, knocking into a stack of hay. The force had the entire structure moving, and in his attempt to catch his balance, he grabbed onto the bed of the trailer, releasing the lock. The top bale rolled off, now freed from its restraints. Realizing what was happening, I dove, taking Noah with me.

Looking up, my eyes met Adam's blue ones. They'd once been soft, reassuring even, but were filled with nothing but crazy possessiveness now. He'd recovered from the punch, and was moving toward the gun, his focus solely on me. His obsession would be his downfall as the massive bale rolled, landing on the hooded man first, knocking him to the ground. His screams were muffled, which I assumed was why Adam didn't hear them. That or his fixation had made him blind to anything else.

Locking eyes back with him, I debated what to do, if I should warn him. His eyes held mine, the crazy tangible as he lifted the gun straight at me, a devious grin on his face. There was no doubt in my mind that he would pull the trigger. He'd take the chance to hit me or Noah, whichever allowed him to live out his deluded fantasy.

Decision made, I covered Noah, squeezing my eyes shut as the bale began its trek, crushing everything in its path. The air moved past us as it continued, rolling down its course. The force had been so strong, my hair lifted off my face.

"Physics," I muttered. "One of these days, people will learn to respect the laws of nature."

Noah looked at me weirdly. "Can you get off me now?"

"Oh yeah."

Rolling off, I poked my head up and took in the scene. Hay rained down all around us, causing me to sneeze multiple times. When I could finally take in my surroundings, I quickly covered Noah's eyes and looked away.

Flashlights began to get brighter as they drew closer, and I could make out shouts.

"Over here!" I yelled, hoping my voice carried. It

seemed the gunshot had at least given them the direction to go in.

Standing, I pulled Noah with me, making sure to keep my back to the gruesome scene behind us, not wanting to expose him to it. Within seconds, my dad, Slade, Simon, Zane, and even Bubba descended on us.

"We're okay. We're okay."

We were engulfed in a massive hug as they all tried to check us over at once.

"Is *that*?"

"Yep," I nodded, "not looking, though. Can we maybe move away from the allergy-inducing nightmare scene?"

The men nodded, grimacing as they realized what had happened.

"Yeah, you guys go upfront. Send Officer Willis this way. We're gonna need some lights and, um, body bags," my dad trailed off. I gave him a look, covering Noah's ears, and he nodded solemnly. "Bubba, can you see if they can get a tractor over here…." My dad trailed off as the two of them moved more toward the crime scene.

"Peach, I'm so mad at you for going off on your own, but I'll let it slide this time because only you could evade kidnapping by some freak chain of events."

"Love you too, Tatzilla."

"Eww," Noah commented, reminding us we weren't alone. "Can we get candy now?"

Laughing, I relaxed, knowing it was finally all over. "Of course, bud. You can have all the candy you want tonight. Make yourself sick."

"Yes! You're the best sister ever, Lennox." He

hugged me and I melted, trying not to think about the fact I could've lost him again. He tugged on my sleeve, motioning for me to bend down. "I'm glad the scary guy is gone. I like the new one better anyway. Since you have three boyfriends, does that mean I get three presents on my birthday from them?"

Snorting, I ruffled his hair. "Absolutely, it does." He smiled, running ahead now that we were back in the central area. Simon nodded, indicating he'd go after him, wanting to keep him in sight even if the danger was gone. Standing back, sandwiched between the twins, I watched my brother show no signs of fear as he went table to table, grabbing candy.

"It doesn't seem real."

"I imagine it will take time for it to," Zane offered. "It's not every day people are crushed by bales of hay."

"Actually," I started, "an average of 18 people die each year from them. They can weigh up to 1200 pounds and when they fall, get up to dangerous speeds."

"Peach, I don't even want to know why you know this."

"I did a presentation on it for my 11th-grade physics class after seeing it on the news. Mr. Jefferies told me it was the most pointless use of physics he'd ever heard. Well, take that, Mr. Jefferies. Physics just saved my life. Bet he can't say that."

The twins looked at one another over my head before breaking out in hoots of laughter. We walked off, following Simon and Noah, hand in hand, and I knew things could only go up from here.

"Did you hear that they almost made those circular

bales illegal?" I asked once their laughter had died down.

"No, Peach. Can't say I'm up on my hay knowledge like you."

"Yeah, well, they were afraid the cows weren't getting three square meals a day."

"Seriously?" he snorted, shaking his head.

"Oh, what about this one? Why shouldn't you order your hay off Amazon?"

Slade stubbornly refused to play along, but Zane succumbed to me, stupid jokes a thing of our past. "Why's that?"

"A few days later, they ask for their feed back."

"You're killing me, Peach."

"Not as much as that hay did to Psycho Thane. You could even say it crushed it."

Slade couldn't hold it in any longer, and we all three laughed hysterically at my lame attempts to make the situation okay.

"Oh, I know..."

When life gave you stalkers, it was best to laugh about it. At least I didn't hit my head this time. It would've sucked to wake up to everything and have it all be a dream. Life might be gritty, but it was mine and I wanted to live it out in the open.

Dear Lemon Drop

SINCE SLADE IS WRITING YOU LOVE LETTERS, I FIGURED I BETTER UP MY GAME AND DO ONE AS WELL. IN SOME WAYS, OUR RELATIONSHIP IS DIFFERENT NOW, I MEAN OF COURSE IT IS, WE SEE EACH OTHER'S PRIVATE PARTS AND ROUTINELY PUT THEM IN OUR MOUTHS NOW.

THAT'S A LEVEL OUR FRIENDSHIP HADN'T BEEN BEFORE. I MEAN, WE WERE AT 'I WOULD PEE ON YOU IF YOU WERE STUNG BY A JELLYFISH' LEVEL, SO IT'S NOT A HUGE LEAP TO WANTING TO LICK EACH OTHER ALL OVER.

AND NOW I'M HARD AND HAVE DIGRESSED FROM MY INTENTIONS OF THIS.

WHAT I'M TRYING TO SAY IS, DESPITE KNOWING ONE ANOTHER BETTER THAN ANYONE ELSE, I'M NOT GOING TO TAKE THAT FOR GRANTED. JUST BECAUSE I KNOW YOU, DOESN'T MEAN I'M NOT GOING TO STILL GET TO KNOW YOU. I KNOW YOU AS LENNOX MY BESTIE, NOT LENNOX MY GIRLFRIEND. WHAT I'M REALIZING THOUGH IS I SUCK AT WRITING WORDS, SO I HOPE YOU ACCEPT THIS LETTER FOR WHAT IT IS.

I'M GLAD WE MADE IT THROUGH EVERYTHING AND ARE HERE TO KEEP PUSHING THROUGH TOGETHER. I KNOW LIFE WILL BE DIFFERENT NOW. FOR SO LONG, IT'S BEEN THE LENNOX AND SIMON SHOW. I DIDN'T MIND THAT YOU DIDN'T REALLY HAVE SERIOUS BOYFRIENDS BECAUSE IT MEANT I GOT TO BE THE MAIN MAN IN YOUR LIFE. BUT NOW, NOT ONLY DO WE HAVE TO FIGURE OUT OUR RELATIONSHIP, BUT US WITH SLADE. AND THEN YOU AND THANE. I KNOW I CAN'T HAVE ALL YOUR TIME ANYMORE. THAT MAKES ME SAD, BUT ALSO EXCITED FOR YOU.

IT'S ALSO GOING TO BE A NEW EXPERIENCE HAVING A BOYFRIEND. THAT'S SOMETHING I'VE NEVER HAD. WHAT DO I EVEN DO WITH THAT?

LIFE HASN'T ALWAYS BEEN EASY, BUT IT'S ALWAYS BEEN YOU AND ME. I WANT THAT FOR THE REST OF OUR LIVES. YOU, ME AND THE GRUMPY ONE. I LOVE YOU LENNOX.

BEST FRIENDS MAKE THE BEST LOVERS. NEVER FORGET WHO MADE YOU SQUIRT.

love,

Your dork

Chapter Eighteen

LENNOX

THE PHONE RANG, rousing me from my daydream, and I blinked before looking at the caller ID. Smiling, I answered quickly.

"Hey, Mom. What's up?"

"Hey honey, I was just calling to see how you were doing?"

It was almost a week after everything had happened with Adam and for the most part, I was dealing.

"I'm okay, still a little paranoid at times, but it's lessening. The reporters are a bit much, but yeah, you know. The guys are awesome though. I'm glad I have them."

"That's good to hear, sweetie. The media's been camping out here too, the vultures. It just makes me worried for you. Though, I'm selfishly glad you're back. I've missed you, honey."

"No need to worry, Mom. I promise I'm better. I've missed you too. How's Noah? Anything to worry about there?"

"Oh, he's fine. He's been telling everyone how his sister is a hero even if she is rainbow. I swear," she laughed, "the things he comes up with. You're the talk of the middle school."

"For Pete's sake!" I laughed. "I had enough of that when I was there."

We talked for another ten minutes about a new project she was working on, and Noah's current obsession with ant farms. I made plans to go over later in the week for dinner. I'd been surprised how well they'd taken the foursome I'd found myself in. But being the awesome parents they were, they accepted it without question.

Setting my phone back down, I was surprised when Slade came into the room a few seconds later and picked me up. A yelp left me, but Slade didn't say anything, just scooped me up and hauled me from the chair I'd been sitting in most of the day.

I'd been a bit lost lately, not knowing how to act after everything. I didn't currently have a job since it had caught fire, and leaving the house to do anything had become a nightmare, with everyone and their brother wanting the inside scoop on my stalker.

Even Shelley had reached out, wanting to see how I was, only to minutes later probe me for the inside scoop. She was a reporter, so at least it made sense. The lady at the checkout line? Not so much. Everyone wanted something from me, and not all of it was good. That was one of the things about small towns I hadn't missed while living in Nashville. No one knew you there, and if they did, they minded their own darn business.

Slade continued carrying me without saying a word until we made it to the garage. "We're going out, Peach. No more sulking, no more sitting around staring at the window and sighing, and especially no more hiding out in this house. We're going out."

"Well, when you put it that way." I smiled, my hands naturally grazing the hair at the nape of his neck. The grin he leveled me with had me squirming. Glancing down at my outfit, I figured it would work. I had on a band tee that I'd knotted on the side, a long tulle skirt, and a pair of chucks. It was comfy and made for a good sitting around the house and looking forlornly out the window.

A door opened behind me, and I was placed in the arms of Simon, who was sitting in the backseat.

"I can walk, you know? I'm not going to run away. I'm good with this plan."

"We know, Lenn. It's just more fun this way."

"You're so weird."

"Yep, proud of it too," he bragged, sticking out his tongue.

The other doors closed, and I turned to the front, seeing the twins buckling themselves in. I scooted off Simon's lap and latched my seatbelt excitedly.

"So, where are we going?"

"Where else does one go on Saturday night in this town?"

"The Whistler?"

"Yep!" Simon beamed, and I began to dance in my seat in excitement.

They were right. It was time to get out of the house and do something. There was a media van on the side of the road, but they were temporarily distracted by a few bikers. I giggled when I saw Bubba talking to the reporter, hitting her with his swagger, so she didn't notice our car driving by.

We pulled up to the old bar a few minutes later, and I could already feel the music playing from inside. The bar was dark as we entered, but our eyes adjusted quickly, and we followed Slade as he made his way to an open table. He barrelled his way through the crowd, no one daring to stand in his way. Zane shook his head, but we all followed, his method effective.

Sitting down, I looked around to see who was all here. It was a local joint, and it was well known for two things: chicken wings and Karaoke. And on Saturday, it was their 2-for-1 special on wings Karaoke night. It was the closest thing to an open mic this town had, bringing in all the local crooners. I waved at a few people I saw and realized that with Slade present, they were keeping their distance.

"Tatzilla, I think you're going to become my new accessory."

He looked at me, a question on his face as he raised his eyebrow at me. "Why's that, Peach? Not that I mind if I get to stick to you."

Fanning my flushed face, I grinned and pointed at all the people around us. "Because you're like nosey people repellent." He rolled his eyes but didn't deny the fact.

An hour later, we'd filled ourselves with wings, beer, and other fried appetizers that had me moaning in ecstasy. "Good gravy, their food is so good."

"I have to say, those were amazing wings," Zane agreed, wiping sauce off his face. I went to tease him that he hadn't tried anything yet, when my name was called from the stage, surprising me.

"Lennox James? Get your cute butt up here, darlin'."

Jumping up, I didn't even wait to see what the guys thought and raced up to the stage, the beer and adrenaline erasing my stage fright. Wrapping my arms around the bearded ginger, I smiled up at him. "Hey Bubba, thanks for the assistance earlier. Do I get to sing?"

"Of course, sugga." He kissed my temple before turning back to the front. The Whistler had a long waitlist to sing, usually requiring weeks to a month to get on it. So to get the chance tonight was a dream come true.

"What do y'all think, folks? We wanna hear our country darlin' sing?"

There were a few disgruntled people in the front, and I didn't know if it was because three hot guys paid them no attention, or because I got to sing, but I didn't care. Most of the crowd cheered, their uproarious noise bolstering me as I took the microphone. Despite the packed bar, my eyes only noticed the three who'd captured my heart—my bossnemy, my first love, and the one who'd gotten away.

I smiled and felt as if hearts had to be coming out of my eyes as I stared at them. Once I thought my love life was cursed, and I'd never have a happy ending. But I realized now, in order to get there, I had to embrace the middle and all it had to offer.

There would be trials and tears along the way, that was part of life, but it didn't have to keep me from living. I wasn't cursed, just human. There would still be times I was scared or feared facing the future, but at least now I had people to face them with.

Our love story had begun with letters, innocent confessions shared between lost souls, forging a connection of friendship until something more mature developed. It had gotten a little messy along the way, but I had faith the next chapter would be better than we'd ever dreamed. With a soft smile on a stage surrounded by strangers, I made a promise to always tell them how I felt. No more lies, and definitely no more misperceptions.

Turning to Bubba, I whispered my song choice, and he nodded. The music started a moment later, the upbeat guitar picking sounding out, and I raised the microphone, singing with everything from my heart. As the words "Glad you exist" by Dan + Shay fell from my lips, I swayed to the music and sang my love to Slade, Simon, and Thane, my Zane. The three smudged lines on my heart had now transformed into a permanent mark, tattooing themselves on my heart forever.

I didn't need to be scared anymore, not when my love story was just beginning.

Epilogue

SIMON

DECEMBER 31ST

The music played over the speakers, and I swayed to the beat, goosebumps breaking out over my skin. It was nearly impossible not to love this song, and when Lennox sang it, I was a goner. Her hope and beauty were pure in each word as she belted, "Don't give up on me" by Andy Grammar. It was one of those songs where you wanted to throw your hands up and sing along, dancing in circles as you belted it out.

Which was what I found myself doing.

Thane laughed next to me, but he wasn't fairing much better, shaking his hips back and forth. Over the past few months, we'd all grown closer, and Thane had become a brother to me and a dear friend. The relationship between him and Slade had improved tremendously. Life had been good post-Adam, and I knew it would be even more each year we were all together.

My parents had taken a little time to get used to the idea, but they were on board now, having fallen in love with the twins as much as Lennox had. Robin and Eddy had been on board from day one, reminding me how amazing of parents they were despite what the pearl-clutchers said.

The media circus that had developed after every-

329

thing that had taken place with Adam took a toll on Lennox and Robin. Her mother had a small episode right before Christmas, the stress getting to her routine. In all honesty, it had been a good thing because it made Lennox focus on things closer to home instead of trying to handle everything else. She was too kind, sometimes taking on too many things she didn't need to. We'd need to do better at making sure she didn't in the future.

"You think she'll like the new tattoo studio?" Thane asked.

Nodding, I smiled. "Yeah. She's going to love it."

Equinox and Emblazed had undergone extensive renovations and were set to open in the new year as Tattooed Hearts. It felt fitting to rebrand everything and give both places a fresh slate clear of Adam. Slade had caved and designed Lennox her own studio, though I think his play acting was only so she didn't know how he'd already had it planned, the big romantic. He hadn't let her see it yet, though. To christen it and the new location, the first tattoo would be the one Slade had promised Lennox all those months back before Adam had blown everything up. Literally.

Lennox jumped off the stage into Slade's arms, and he spun her, carrying her back to our table where we stood in the banquet hall. If they weren't so cute, the grumpy-tatted guy and the quirky sunshine girl, I'd probably be jealous. But all I saw when I looked at them were the two pieces of my heart. Them being happy made me happy, and I finally understood that statement Lenn had made. Love didn't take, it gave. Loving them was easy, and it had doubled the love I had.

"Amazing as always, Lenn."

"Thanks, Si." Slade put her on her feet, her customary dresses and hair back to her usual standards. Tonight she wore a navy dress with the zodiac on it, and star stockings. It was beautiful on her, and she kept twirling, the satin skirt of it swishing with each motion.

"It's about that time, folks. Grab a glass and raise it with me as we prepare for the countdown."

We grabbed ours off the table, smiling at one another as the countdown started. It wasn't really midnight, only about 7 pm, but we were counting down with Europe, the event wanting everyone to be home early and safe before actual midnight. Altogether, we began counting down. "Ten, nine, eight, seven, six, five, four, three, two, one."

The music played, and squeakers blared as everyone shouted, "Happy New Year."

Slade grabbed Lennox, kissing her deeply before releasing her to his brother. She wrapped her arms around his neck, and he dipped her, causing her to laugh as he brought his lips to hers. I'd been watching them, so I missed Slade's approach until he grabbed my neck, pulling me to him. "Don't think you don't get one too, Si." He slammed his lips to mine, the taste of the champagne still on his lips as our tongues danced. His grip tightened on me, and I moaned at the action.

"Fuck, I want you," he murmured, pulling away from me, our breathing heavy. We stared at one another, and I kissed him gently, touching my lips to his. "Then take me."

Moaning, he kissed me back before releasing me and turning. "We can leave now, right, Peach?"

She was fanning herself, apparently enjoying the show we'd just given her. "Uh-huh."

"Good. Make your goodbyes. I'm ready to be home."

She smiled, kissing me quickly and then did as Slade had demanded. Thane rolled his eyes at his brother, but held Lennox's hand as she pulled him to say bye to her parents and Bubba. He'd given us all the third degree, but had finally accepted our relationship with her. I'd never realized how much of a big brother he'd come to be for Lennox.

Slade grabbed mine, pulling me through the banquet room we found ourselves in. We'd been invited to some function at the college, Lennox's semi-famous status getting us all sorts of invitations. We'd all agreed to go tonight because her parents had wanted to attend. Anything that made Robin excited was something we all desired to give her. Noah had been upset he had to stay home, but when we left, he'd seemed fine with the pile of video games and junk food he had around him at my parents' house.

Slade pulled me hard through the people, not caring if they got out of his way or not, bulldozing as he did through whoever. The air hit our flushed skin as we left the upper doors. The night air was cold but felt refreshing at that moment. Slade kept walking, not stopping to wait, and I figured he wanted to pull the car around to the other entrance.

Except when we got to the car, he shoved me up against the door, kissing me. His hands were in my hair, tugging as he rocked into me. Puffs of air could be seen around us as we battled the elements in our frenzy. His hand slipped down between us, slipping into my pants, and I moaned as he squeezed the head of my cock.

"Shit, babe."

"If it wasn't colder than a witch's tit out here, I'd drop to my knees and bring in the new year with head, but I don't think you want your balls freezing off."

"Uh, that's a no." I laughed, shaking my head. "Come on, let's get the other two and we can be home and resume this."

"Fuck, you're hot when you're all logical and shit."

Slade opened the door for me, winking as he shut me in before he jogged around to the other door, sliding in. Rubbing his hands together to gain some warmth, he started the car and drove over to the front entrance. Lenn and Thane rushed out when we pulled up, not wanting to be in the cold any longer than necessary.

"Holy guacamole, it's so dang cold."

"I'll keep you warm," Thane mumbled, making Slade gag upfront. He'd accepted them being together but enjoyed making comments about it to tease them.

"You're just jealous, Brother."

"Hmm."

Snorting, I sat back, enjoying the normalcy our little unit had found.

Ten minutes later, we pulled into Slade's house, but it really was all of ours at this point. Thane had officially ended his job at the clinic, moving all of his belongings here over Christmas. Lenn and I had closed out our lease as well, and we'd made a cozy home together. Slade parked in the garage next to Lennox's new car, the one we'd all surprised her with for Christmas. It wasn't yellow like she'd had, but it was a baby blue, and we offered to have it painted if she wanted it to be yellow again. In the end, she decided to keep it blue, and it had been dubbed Buddy Blue in honor of Slade's Halloween costume.

He acted affronted by the joke, but I knew he secretly enjoyed it.

"Last one inside is a rotten egg," Lennox challenged, opening the door and taking off. The three of us looked at one another and then took off, not wanting to find out what being a rotten egg would entail.

Her giggles led us to where she was hiding, though the trail of clothing was also a good clue. By the time we made it to the master bedroom, I'd spotted her underwear and bra on the floor. The only lights in the room were from the Christmas tree, the soft white and color bulbs twinkling. Lennox had insisted on having three Christmas trees, and at this point, we couldn't deny her anything. She was lying on the bed, her legs kicked up as she watched us enter. When we were all in the room, she held up some mistletoe and winked.

"Who's going to get caught kissing me under the mistletoe?"

Slade, never one to wait, pounced. He'd already taken off most of his clothes, his pants the only thing left, and they were already unzipped. I watched as he walked forward, his eyes on Lennox.

"I'll see you guys in the morning," Thane mumbled, stepping back, and I grabbed his arm.

"He'll get over it. You belong here just as much as us. Stay. I know Lenn wants you too."

Thane looked between all of us, swallowing before he nodded. "Okay."

Dragging him over. I left him at the end of the bed as I stripped out of my clothes, climbing onto the bed. I knew Slade wouldn't be able to handle anything too close, but with her laying like this, I knew we could find a way to make something work. We'd tried several positions over the past month and weren't scared to try any combination now.

Sidling up to her free side, I stole her chin and kissed her. Slade grunted, but he didn't stop me. Sometimes, I just had to remind him he didn't get her to himself, despite his attempts. It was always easier for him when it was the three of us, but I knew he didn't begrudge his brother for loving the same girl anymore. It was just hard for him to share.

Thank fuck, Lennox had fallen in love with people he cared about, or I didn't think she'd have three boyfriends if she'd chosen to be with the possessive fucker. Though, since that possession also included me, I wasn't going to complain. When Slade went all domineering on me, I caved every time to his demands. He called us both brats, but we just liked seeing him take charge. It was his fault for being too sexy while doing it.

Letting go of her mouth, I kissed down her neck, finding my way to her breasts. Like I hoped, she'd tilted her head back and was now licking Thane's dick. Slade narrowed his eyes but didn't say anything, going back to his favorite activity between Lennox's thighs.

Rubbing my thumb over her nipple, I almost jumped when I felt someone grab the base of my cock. Looking down, I found Lennox's hand. Closing my eyes briefly, I relished in the pleasure her touch sent through me. Focusing back on her tits, I sucked her nipple into my mouth, twirling my tongue around the taut peak. I could hear her moaning around Thane as he gently moved in and out of her mouth.

Lavishing wet kisses on her nipples, I kissed all over her flesh, trailing myself down to meet Slade. For a few seconds, we kissed, our tongues tangling over her clit, touching it in small amounts until the controlling fucker emerged. He pulled my face entirely to him, devouring me as he continued to plunge his fingers in and out of Lennox at a fast pace.

Letting go to catch my breath, Slade dropped, taking my dick into his mouth now. Throwing my head back, I tried to stay in the present and not blow my load in his mouth. When his finger started to work me over further down, I gave up, falling back on the bed. Slade pulled off me, his smirk growing as he pulled some lube out of practically thin air and began to lube up my back door.

Grabbing the base of my cock, I tried to keep myself from cumming, not ready to stop the fun we were bound to have. When Slade had me ready enough, he turned me on my side before he slid in. For a few seconds, we both laid there, panting as we adjusted to the tightness.

"Fuck, Si," he breathed.

"Lenn, move over." Grabbing her hip, I pulled her closer, draping her leg over my thigh, and waited for further instruction.

Slade swallowed a few times before directing his brother. "You can choose her mouth or ass, brother. As long as you're far away from me, I don't care. I just don't want to see your balls swinging anywhere near my face, got it?"

Thane snorted but nodded, moving to the bed. Slade handed him the lube and he started to prep Lenn while I slid into her front. Kissing her, I helped distract as he positioned himself behind her. Slade hadn't been patient and had already begun to make small thrusts, pushing me deeper into Lenn.

Our moans filled the room as the Evans brothers fucked us, Lenn and I hanging on to one another, our foreheads pressed together as we looked into one another's eyes. Slade had grabbed her leg, using his advantage to pull himself as deep as possible in me, causing a similar motion for her. With everything, I couldn't hold it back anymore, and I erupted, grunting as I came, Lennox following me as she tightened around me, extending my orgasm. Slade and Thane followed soon after, their moans joining our own.

We all lay there panting. The silence was pleasant as we celebrated the new year all together.

"Now that's what I call a double double-dip," Lenn snorted. "I can't believe I just got that." Her laughter had us all joining in, then groaning as the move had us tightening in places.

"Yes, Peach, that was a double-dip. Now, be still, or you'll wake snakezilla, and I'll have to fuck you more."

"Did you just name your cock?"

"Well, it only seemed fair."

"I did think it was like a snake charmer the first time we had sex," she giggled.

"Wouldn't he be the snake charmer, and his dick the snake?" Thane mused drowsily.

"Brother, don't talk about my dick."

"You're the one who brought it up. Blame yourself."

"I pretend you're not here. It's not my fault you overhear my private conversations."

"Tatzilla, admit you love your brother already. I'm tired of this fake fighting."

"It's not fake! I barely tolerate him."

"Bless your heart, Slade."

"What's that mean, Peach? I feel like that's one of those things you say that doesn't mean what you say."

"Southern for 'you're dumb' or 'you're cute, but you ain't got a clue'."

"At least you think I'm cute," he pouted.

Laughing, we eventually got up, cleaned, and put on some clothes before all getting back in the bed; Thane included and watched, you guessed it, Real Housewives of Beverly Hills. After months of griping about it, Slade had caved, and admitted he 'sorta' liked it.

And that was how we brought in the new year, snuggled under blankets and watching TV. It was the best New Year's of my life, even if Slade was snoring logs in my ear.

At one time, our love story had been riddled with lies, smudging the lines of our inked confessions. We'd all fallen into the trap of believing the lies, too scared to step out into the light to find the truth. Despite the attempts to break us apart by sending chaos into our lives, we'd bonded together stronger, shedding the weight of the past. We'd learned to trust, to have faith in one another, and to love without fail.

None of us were perfect. Far from it.

Thane struggled to believe he was good enough. Slade struggled to share, afraid he'd lose the things he cared about. Lennox struggled to believe in herself, and the power she had on her own. And well, I struggled to believe in 'the more' life had to offer, afraid I didn't deserve it. Together we found a way to soothe the hurts and broken edges, to bend and weld them until we all fit together. Our jagged edges transformed into gold, creating something more beautiful than we ever imagined. We'd irrevocably tattooed our love on one another's hearts, and we weren't ever letting go.

The End... for now. 😊

Letter from the Author

This story grew into a beautiful tale, and I couldn't imagine it any other way. I'm so glad that I decided to give them their story. I fell in love with Lennox, Slade, Simon, and Thane/Zane. Not to mention Darcie and Bubba are near and dear to my heart. Though, I might've screwed myself over by making my first true Alpha-hole so damn perfect. Slade, you are one in a million buddy, and I will always carry a torch for you. Le, sigh.

Just in case you're wondering why Lennox didn't pick up that Blaze was two people, you have to remember that you're only reading the letters I chose, not all the letters and emails passed between them over an eight year span, so there were times when she would question Blaze, and even with Adam messing with messages at times, she started to chalk it up to not remembering correctly, or having read into something differently. With all the things going on in her life, she figured it was her, not him. It's why at the end, she was able to accept Thane/Zane so easily because she'd known him. Hopefully, that makes sense to you, and you won't fault Lennox her misgivings.

If you didn't catch that little tease at the end, I do have plans for another story for Lennox and her hunky men. The nice thing about duets is I can write shorter adventures for them and never get bored. I also have a story brewing for Darcie, and I already know how it will begin. ;) So, if you love them as much as me, let me know what you'd want to see.

And have no fear, there will be a completed duet coming in paperback soon with a bonus scene of Lennox getting her tattoo, and the lead in to the next book for them. Make sure to join my reader group or newsletter to stay up to date on all things Lennox, or you just might be crying out fiddlesticks!

Emma, as always, you're my bae.

Kayla, thanks for being the best cheerleader.

Thanks to Jillian for stepping in and saving my ass. You're the best and the absolute sweetest.

Thanks to all my girls who rallied for Lennox and her story, and panted for Slade, laughed with Simon, and swooned for Zane/Thane. Tory, Jess, & Becki, thanks for helping me see what I needed to add, especially chapter 18. Brenda, Megan, Amber, and Amanda, thanks for shouting for her story, and giving me all the amazing feedback. Reading your comments was the reassurance I needed that the story didn't suck!

To readers new and old, I hoped you love this story and will check out the rest of my books. Links to join my newsletter and reader group are on my website.

Also by Kris Butler

Dark Confessions Series

Dangerous Truths

Dangerous Lies

Dangerous Vows

Dangerous Love

Tattooed Hearts Duet

Riddled Deceit

Smudged Lines

The Council Series (completed series)

Damaged Dreams

Shattered Secrets

Fractured Futures

Council Christmas Novella

Bosh Bells & Epic Fails (Christmas Wishes Anthology)

The Order (Council Spinoff)

Stiletto Sins

Summer 2022

Sinners Fairytales Rapunzel Retelling (standalone)

Pride

Kris Butler

Kris Butler writes under a pen name to have some separation from her everyday life. Never expecting to write a book, she was surprised when an author friend encouraged her to give it a try and how much she enjoyed it. Having an extensive background in mental health, Kris hopes to normalize mental health issues and the importance of talking about them with her characters and books. Kris is a southern girl at heart but lives with her husband and adorable furbaby somewhere in the Midwest. Kris is an avid fan of Reverse Harem and hopes to add a quirky and new perspective to the emerging genre. If you enjoyed her book, please consider leaving a review. You can contact her the following ways and follow Kris's journey as a new author on social media.

Manufactured by Amazon.ca
Bolton, ON

26784876R00206